Slow Work

A novel by

Tim Farrington

Born Laughing Productions

Copyright © 2018 Tim Farrington

ISBN-10:1987661206
ISBN-13:978-1987661200

for my grandfather, Francis Xavier Farrington
1903-1997
with love and gratitude

Eternal rest grant unto him, O Lord,
and let perpetual light shine upon him.
Amen.

Therefore thus saith the Lord God: Behold,
I lay in Zion for a foundation a stone, a tried stone,
a precious cornerstone, a sure foundation:
he that believeth shall not make haste.
Isaiah 28:16

CHAPTER ONE

It was my grandfather who taught me to work with stone. Edward Tremaine was a mason and a stonecutter of the old school, and even did his own quarrying at times, but his real love was monuments to the beloved dead, and his style on tombstones was plain and sturdy and full of serene dignity. I believe he would have liked to pass it all on to my father, who had a gift for the work as well, but Korea intervened, and then the Cold War in general: my father enlisted at seventeen in 1951, and like so many of his generation devoted himself thereafter to the fight against Communism. For his son's heroism, my grandfather achieved a baffled and wounded sympathy that never quite healed fully into approval; he was less fervent about historical things. Perhaps it was just as well, though—beyond his passionate defense of American freedoms, my father had a streak of deep black humor that might not have gone well with the art of *mementos mori*. His irony eventually found its most adamant challenge in Vietnam, and in the fact that his oldest son came to doubt the American truths he spent his life fighting for.

Long before I found my way into the agony of that doubt, it turned out that I had something of a way with stone too. While my father fought the wars of the second half of the twentieth century, I spent a lot of my childhood summers with my grandfather in his big, bright workshop in the foothills of the Appalachians, just down the road from the Shenandoah Springs Cemetery, at work and at play in the lazy slow Virginia air, in gradual initiation to the miraculousness of granite. Later, to be sure, it became clear that I had come in for my own share of my father's black humor as well, and so I have spent much of my life trying to reconcile the depths of contradictory gifts and suffering the collision of antagonistic devotions. But I think of those early summers as idyllic.

My grandfather's workshop had no sign and no telephone. Indeed, it was many years before I realized that he was in business at all. To me what he did seemed as natural and inevitable as the progression of the seasons; when work came he embraced it with such quiet matter-of-factness that it never occurred to me it was anything but what he wanted to do most.

Which, of course, it was. He built walls, houses, sheepcotes, and the occasional church, and was much in demand on both sides of the Blue Ridge for his masonry, but as I said, his real love was for gravestones, and that is where his character showed most clearly.

He never advertised, but people would always find their way to the shop. They would sidle uncertainly into the little yard with its gardenias and azaleas and the rose bushes at the far side by the weathered fence drenched in honeysuckle, and stand there amid the heaps of hewn stone looking dazed and undone. Often they were in black, but often too they were simply in their best clothes, farmers in ties and stiff-looking suits, fingering their collars, women in soft, sad, subdued patterned dresses, holding purses shiny with disuse and empty of normal accumulation: people in the grip of unpracticed solemnity, tentative and more than a little at a loss in the sudden mystery of ordinary things.

My grandfather's real gift was in meeting these people and setting them at ease without in the least diminishing their awe. He was at home in awe himself as a result of his peculiar relationship withh stone. "It's slow work," he would always tell me, speaking of granite, but he did the same slow work with the bereaved. He would join them in the vast new country of their grief without pretension or fuss, and it was wondrous to see the effect his natural company there had. Gradually their jaggedness, the razor edges of their freshly broken places, would soften. My grandfather would offer coffee, or the apple juice my grandmother made, or cider— sweet or hard, as the situation seemed to call for—or even in certain cases Irish whiskey and peanuts.

When things had settled to a peaceable calm he would bring out chairs and they would sit in the yard in the sight of the mountains and begin to talk of what had brought them together. Often people had extravagant ideas of their obligations to the dead, or extravagant ambitions as mourners. They wanted mausoleums, shrines, grand statuary—pyramids even, wild flailings of inflated remembrance. My grandfather would just listen, would nod and quietly listen, listen, listen. It was his deepest belief that anything set in stone should be done with love, and love alone, and so he listened through the extravagances that were born of guilt or fear or anger until he heard the clean note of real love. This was, most often, a smaller project than the people had in mind, but one more in proportion to their resources and more faithful to their hearts.

It was fascinating to watch someone arrive at this realization. Often, up to that point, their extravagance had protected them against the further reaches of their pain. My grandfather would sit quietly with them as they wept afresh, or even for the first time. Sometimes that moment took hours, or days, to reach, but my grandfather never hurried. He would not work anywhere but on the ground of love.

This limited his clientele, inevitably. There were those who persisted in wishing to commission some grandiosity, and it was almost as interesting to see it dawn on them that my grandfather would not do it. They always thought at first that he was holding out for more money. "I don't do this for the money," he would tell them; and in fact he barely covered costs on most of his monument jobs, to my grandmother's humorous dismay. But this was incomprehensible to those my grandfather refused. They would, most often, get angry and accuse him of exploiting the bereaved. He would refer them to a mortuary outfit in Richmond that welcomed spectacular griefs.

* * *

My grandfather never thought I should go to California, of course, just as he had never thought his own son should go to Korea or Vietnam. He felt every break in continuity keenly. His own father, and his father's father, had been carving the gravestones in Shenandoah Springs since 1848, when my great-great-great-grandfather Jacob Tremaine and his brother Esau fled what my grandfather still called *An Gorta Mór*, the Irish potato famine, and came to Virginia from County Cork with nothing but a few ball-peen hammers, some wooden mallets, and a handful of cold chisels. You can walk through the vast old cemetery down the road from my grandfather's shop and find Tremaine work from well before the Civil War. It is an impressive cumulative heritage of careful, loving work. But when I took off for California, I had ceased to care about that: like my father, I fled Virginia early, at eighteen, to fight wars my father could not comprehend.

I never blamed Dad for that failure of comprehension, much as it pained me. How could I? I didn't understand myself. My father fought the Red menace, very simply, defending American's straightforward freedoms without a second thought; while my struggle for many years was vague and even blind, a flimsy rebellion against an obscure vastness, a wrestling not against flesh and blood, but against principalities, against powers, against the rulers of the darkness of this world, against spiritual wickedness in high places. In my mind, I had left Pharaoh's Egypt for a promised land, intent on laying down my sword and shield by the riverside and studying war no more. But like most of my generation, I was brutally unprepared for the realities of the wilderness; and in

California, golden calves abounded. It took me almost twenty years, and a massive drug overdose, before I even began to come to grips with the nature of that desert wilderness at all, and with the truth of how lost I really was.

* * *

They tell me I was actually dead. Certainly it was obvious enough to me at the time, clinical considerations aside. I know that I left my body and was circling the earth in an orbit just beyond the moon's, talking frankly with the angels and the saints, the demons and the damned. I got farther and farther away, the sun dwindling beneath me like a campfire you leave behind in mountain night until it was just another bit of starlight, and then there was the tunnel, just like they say, though less dramatic somehow than I had been led to expect, and beyond that an atmosphere that was nothing but light, warm and rich and modulated by presences I knew were souls. I was filled with joy and just beginning to settle through the sweet depths of radiance into God when I was revived by the heroic doctors in the emergency ward of St. Francis Hospital in downtown San Francisco. Two beds over, a guy with massive gunshot wounds had just died, defeating all their efforts, and I envied him the thoroughness of his departure.

For weeks I lived in chronic dismay of the unreality of everything I had been dragged back to. I could see auras—everyone had one—and it was not pretty at all. It was all so much aggravation. The only things I could see that made unpainful sense to me were bricks and stones and the occasional tree. Their unhurried auras were calm, clear, and mercifully without glare. Everything else was like a bad Charlie Chaplin movie, frantic slapstick in frenetic black-and-white. It was plain to me that it was all only temporary, and at last I got myself a slab of granite with a particular appeal and went to live in the country, in the foothills of the Sierras near Grass Valley.

Every day I sat with that granite, as with an anchor to

everything real. For months, I believed the stone would begin to speak, and clear everything up for me. Eventually I realized it didn't work that way, and at last I got myself a mallet and stone chisel, with the intention of carving the rock to serve as my tombstone. That, at least, made sense to me. It was a project I could relate to. But after weeks of chunking, sanding, and scouring a face onto the stone, I chipped the first letter, trying for a serif, and chipped the second too, trying for a point. By then I was so struck by the immensity of what I had yet to learn that I retreated in an apprentice humility to the east coast. There I found my grandfather in his shop, faded with age a bit but recognizably present, like bricks and stones and trees.

He acted as if the decades I had been gone were nothing. When I mentioned the angels and galaxy stuff, the tunnel and the light, he shrugged.

"The main thing is to do the work God sets before you with love," he said. "The rest takes care of itself."

"I can't love anything," I told him. "I can't even really *see* anything. It all looks phony and two-dimensional. The only things I can see that look real are bricks and rocks and trees. And you."

"It's a start," he said.

He had a little job that had just come in, a simple marker inscription:

ROBERT HENRY PRESTON
BELOVED HUSBAND
BORN APRIL 8, 1913, DIED JULY 12, 1991
'HE IS WITH GOD NOW.'

My grandfather had already prepped the stone, inking out the letters in advance with a medium-edged calligraphy brush on the small rectangle of dark Virginia slate, and he put me to work on it. I was cleared only for certain letters in the simplest glyptic style: my thick lines and my thin lines were still inconsistent, I couldn't hold a curve, and something like a "K," which involved a very fine dance between a point and an angular junction, was out of the question. It took me almost a month to do the epitaph, about a letter a day, with my grandfather talking me through the tricky cuts and occasionally stepping in to touch up a junction or clean out a valley that was threatening to get out of hand. But there was no hurry, it seemed. And when Robert Preston's widow, Alma Lynn, came in to see the finished product and winked at me, a slow conscious wink, so pleased was she with the stone, I realized that I could see her too: like the stone itself, she was lit from within by the simplest unhectic light; and I began to understand a little more how my grandfather had been at home in wonder for so long.

* * *

My grandfather understood my more or less catastrophic California odyssey. It even made a sort of deeper sense to him. I had been looking for God, he always said, translating things into his own language. Since God, for my grandfather, was always as close as the next chisel stroke, or the next mourner, it was a stretch for him to grasp why someone would have to leave home, much less cross the country, abuse substance, worship idols, and lay waste to relationships, to look for Him; but he was prepared to concede that it took all kinds. He even told me once with a slightly confidential air that Jacob Tremaine's brother Esau had gone to California, too, in 1849. I had the feeling of being the repository of a family scandal that continued to merit circumspection. The two Tremaine brothers had come over from Ireland on the same boat and traveled west across Virginia together, but Jacob only got as far as the foothills of the Appalachians. The standard family line was that he fell in love with the Blue Ridge. Actually, my grandfather said, deepening the revelation, Jacob Tremaine fell in love with Margaret Mary Peterson. Esau, though, had already heard about the gold to the west, and he went on.

"So I suppose you've got a bit of the brother in you yet," my grandfather concluded. "Your father had a bit of the brother in him."

There was wistfulness, in that. We were drinking Jameson's

whiskey and eating peanuts, and it was a moment of particularly deep confiding. My grandfather had never found a bit of that Tremaine brother in himself his whole life. To him, that bit was like papayas, or a color he had only heard about, or a fever he had never had.

What was stranger was that by then I already knew about Esau Tremaine. I had found my great-great-great-grand-uncle's grave by pure cosmic coincidence, in a tiny miners' cemetery northeast of Grass Valley, not long after my own botched death. My grandfather had never breathed a word about that black sheep Tremaine's pilgrimage west through my entire childhood, but I had recognized the granite of the monument at once. It was the nearly flawless, dense-grained rock, almost silver-colored, with purplish streaks and a faint suffusing glow of rose, from the Big Rabbit quarry near Richmond. And if that, and the name on the grave, had not been enough, there was no mistaking the style of the inscription. I knew that granite script from before I could read. Jacob Tremaine himself had carved his brother's stone.

ESAU TREMAINE
B. MARCH 18, 1823 COUNTY CORK, IRELAND
D. ? 1850 CALIFORNIA
I PRAY THEE, MY BROTHER,
IF NOW I HAVE FOUND GRACE IN THY SIGHT,
THEN RECEIVE MY GIFTS: FOR THEREFORE I HAVE
SEEN THY FACE,
AS THOUGH I HAD SEEN THE FACE OF GOD.

Standing there at my unacknowledged ancestor's grave in the autumn sunlight, with ravens squabbling in the gnarled oaks nearby and the Sierras to the east already cowled with the season's first snow, I felt the mystery of fate. I had been raised on the solidity of the Tremaines, the flawless stone of an uncompromising lineage, and here was a streak of unsuspected vagary in that bedrock, like the rusty veins in limestone where groundwater infiltrated the compacting sediment and set a weakness in it. I could never be sure again after that day how much I owed to the one in the grave, and how much to the one who lived to do the slow work of grieving, and to carve love's memory into the rock, working carefully, as always, around the flaws in the grain. Obviously, it was way more complicated that I had been led to believe. Much as I loved my grandfather, I had to wonder what else he hadn't told me.

* * *

On the strength of that same bottle of whiskey, my grandfather also confided in me that he had known I would get into stone work from the time that I was five, but that he hadn't wanted to seem pushy. I laughed, because I had only become sure myself of my vocation so much more recently, and in such an appallingly roundabout way. But it was a blessing of sorts. He gave me a complete set of his second-best tools that day and I drove home with them in the back of my old '73 Chevy one-ton. The hammers, chisels, mallets, drill bits, and polishing disks rattled in their tool boxes every time I hit the smallest bump, but that was okay with me. That truck could sound like hell in even the best of times.

* * *

My own shop here in the Back Bay, in the tidewater country just south of Virginia Beach, is a lot like my grandfather's, though I have made certain concessions to modern communications. I have a telephone, for instance, though I must confess that last spring the phone company turned it off due to a certain laxity in my payment of the bills. That was not long after Dominion Power turned off the electricity. I managed to keep the water running, but it was a tough period. This business is no more lucrative now than it was in my grandfather's prime, and in the decade or so that I've been at it on my own I have barely begun to rebuild the kind of local recognition he had in Shenandoah Springs.

I tried to complain to him about this once, but my grandfather had no sympathy for it.

"I've never needed a phone," he told me.

Which was true, of course. If God had work for him to do, God would send it. And in my grandfather's experience, God didn't need a telephone. God was a walk-up.

"You're rural, and I'm practically suburban," I pointed out. "And you or some Tremaine or another has carved gravestones for half the people who died in that county for a century and a half. You've got word of mouth—uh, so to speak."

"You'd have word of mouth too, if you weren't always charging off somewhere and starting from scratch," he said.

* * *

The local trash company stopped the garbage pickups at my shop last April, too, pending me paying the bills, and so it was that on a bright Saturday morning toward the end of Lent, with the air just beginning to thicken toward warm and the fruit trees budding, I happened to be wrestling an overloaded can of trash onto the bed of my truck, to take it to the dump myself, when a couple in a cream-colored Mercedes turned off the dirt road and pulled into my gravel driveway. The guy got out of the driver's side and my brain said, *Lawyer.* He was forty-ish, about my age, much better outfitted and equipped, but not obnoxiously so: Banana Republic, basically, nothing showy. His wife, a brunette costumed companionably in Anne Taylor Loft, disembarked more slowly, perhaps even reluctantly. She was quite tall, and took a moment to unfold her willowy frame, but when she straightened, her steady brown eyes held mine for about three beats; and then a fourth. And then time stopped completely and my brain said, in the sudden hush, *ohmygod Jocelyn Page.*

Chapter Two

One reason stone carvers work so slowly is that mistakes are so easy to make and so brutally hard to fix. However impatient and impulsive your nature, by the time you've screwed up a few times late into big jobs, you begin to learn to read the grain of the stone with the attention of a suitor and to make your cuts with a lover's tenderness. My grandfather used to pause over certain crucial chisel taps like a golfer with a twelve-foot putt to win the U.S. Open. He would get so still that the world seemed to hold its breath, standing there poised and attentive to something entirely mysterious, waiting for some inscrutably ripening intimacy between him and the stone and God and history and the weather and God knows what else to move him; and when the stroke fell at last, it always seemed to fall in a time entirely of its own choosing, as spontaneous as an apple from a tree.

The most intense pressure comes in working on stones that are already in place. Standing on a scaffold above the vestibule of a cathedral, shaping the face of a massive piece of limestone that will be there until the church walls themselves come down, you just don't want to screw up.

And yet even the best do, sometimes. My grandfather delighted in taking me around the National Cathedral in D.C., where he had spent much of his life working on and off, pointing out to me the fudged strokes and errors of proportion, the shims and scrapings and ad libs, the place on the façade that was a quarter-inch shallower than the rest because they'd had to grind off some blunder or another. It was an ongoing lesson in the fundamental values of patience and humility; but it was also heartening to know that certain inexplicable curlicues and adornments in various stone works probably had their beginnings in a master, deep into the work on an important piece, steering with the skid of a moment's lapse, a bad chisel stroke, a tricky spot in a hard stone.

And sometimes the mason dies, or the cathedral makers run out of money; the plague hits, or the revolution comes: the work is abandoned, for one reason or another, and the mistakes no one ever got around to doctoring abide there in the stone through the ensuing centuries. Given hundreds of years to grow accustomed to the incongruity, something like that can even end up looking like style, like a defining touch of flair or some outrageous artistic statement made far ahead of its time. But usually it just looks like somebody screwed up.

In the cathedral of my life, Jocelyn Page was the ruined cornerstone, an immovable twenty-ton block of limestone that I had botched early and made worse through elaborate years of futile attempts at repair, adding discrepancy to miserable incongruity to outright lie, until finally the aberration was reflected through every surface of the entire structure. I'd never had the chops or vision to fix the damage and I hadn't really learned to live with it either. I had just given up, I suppose. But I should have known she would come around again eventually. She always did.

* * *

On that spring day after she got out of the Mercedes in my driveway, I could smell the new blossoms of Carolina jasmine that flanked the shop's entrance and entwined above the door, a sweetness in the April air. Jocelyn held my eyes as she had always held my eyes, for as long as I could stand it. There are things you cannot even begin to remember until you are experiencing them again, subtleties of consciousness that simply disappear beneath the surface impacts of daily life: the immediacies of awe, of grief or love, or the pain of childbirth. We forget, because there is no place in our usual minds to keep the memory. And then, when the reality comes around again in its fullness, like new water in a dry streambed, we marvel, because it seems like the most obvious thing possible, like the only unforgettable thing. And we think, What in the world have I been *doing* all these years?

The man I took to be Jocelyn's husband approached first.

"We had a helluva time finding this place," he said cheerfully.

"It's a bit off the beaten track," I conceded. I was still clinging to the handle of the trash can, conscious of my heart in my chest, an ache with a beat.

"Seriously. You're not even in the Yellow Pages."

"I believe in destiny," I said. It seemed superfluous to tell him that my phone was disconnected anyway. Or that the main reason I believed in destiny was his wife.

He laughed and gave me a wink. "Destiny doesn't pay the rent, amigo."

I considered disliking him, then let it go. He meant well, it seemed, on his own terms; and you can't blame the bull, that the china shop is full of glass.

As I stood there quashing sharp retorts, he put out his hand. "Bill Sherman."

"Eli Tremaine." I let go of the trash can handle and offered my hand in return, conscious of my calluses, stone-rough against his clean smooth grip. His handshake was everything you'd expect of a man prepared to give career advice to strangers, firm, vigorous, and a bit too robust. A handshake that paid the rent.

Sherman's wife had drawn near now, and he turned to include her in the introductions.

"And this is—"

"Hello, Jocelyn," I said.

Her eyes narrowed, a gentle fan of lines deepening at each corner. Someone else might have taken the expression for sternness, but I recognized the early stages of a smile, somewhat suppressed. I had always felt the study of Jocelyn's face to be near the heart of my life's calling, and knew the stages and variations of her dawning smile the way early risers know the softening of a night sky into sunrise. This look now was something like the first gray as the stars begin to fade, but touched with sadness, as with high clouds backlit by a hidden moon.

"Hello, Elijah," she said.

Bill's smile turned uncertain. "You two know each other?"

"We were best friends in the fourth grade," I said. "We were, uh—"

"Friends, right through high school into college," Jocelyn said preemptively. "It's been a while, Eli."

Twenty-two years, eight months, two weeks, three days, and fifteen hours, I thought. Give or take a few minutes. But I just nodded. She had obviously never said a word about us to her husband. And why should she have? The charitable reading was that we'd had our teenage moment and we'd let it pass. It was as if Romeo and Juliet had not burned up properly in their passion like twinned moths in a flame, but had faltered, had lost their nerve and renounced their mad and unearthly love, brought to their senses after all by rude social reality. You could even look at it as having worked out for the best. Juliet, as far as I knew, had gone on through the standard four university years, and then grad school, and then—it seemed—had married well. Romeo, after a certain amount of superfluous melodrama and a breakdown or two, had settled down and learned a trade.

Bill Sherman gave his wife a mildly admonishing glance, like *You might have mentioned . . .*, and she gave him a charming shrug of reassurance: *Ancient history, honey. No big deal.* He seemed content enough with that and settled back politely to give us an opportunity to say all the high school reunion things and do our prosaic exclamations about time flying; but reducing a quarter century of grief and bafflement to small talk seemed a kind a blasphemy to me, and I held my tongue. I began instead to quietly pray, nothing fancy, just the basic plea of the undone:

Oh God, oh God, oh God. Help.

Jocelyn too said nothing, and we all just stood there for a moment. A Celtic cross of rough pewter hung around her neck, nestled in the hollow at the base of her throat. Strung on a delicate gold chain, it looked like it was a thousand years old and had been made in a forest. The incongruity was so keen that I met her eyes again. They were as they had always been, an unfathomable brown, rich as dark chocolate: the color of warmth, and of a delicious quiet.

"Small world," Bill Sherman pronounced at last, a little tentatively, as the silence threatened to grow awkward.

"Not that damn small," I said, not quite sure what I meant; but apparently the tone was right and we all chuckled vaguely. And then to everyone's relief we were past it, practically speaking, and I said, as if I were running an actual business and they were simply customers, "What can I do for you folks?"

"You did my grandfather's, um, headstone a couple years ago—" Sherman said.

"Sherman . . ." I said dubiously. I knew that I had never carved a stone for anyone named Sherman. It's not the kind of thing you forget.

"My mother's father," Sherman said. "Jerome Hartley?"

"Oh my God," I exclaimed. "Of course." Sherman's grandmother, Marietta, a doughty little woman with sea-green eyes, had handled all the arrangements. The stone had proven to be a chore of the most delightful kind. Jerome Hartley's instructions for his epitaph had been a request simply for "something from Yeats," and he'd left it to his widow to pick the verse. She and I had spent three long afternoons and part of a crucial rainy evening with the Irish poet's collected works, and I remember that it was like a slow light growing in both of us. Marietta read everything aloud, often two or three times with varying emphases, in a quavery old tidewater accent. Sometimes she would glance at me conspiratorially and smile, a fierce, quiet smile accomplished mostly in the depths of those deep cat's eyes. Toward the end she narrowed it down to the speeches of Crazy Jane; and at last, chuckling to herself, she chose,

> "That lover of a night
> Came when he would,
> Went in the dawning light
> Whether I would or no;
> Men come, men go,
> *All things remain in God.*"

It was the first time I had ever tried italics in granite without my grandfather pre-writing the letters on the stone in water color, but the work came off. The stone, I vaguely recalled, had caused something of a stir among the immediate relations, but Marietta Hartley had held her ground. Remembering the mutterers now, and the way she walked away from the grave that day in her stocking feet on the grass, with her shoes held dangling, one in each hand, I smiled. I believe Jerome was a lucky man.

"How is your grandmother?" I asked.

"She broke her hip last year, I'm afraid, and hasn't walked since. She's very frail."

"I'm sorry to hear that. She's a wonderful woman."

"She's actually gotten a little eccentric," Sherman said. "She's begun to re-use all the junk mail envelopes she gets, for her personal correspondence."

"It could be a fashion statement," I said, determined to defend the old gal.

Jocelyn said, apparently to forestall further dispute, "She

recommended that we use you. She insisted, actually."

"'Use me?'"

"We're here because our daughter died."

I realized that I had somehow taken hold of the trash can's handle again during the conversation and was clinging to it like a storm-blown sailor to a railing. I gave the can a shove to get it on the truck bed more securely, and let go. I felt deeply foolish; I had been sure from their demeanor that they'd come to order a sidewalk or a patio, or even that they were here to file one more complaint about the Crazy Jane verse on the Hartley stone. A number of the relatives had already called in the years since the placing of the monument to vent their displeasure, having found no satisfaction with Marietta. That much, at least, was clearer now—probably the old gal was answering their gripes with feisty bits and snatches from Yeats, in recycled junk mail envelopes.

Still, I knew I had missed it badly with the Shermans. My grandfather would have seen the whole thing coming, somehow, reading a hundred clues that I had failed to see, and offered refreshments long since to make a space for the deeper issues.

"I'm so sorry," I said.

Bill Sherman shook his head helplessly and looked at his hands, and then at a spot somewhere near the shop's entrance. His blue eyes had filled, and I noticed for the first time that they had a dilute streak of his grandmother Hartley's warm green running through them, like the Gulf Stream fading into the North Atlantic. It made my heart hurt. I had been wild for his grandmother's eyes.

I looked at Jocelyn and found her considering me unflinchingly, dry-eyed and even coolly, registering my shock, but showing nothing else. The trash can was emitting a putrid stench that she probably associated with me at this point, and I saw myself for an instant as she must have, as a dumpy guy in his forties, with a close-cropped haze of dwindling dishwater blond hair, a three-day growth of beard graying at the tips, my grandfather's blue eyes and Roman nose, broken once like an Irish boxer's, and an obvious attitude problem. Rode hard and put away wet, as my father used

19

to say. Certainly nothing that might cause her to rue the choice she'd made, all those years ago.

I wondered what my grandfather would have done in a case like this. He always saw his work as one of the healing arts; he believed that everyone who came to him was a soul in particular need, and in his modest, gentle fashion he almost always found a way to meet that need. But I felt utterly inadequate here. I was way too stuck on issues I should have resolved as a teenager.

I said, "Would you like some apple juice? My grandmother makes it special." And, as neither answered, "I've got cider, too." Still no response. "I've got, uh—"

"Do you have Scotch?" Bill Sherman asked, his eyes returning from the Carolina jasmine.

"By the grace of God," I said.

Chapter Three

My shop is roomy, but unimpressive. It's really a sort of glorified shack held together by windows and good work habits. I lease it month-to-month from an ornery farmer named Mitchell who is always threatening to throw me out. But I think he knows he would have a hard time finding anyone else to take the place. It's just south of the green line, off a dirt road running between a soy bean field and a salvage pit, but the lot is zoned commercial, and while the commercial value of my activity is not always evident, I've never been more than three months behind on the rent. Mitchell figures he can live with that rather than let the place sit empty for a couple of years while he tries to find another person foolish enough to believe he can do business here at all.

The place is drafty, and it tends to echo. The ceiling is high, with a half-hearted skylight like a rip in the roof, and the original dirt floor is buried beneath half a foot of packed stone

21

dust. The only real neighbors are the seagulls circling the ripening crops and an Armenian widow a hundred yards to the east who is constantly leaving me baked goods and sweets in an effort to take my mind off of death. Her baklava is extraordinary, but I find her cookies dry. On days with a north wind I can hear her playing rousing gypsy carnival-like tunes on her organ.

Inside, I leave a lot of room to pace between the work benches and the granite in varying stages of refinement. The place is neat enough, for a working shop. From the east window you can see the widow Sofya's house and, beyond it, intimations of suburban Virginia Beach, the malls and pizza places creeping toward the green line; but the west window looks out onto pure Pungo and you can see nothing but a sea of young green soy beans with a tiny island tree in the middle, guarding one of the old farm family burial plots.

Jocelyn went to the east window as soon as she came in. She stood looking out, her back to me while I poured the drinks. I am not normally a Scotch drinker; my grandfather's preference for Irish whiskey shaped me radically. But I keep a bottle of Cutty on hand for high ceremonial occasions and medical emergencies. It is important, after all, to be able to address the tastes of every sort of mourner: blessed are those who drink Scotch, as well.

"No ice cubes?" Bill Sherman asked.

"I could run up to the 7-Eleven."

He shrugged. "Neat's fine."

I poured drinks for him and Jocelyn and, after a moment's hesitation, one for myself. I knew Jocelyn to be a woman who did not suffer dilution lightly—in our day we used to drink straight tequila shots with Corona chasers—but I splashed a perfunctory bit of water into my glass to establish a sobriety scale, handed Bill Sherman his drink, and carried Jocelyn's over to the window. She accepted the glass without enthusiasm, examining it a little dubiously. It was a jelly jar, and I couldn't really blame her. But it was clean, and it was the best I had. We'd drunk out of worse, all those years ago.

Drinks in hand, we all hesitated. I felt the dead child in our silence, and was humbled and quieted by that. It's what keeps me honest, amid the confusion of the survivors' emotions, and my own confusions.

Jocelyn had half-turned back to the window, as if her participation were provisional. I felt by now that it was risky in the extreme to meet her eyes, and instead studied the exposed joists where the shop's ceiling should have been. There is a sparrow's nest up there and sometimes in the springtime you can glance up and see bright little eyes looking back at you. But this year's brood hadn't hatched yet, and the nest seemed empty.

Patience, my grandfather always said. Patience, and humility. Those are the virtues stone teaches you. I would have choked before I said a word at this point; I had no idea what was supposed to happen here. It was Bill Sherman's move.

"We're thinking of something with cherubs," he said.

* * *

He knew pretty much exactly what he wanted: a sort of neo-Victorian shrine to tragically quashed innocence, with chubby guardian angels, a lamb lounging beneath a dwarf cherry tree, and an eternal flame. He had a sketch of the whole thing, done by an architect friend. Embedded in the stone itself would be a porcelain photo of the little girl.

I stared at the snapshot he handed me: a three-year-old with a mass of unmanageable dark curls, her mother's rich brown eyes and the same air of secret knowledge, and precise little hands, like a miniature pianist's. She was posed formally, in a blue velvet dress with a lacy white collar, holding a stuffed Tigger in front of a photo studio backdrop painted to look like the House at Pooh Corner. The kid looked somewhat bemused by the whole set-up; I had the sense she had probably jumped off her stool the moment after the photo was snapped, to see what was behind the elaborate facade. Her name was Ariel. She had died the previous December.

"Congenital LVHS," Bill Sherman said. And, as I must have looked blank, "Her heart. The left ventricles never developed properly."

I nodded, for lack of anything else to do. My antennae were straining toward Jocelyn, but she remained beside the window, monitoring our exchange inscrutably from the edge of my peripheral vision. I had no idea what she was feeling. I would have been uneasy by this time at the lack of synergy between the Shermans on their daughter's memorial even if I had never met either of them before, but with Jocelyn's silence, I was close to panic. Something inside me was dizzied, and keening; but I couldn't tell where the grief was coming from, or what the lamentation was for. It was all too much for me, really. I was out of my depth.

"Can you do that in color?" Bill Sherman asked.

"What?" I said.

"The porcelain photo—is it possible to get that in color?"

"Sure. Yes. It's pretty easy now." I hesitated, then said, "Look, Mr. Sherman—"

"Bill. Please."

"Of course. Bill. I'm really not sure. . . I mean . . . " I trailed off. His eyes tracked me anxiously, the blue still watery with his recent tears, the green crisper somehow, a sort of coolness, and I thought again of his grandmother, sitting on the beach with Yeats. It was the only solid ground I felt I'd come across yet.

Sherman's glass, I noted, was empty already. "More Scotch?" I suggested, trying to slow things down until some of the mud settled out of my inner water.

"It's all right, Eli," Jocelyn said suddenly.

I turned and met her eyes and it was as if we were alone. We had always talked so, skipping three or four steps to start our conversations as if they were works long since in progress. "Is it?"

"Yes."

I nodded. I didn't believe her, but I didn't necessarily trust my gut on that. It was my damn gut and its vagaries that had wrecked us in the first place. My gut and I had issues.

"What?" Bill Sherman said.

"He's afraid I've got some sort of problem with the memorial, because I haven't said anything," Jocelyn translated. And, to me, "It really *is* all right."

I didn't even bother to nod this time. Her daughter had just died, for God's sake, and she was standing here in the light of God and history with her husband and her ex-lover, discussing the cemetery arrangements. And that was just for conversational openers.

But apparently "all right" was going to have to do here. Any further exchanges between us were strait-jacketed, like the worst of a Houdini nightmare: handcuffed by past and present, bound, boxed, and buried beneath every choice we'd made for the last twenty-five years and everything our lives were now. And maybe, I thought, that was even for the best. God knows what I might say, if our talk actually broke free.

"Can you work out some kind of estimate on this?" Bill said. "I mean, price is no object, frankly, but just some kind of ballpark figure. I can leave the sketches and—"

"Sure," I said, to keep him from going on. It was starting to sound too much like a car repair.

Sherman set his empty glass down on a block of limestone, then thought better of it—perhaps it struck him as vaguely disrespectful to use someone's future gravestone as a bar—and shifted it to my workbench. Jocelyn promptly set down her own drink, barely sipped, on the windowsill. They were done, it seemed. I felt like we had barely started. But Bill Sherman already had his checkbook out.

"No need for that right now," I said.

"Just to get you started," he said, already writing. "Tremaine, right? Elijah Tremaine. . . . It's crazy, you know, that you're not in the Yellow Pages."

"My grandfather taught me the business. He didn't believe in the Yellow Pages."

"How medieval," Sherman said. His script was brisk and precise, with competent neat loops and bold crossing strokes. He signed the check with a small flourish and tore it out with a practiced motion to hand it to me. I accepted it uneasily.

"Can you come by the house—tomorrow, maybe?—after you've worked out the estimate?" he asked. "We can go over the details then." And, as I hesitated, "Unless of course you're stacked up with other business for tomorrow?"

His glance around the shop indicated that he had long since made a realistic estimate of the likelihood of that. If I'd had a pocket calendar or something, I might have taken it out to check it, for dignity's sake, but I keep all my jobs in my head with room to spare. I said, "I've got to run up to Big Rabbit Quarry tomorrow morning to pick up some limestone. But tomorrow afternoon is fine, toward the later side."

"In the afternoon, then. Four-ish, say?"

I felt the job's underlying complexities again. It was all moving too fast, somehow. But I hated to seem gratuitously recalcitrant.

"Sure," I said.

Jocelyn relinquished her spot by the window, apparently sharing Bill's sense that we were done for the moment. "Thanks for the drink, Eli."

"You hardly touched it," I said, but she and her husband were already striding out. I watched Jocelyn's ankles go wobbly on the gravel drive, and considered, in spite of myself, the sway of her hips. The two of them gave the trash can on my pickup a conspicuously wide berth. The car doors thunked, the diesel engine roared; I listened to the crunch of tires as they drove off, until it faded and the shop was quiet again. I felt like a fool, thinking over every stupid thing I'd said and every thing I'd failed to say, stupidly.

The check was for a thousand dollars, on the account of William H. and Jocelyn P. Sherman. I set it down on an unworked stone, reached for my Scotch, and drank the last of it off in one shot. Jocelyn's glass was still on the windowsill, its rim smeared with pink rose lipstick from the one touch of her lips. After only the slightest hesitation, I finished that off as well and gasped for breath.

Patience and humility my ass, I thought. I am, at best, the imperfect representative of a fine old tradition. I walked to the truck, and wrestled the trash can the rest of the way onto the bed. I felt like crying, vaguely; but I also couldn't help thinking that if I got to the bank before it closed and cashed that check, I'd be able to pay the dump fee after all.

CHAPTER FOUR

The Bank of Southeastern Virginia kept mercifully late Saturday afternoon hours, to allow the farmers to get in. Susie, the teller, seemed surprised to see me, and more surprised that I was not there to explain a check bouncing or some other financial failure. She studied Bill Sherman's check for a long moment as if she suspected a scam, then made a few keystrokes on her computer.

"I can't cash this," she told me. "You have a negative balance of $17.73."

"That's sort of the point of wanting to cash the check," I said.

"You can deposit it, that's no problem—"

"The guy at the dump prefers cash."

"—but it will be three working days before the funds are available."

"Three days!"

She shrugged and gestured vaguely at the computer, invoking its authority. "We have to wait for it to clear."

"I thought things cleared in nanoseconds now," I said.

Susie shrugged again, and had the grace to look mildly distressed. It was a stand-off. I stood there with my driver's license on the counter and she continued to draw strength from the computer screen. The people behind me in line discreetly craned their necks, to see whether they should be worried about stray gunfire from a botched robbery, or just annoyed.

After a long moment Susie said, a trifle plaintively, as one human being to another, "There's really nothing I can do."

I considered the irony of compassion in this instance, briefly weighed my felony options, then conceded, "I guess I'll just deposit it, then."

She smiled in relief. I filled out the deposit slip, slid the paper toward her as ungrudgingly as possible, and accepted my receipt. She told me to have a good day and I nodded and left the bank. The smell of the trash can in the back of my truck had not improved with its time in the sun. I could live with that, I supposed. But I had really been hoping to be able to get to a bar. All the gravestone shops in all the towns in all the world, and she walks into mine.

* * *

Jocelyn Page and I rode the same bus home from school in the fourth grade for almost a year before we ever said a word to each other, but I was in love with her from the moment I saw her as only a nine-year-old can be. There were two fourth grade classes at Woodstock Elementary School, in the Kempsville region of Virginia Beach and she was in the other one, which I took as fate. But I had the bus ride. Jocelyn got off three stops before I did and I waited all day long for that moment in the afternoon. I would always sit at the window seat at the extreme right rear of the bus and watch her from the moment she hopped down onto the street with her book bag and her patent leather Thom McAn shoes. Her rich brown hair was long and straight then, and usually tied back in a pony tail. Sometimes she wore it in a French braid, held up with bobby pins, which I thought made her look like a princess.

Mine was a simple adoration. I loved her brown knees, set off by white knee socks. I loved her face. I don't know why it is that certain faces are magical for us, why a particular set of features should seize us with the conviction that all of love and meaning can be found in the way a particular eyebrow lifts, or the way the corner of a mouth—of just that mouth—tucks in to suggest a smile. But Jocelyn's face always seemed like a miracle to me.

We never exchanged a word or even a glance. If I passed her in the hall at school, I lowered my eyes like a commoner before nobility. But I lived for her presence. She only missed one day of school all year and the bus ride that day was so empty that my life seemed to have passed into a desert; and when she was back the next day as usual, I felt that water was running again in dry stream beds and the flowers could bloom once more.

The only time the fourth-grade classes were lumped together was on Field Day that spring, when we all competed in various athletic events. I was the fastest runner in my class, by enough that it had never been an issue, but it turned out that Jocelyn was the fastest kid in the school. In the final heat of the fifty-yard dash, I was surprised to find her two strides ahead of me, her ponytail bobbing. Truly, I was happy just to be that close. She gave me a smile after the race, of camaraderie more than triumph, which seemed exceptionally kind to me, since the two of us going head-to-head had inevitably turned into a class pride thing and all her classmates were cheering her win as if a crucial issue had been decided, while my classmates were downcast by the loss. I ended up catching a certain amount of teasing for having lost to a girl, but that didn't bother me in the least. Jocelyn had beaten everyone, after all. She had a film of sweat on her smooth tan forehead, but she wasn't even out of breath.

She beat me in the standing long jump too, by almost half a foot, but that was an event that did not involve interaction and so was wasted as far as I was concerned. The final event was the jump-and-reach, in which you reached up flat-footed to make a chalk mark on a high green board, then jumped and made another mark at the top of your leap. The teacher officiating the event left all the chalk marks on the board, and when my turn came up, Jocelyn's mark was already there, in rose-colored chalk, four inches above the field. It seemed well within my range, but for some reason I was loath to beat her, and when I jumped I simply crossed her mark with my blue chalk as if completing an X. I miscalculated slightly, however, and the judge felt that her mark was higher, so when the ribbons were given out, Jocelyn got the blue one again, her third, while I ended up with another red.

On the bus after school that day, I made my way as usual to the right rear, taking my seat by the window. Jocelyn got on a moment later, with her little pack of friends. She was quite popular, the center of her circle and an effortless trend setter, but she never let that go to her head. Even then, I was solitary as a wolf for the most part.

She and her friends always sat about three seats back from the front of the bus, more or less out of range of the barrages of spit balls, paper airplanes, and chewed gum that the boys in the far rear tended to toss forward. Today, though, Jocelyn walked past her usual seat, continued straight down the aisle with an ease that suggested she'd been doing it since September, and slid into the seat beside me.

"Hey there," she said.

There was a moment's stunned silence in the usually boisterous rear. No girl had ventured farther than halfway back on the bus all year, so this was quite an event. It had happened so quickly that I didn't have time to panic or plan, but I was keenly conscious of the boys immediately behind us in the long bench seat that stretched across the rear of the bus, the hardest of the hardcore rowdies. I was afraid that they were going to start pulling

31

Jocelyn's hair or snatch her backpack or otherwise get crude and stupid with a girl back there, and that I was going to have to waste this grace, this obvious gift from God, by getting into a fight.

But Jocelyn's perfect aplomb carried the moment through. The backrow boys were briefly baffled into quiet—not awe, but something close—and then through some collective animal decision they just started punching each other again, knocking each other's books on the floor, and throwing things with renewed vigor toward Jocelyn's friends up front, who were all giggling and tittering with their own heightened electricity by now, their girl radars alive to the extraordinary developments in the rear.

Relieved of any need to defend her honor, I was free to meet Jocelyn's open brown gaze and begin my lifelong study of her eyes. I was astonished to find myself not only at ease, but filled with a blossoming warmth. It was as if my real self had just been waiting until it was touched by her look to make itself felt, like one of those plants whose leaves curl up at night and open at the first touch of sunlight. It turned out that my life until that moment had been a kind of twilight, the gray hush just before dawn.

"Hey," I said.

She reached into her book bag, took out her math book, and opened it. Lying inside the cover was the blue ribbon for the jump-and-reach. I saw that Jocelyn had cut it neatly in half, lengthwise. She met my eyes with a smile that even then seemed to know everything important and held out one of the halves to me.

"I think this is yours," she said.

I got off the bus that day at her stop instead of mine, and after that, the two of us were inseparable. Jocelyn could run faster and jump higher than I could, of course, and it turned out that she could hit a baseball better too, until well into junior high school. She was even smarter.

But somehow I did not mind. She never rubbed it in. We were best friends from that first day and everything we did was lit with the joy of doing it together. Every afternoon after school, we would do my paper route with Jocelyn sitting on the handlebars of my sturdy blue three-speed Schwinn, tossing the papers into the driveways more accurately than I ever had. That done, we would take off for the woods and be explorers, or ride our bikes as far as we could go and still get back by dinnertime, or collect bottles along the side of Providence Road to turn in for the deposits to fund our various grand projects, such as magnifying glasses and other evidence-gathering tools for our detective agency, or a cheap Kodak Instamatic during our nature photography phase, or the walkie-talkies we had for a while, wearing out sets of batteries until we got busted for using them in school.

I believe both sets of parents were briefly concerned, but the essential innocence of the thing prevailed. It was understood between Jocelyn and me that we loved each other, but the word was too gooey for either of us to say anything to that effect until the summer after fifth grade, when our fifth grade teacher got married. All the kids were invited and it was an occasion of some awe for us. At the reception afterward, inspired perhaps by the high solemnity of the event, I gave Jocelyn the second Get Smart Decoder Ring from a set of two I had acquired, and a note that said "EHKRAUKABKNARAN."

She used the ring to decipher the message as "I love you forever," folded the note carefully and stashed it in her pocket, then slipped the decoder ring onto her finger and met my eyes.

"Does this mean we're engaged?" she asked.

"Yes," I said. "I mean, if that's okay with you."

"Of course," Jocelyn said. "I love you forever too."

CHAPTER FIVE

I slept badly the night after Jocelyn and her husband showed up at my shop. I consider my frequent insomnia a professional failure. It is my business, after all, to be at some peace with mortality. I know my grandfather always slept the sleep of the just, woke fresh, and went about his sorrowful business as if the joy of eternity were as certain and immediate as the stone he worked with. But death keeps me awake.

The clock read 3:30 when I surfaced from the murky dreams of my latest sweaty doze: something about a weeping marble lamb. I closed my eyes again, determined to not dwell on it, and found myself obsessing instead about Jocelyn Page Sherman: standing by the window in my shop, the afternoon light gentle on the fine high bones of her perfect cheeks. Dry-eyed, her daughter dead, and her husband weeping before writing the check. It seemed wrong that, amid such intensity, all I could really think was how beautiful she was.

I tried to read for a while, but didn't get much past the fact that I was still using that half of the blue ribbon from the fourth-grade jump-and-reach as my bookmark. It had long since grown badly tattered and I'd had to have it laminated at some point to keep it from falling apart entirely.

Finally I just cut my losses and got out of bed. I made a pot of coffee to clear my head, filled my big plastic Redskins travel mug, and got into my truck to drive to the shop, figuring I would just get to work. I was already to the Pungo stoplight before I remembered that the shop had no electricity. I had kerosene lanterns and flashlights, and even a portable generator I could have fired up, but the thought of all that bad light and noise was just too much for me and so I turned left at the light instead, and drove out through the swamps along the Northwest River, heading west and then north toward Surry County.

* * *

Awe, Virginia is a town that never quite happened, but it took such a good run at becoming someplace that, more than three hundred years later, it is still almost, but not quite, happening. There are no signs to the place anymore, if there ever were, but if you drive north through Isle of Wight County and take the right turn off Highway 10 at the Bacon's Castle Store toward Hog Island, and then turn north onto Hog Island Road and follow the signs toward the nuclear power plant at Drewry Point, you're in the neighborhood.

About a quarter mile past Olde Brickyard Road, there is a left turn, west toward Lower Chippokes Creek. The road is unpaved but graveled at the low spots, and it runs southwest between some peanut fields into a thin forest of loblolly pines interspersed with witch hazel and cinnamon ferns. You can smell

the skunk cabbage in the marshier areas and catch whiffs of
trumpet honeysuckle during the summer.

After half a mile or so, there is a slight rise in the road,
then a last, sharp turn, and suddenly you are clear of the trees and
standing before you is what at first glance appears to be some kind
of ancient ruins, a facade of limestone blocks, with intricate lintels,
tympani, and pointed archivolts on the empty bays that were
intended to be populated by angels and saints. Across a limestone
porch, smoothed by more than three centuries of rain, the three
doorless portals of the entry are flanked by uncompleted stone
towers. Beyond these, an unroofed nave is enclosed by weathered
stone walls, almost forty feet tall in spots, just high enough to begin
to indicate where the stained glass windows would have been, and
along the walls on the outside are the massive piers that would
have grounded the buttresses. At the eastern end of the site, the
crumbled brick ruins of a small chapel stand within the circular
foundations for the apse. For half a century, in the late 1600s, the
cathedral of St. Stephen rose from the sands of Hog Island, funded
by a run of good tobacco crops and fueled by royalist politics and
local pride. The project petered out early in the reign of William
and Mary; and nowadays, taken as a whole, the unfinished cathedral
of what was once called Auwe, Virginia, looks something like the
hulk of a stone ark that didn't float for its flood.

I parked the truck near the trace of the old road that ran
on past the building site and down to the creek, along which the
materials had been hauled during the building's active construction
phase during the seventeenth century, and approached the looming
western facade, moving carefully but surely in the dark. I have been
coming to the place for decades now and can move around the site
by the gravity of the stone alone, steering by mass and memory and
only occasionally stubbing my toe.

Passing through the leftmost of the entry passages, I
settled in my usual pre-dawn spot, right about where the font for
the holy water would have been. From here the nave stretched
before me as a long pool of black, punctuated by the deeper

vertical blackness of the chimneylike piers. At the far end, the wrecked brick chapel was nothing but a smudge in the starlight, crumbling around the only altar this place has ever known.

Farther on, beyond the deeper black of the trees and fields and marshes, and the wide place in the James River where it turns south beyond the Hog Island peninsula, the sky to the east was just beginning to lighten. The cathedral was laid out in the traditional fashion, pointing toward the spot where the sun emerges on the summer solstice, and it is possible, on mornings like this, to imagine the rising sun someday searing a great rose window into life in the wall of an unbuilt apse. It is even possible, surrounded by two-hundred-million-year-old stone hewn and laid by men who have been dead with their hopes and dreams for more than three centuries, to believe that all of history is not futility, and to remember, for a moment, without pain.

* * *

Jocelyn Page and I stumbled onto the non-town of Awe and its unfinished cathedral the summer after our sophomore year in high school, during a prolonged birdwatching phase the two of us went through, in lieu of dealing with the unnerving issue of our adolescent sexuality.

We had managed to get through Jocelyn's training bras, armpit shaving, and the onset of her period, and my early erections and wet dreams and interest in the brassiere models in the Sears catalogue, without ever admitting that these things might have an impact on our relationship. We were both late bloomers, which was a break in a way, but you can only defer certain crises so long. I had just gotten my driver's license that summer, so we didn't spend as much time on bicycles, but otherwise we were bent on pretending that we were still best friends in grade school, roaming the dwindling forests of Kempsville with twin pairs of binoculars, the 1947 edition of Roger Tory Peterson's *Field Guide to the Birds of Eastern and Central North America*, and a sort of desperate mutual earnestness. We had always been good together in the woods and the birdwatching kept our attention above shoulder level most of the time. It may have been the last moment in my life when I could see a kingfisher without thinking of the maimed and impotent king of the wasteland in the Grail cycle.

We came upon the cathedral late in the afternoon on a Saturday during the dog days of August, after a day in the wildlife refuge on Hog Island, having turned down the unmarked road into the woods only because we were exhausted by a long day of snowy egrets, green-winged teal, and relentless sublimation, and looking for a shortcut back to Highway 10.

I remember the moment the way you remember how you got a scar. Jocelyn had just told me that Jimmy Benoit had asked her out, to a movie, and that she was going to go. I suspect that she had waited until we were on our way home to break this news because she was as terrified as I was of what it all meant. Jocelyn had gone out on several dates during junior high school, stilted and utterly unthreatening outings, bruising fiascos at skating rinks and dinners at McDonald's where the dollar bills ran short. One guy had tried a few holds of his own after they went to a J.V. wrestling match together, but Jocelyn had eluded him easily enough with a sit-out escape and regained the upper hand without much fuss. "Jocelyn 3, Date 0," as she had wryly summed up the adventure for me the next day.

But Jimmy Benoit was a brand-new thing. He was a halfback on the football team, smart and completely un-dweeby, and certainly the first guy to ask Jocelyn out who had to shave. The end of our innocence had arrived. It was not just that the Get Smart Decoder Rings no longer fit on our teenage fingers, or that I could, at last, throw a baseball better than Jocelyn and take her in a footrace. The knees that had dazzled me in fourth grade, shining above her knee socks or covered with band-aids after one of our frequent bicycle wrecks, now led into long slim thighs browned by the Virginia sun to the shade of a smooth coffee liqueur. I knew every scar on those knees, but they were different knees now. At sixteen, Jocelyn was four inches taller than I was, coltish and almost ungainly, with ankles and wrists as thin and delicate as the bones of a songbird. Her cheekbones had surfaced, her eyebrows had sharpened, and her face as a whole had grown infinitely subtle and so varied in expression that I would never quite catch up again, though it would be my joy and what felt like my true vocation to try.

Perhaps most crucially, though, Jocelyn had breasts—sweet, still compact, and dizzyingly luscious. She had barely begun to awaken to their impact. But I was thoroughly impacted. I had no doubt that Jimmy Benoit had noticed those breasts too, and I was afraid to even begin to imagine what she had noticed about him.

And so I was in a state of quiet but savage despair, and struggling to maintain a working pretense of the just-friends-now supportiveness that seemed to be called for, when the road bumped into Chippokes Creek, indicating that the hoped-for shortcut wasn't going to work out, and then hooked north, confirming that we were a bit lost.

"We should probably just turn around," Jocelyn offered, gently pragmatic, understanding that I was in a bad state of mind.

I nodded obligingly, but did not immediately slow the car. Truly, I was in no hurry to take the most efficient route back to a world in which Jocelyn was going to the movies with Jimmy Benoit.

And so we cleared the last stand of trees and the western facade of the cathedral loomed before us like a sudden cliff, the first upthrust of a newly forming mountain or the last shard of an eroded range, the low-angled sunlight warming the rose veins in the limestone, the stunted towers jutting raggedly at either side like early phases of uncompleted moons.

I felt at once the strange grace of the place. It imposed its own time scale, made moments of years and centuries. I would later learn some of the uneven history of the project, uncovering the scars and ashes of ungrieved tragedies and forgotten farces, the lives spent, aspirations tempered, and ambitions thwarted there;

but that first day the cathedral presented itself as something complete just as it was, an awesome given.

Beside me, Jocelyn had fallen silent too. I stopped the car and we got out without a word. As we approached the ruins, she took my hand, spontaneously. We passed through the center portal and the vastness of the nave opened before us, its space halved neatly into light and dark by the long late-afternoon shadow from the facade. We eased up the center aisle, staying slightly to the right, gripped by an instinctive humility. The stone beneath our feet was ankle-deep in drifted sand, but the pattern of the flooring showed through occasionally and halfway to the central crossing, just beyond the sharp line where the deep shadow of the towered western front gave way to brightness, something glinted in the sunlight. It was a small Celtic-style crucifix of crudely cast pewter, black-gray with age and weather, exposed by a recent rainstorm. Jocelyn picked it out of the sand and held it in her hand as we went on.

My unusual childhood with my grandfather, our many trips together to the National Cathedral in Washington, D.C., had given me a surprisingly vivid sense of the basics of cathedrals and their construction; but my grandfather's cathedral was a museum dinosaur of a church, neatly assembled, serene, and exemplary. The cathedral on Hog Island was raw, a gutted carcass sprawled in the sand, unsettling as a fresh Tyrannosaurus kill, still smelling of blood.

The church's construction had progressed unevenly, with the western facade ending up well ahead of the eastern end, but the columnar piers of the nave's arcade level were all in place, solid chimneys of stacked limestone, forty feet tall, awaiting their structural loads. It was almost eerie to see them so complete and undisturbed: Set up the falsework for the arches, I thought, and you could have started the clerestory level vaulting tomorrow.

The first level of vaulting, in the bays of the arcade, was also complete along the length of the nave, to where the choir would have begun. Jocelyn and I peered into the homely, almost

hut-like, little brick chapel, the tiny mustard seed of this massive
growth. We discovered one of the spiral staircases built into the
wall near the crossing of the south transept and climbed it eagerly,
emerging, breathtakingly, above the arcade.

Here you could walk right along the top of the wall, at the
building's growing edge. Jocelyn and I sat down on the ledge and
dangled our feet into the nave, looking north. From this vantage
point, the cathedral's essential cruciform outline could be seen
clearly, though the transepts were laid out only in their foundations.
Apparently the plan had been to finish the main body of the
church first; and even then they had gotten ahead of themselves
and completed more of the most impressive part, the west facade,
before getting very far with the apse. Probably it was separate
crews and the guy running the crew on the west end was just way
better. They'd probably figured it would all catch up with itself
eventually, in God's time, and then it had all crapped out. It was a
scary thought to a teenager trying to be patient in love.

The late afternoon sun was just slipping behind the
western front to our left and the shade was a sweet relief from the
August heat. I was conscious of the bright sheen of sweat on
Jocelyn's long thighs, and conscious of trying to not be conscious
of that, and so on. She was wearing a white camisole that
sharpened her tan to a rich nut brown and her shoulders and chest
had a light scattering of freckles, each of which I wanted to lavish
kisses on. A single drop of sweat had gathered at the cleft of her
breasts. To touch my tongue to that salty spot would have left me
free to die happy.

"Are you jealous?" Jocelyn asked.

"Excuse me?"

She took a breath. "Jealous. I think you might be jealous."

"Of Jimmy Benoit?"

She nodded patiently, as if to say, Well, duh. She was not
playing games; Jocelyn did not do that. She just really needed to
know. And she seemed as frightened as I was, of what any of the
possible answers might mean.

I considered lying, in a purely tactical sense, or playing dumb, which came naturally enough to me. It certainly wouldn't do to tell her I was jealous of that drop of sweat in her cleavage. If I was going to have to do some long grueling stint as just a friend, I wanted Jocelyn to feel that I was serene with whatever role she cast me in, at any given moment in her life. I just wanted to be around for the long run. But if you're going to count on true love prevailing, you have to count on truth too, and finally I said, "My grandfather always tells me that he fell in love with my grandmother the first time he laid eyes on her. She was a younger woman, in sixth grade then, while he was in eighth—"

Jocelyn smiled, clearly wondering where I was going with this. "Not fourth?"

I shrugged. "He was a late bloomer. He says my grandmother wouldn't give him the time of day at that point. But he was patient, he just let things develop at their own pace, and he kept his cool while my grandmother dated hundreds of boys, through junior high and high school—"

Jocelyn laughed. "Hundreds!"

"That's my grandfather's story, and he's sticking to it. My grandmother says it might have been three or four. She didn't succumb to my grandfather's charm until April of his senior year. They went out for ice cream cones, finally. He had vanilla, she had chocolate, and that was that."

"Happily ever after."

"Amen and forever. I asked my grandfather once if he had ever gotten nervous as all that time went by and my grandmother still hadn't come around, and he just laughed and said, No, not a bit, he trusted God and true love too much to ever doubt it for a moment."

Jocelyn was silent for a moment, and then she said, very quietly, "So you're saying you're not a bit concerned about Jimmy Benoit?"

"No," I said. "I'm terrified. I wish Jimmy Benoit would disappear from the face of the earth. I'm saying I don't know how my grandfather ever made it through high school."

Jocelyn laughed, genuinely surprised. And, to my relief, clearly delighted. I loved her so much that it was always hard for me to realize she could have her own doubts about being loved, and her own terrors within. But she had been scared too.

Our eyes met, for what felt like the first time in ages, in our old deep quiet way. Everything seemed right as it was, just like that, and there was time for everything. I had forgotten what that felt like. The world was simple once more, and my eyes filled with spontaneous tears.

I touched Jocelyn's face, tracing her cheekbone softly, as if it were the edge of a butterfly's wing. It was all I wanted and all I had ever wanted, to touch her so, and then she kissed me and that was all I had ever wanted too and forever. Her lips were firm and dry and delicate as a communion wafer, and her tongue was like a taste of wine. I could feel my heart in my chest, and when her hand came up to touch my face, it seemed to me that it made my skin real for the first time. My grandfather was a natural. But I have had so much to learn.

"You're so silly to think I could ever love anyone but you," Jocelyn said.

* * *

The sun was up now, a sweet cool spring dawn, pitched to the left of the chapel as you looked east along the nave. I stirred, and stretched my legs. In the early light, the cathedral looked much the same as it had in the days when Jocelyn and I first came upon it, but toward the apse there were several layers of fresh limestone in the wall, the unweathered blocks as obvious as new growth on a tree. As far as I know, no one had set stone on stone here for three centuries; but I have been quietly working on the cathedral myself, on weekends and slow days, for almost a decade now. I get the limestone free for the drilling, breaking, and hauling, from a pal who runs a quarry west of Richmond, and just take things one block at a time. It usually seems obvious to me that I am not even keeping up, on the whole, with erosion; but at least it is a work in progress. By my calculations, the church of St. Stephen has been under construction now for about three hundred and fifty years—a bit late on delivery, even by the usual two- or three-century standard of most cathedrals. But I prefer to think of the building as off to a slow start.

CHAPTER SIX

I spent most of the morning and early afternoon working up sketches of little Ariel Sherman's memorial. The process was painful and humbling, and I felt the Shermans' desperate loss throughout it. I kept the photo of Ariel Sherman close, to keep me honest. I actually couldn't imagine what sort of memorial I would have made if it had been my child. Job on his dung-heap, maybe. Lear out in the storm, raging against the elements. Prometheus, chained to a gravestone, with vultures feeding on his liver.

At no point did I let myself dwell on the fact that this grave was for the daughter of Jocelyn Page. There was nothing to do with that. So I did nothing, which was just as well, as I barely had the basic package together by late afternoon, just in time to be slightly late to my appointment with the Shermans. It was only when I got into my truck and started down the dirt road toward town that I thought, *God help me do this right for her.* It seemed as much as my own heart could really bear.

* * *

The Shermans' house was almost to the end of Little Neck Road, a big pseudo-Tudor thing built into a slight hillside among the oaks and pine trees above the Lynnhaven River. There was a three-car garage and a big boat docked out back, but the stone walkway winding up through masses of blooming azaleas to the front entrance was in a state of mild disrepair. They had used an inferior blueish slate and it had aged badly under the traffic. An addition was under construction on the left side of the house, what looked like an extra bedroom, already roofed and tarpapered, with stacks of shingles and siding ready in the side yard. I wondered whether the additional room had been intended for their daughter; but the thought was too brutal to dwell on.

Before ringing the bell, I paused on the broad front step, also of degrading slate, to belatedly consider my attire. I was wearing what I had dressed in at 3:30 that morning, a tee-shirt from Munden's Bar in Pungo, old jeans from which a puff of stone dust would spurt if I slapped them, and my scarred steel-toed work boots, designed so that if I drop a boulder on my foot, the foot will at least be crushed into a regular shape. It was too late to change now; and in any case, if you hire a stone worker, you get the stone worker dressed to work with stone. But I felt that I was on solid historical ground, looking a bit seedy. In 1232, the French bishops decided that the cathedral masons had gotten out of hand and decreed that all stone workers dress better, cut their hair, and shave their beards. All over Europe, masons promptly went on strike, and work on the cathedrals halted. Thousands of stone workers were arrested and imprisoned, but the masons held their ground, and even upped the stakes, threatening to burn the cathedrals unless the dress code was rescinded. In the end, the bishops gave in;

cathedral construction resumed, to everyone's relief; and that was the last time, to my knowledge, that anyone has tried to tell masons how to dress.

I rang the bell and a mellow, three-toned chime resonated within the house. A moment later the door opened and a young boy peered out at me. He was about ten—the same age I had been when I had fallen in love with his mother, more or less. The thought was a little dizzying. His hair was sandy, like his father's, but he had Jocelyn's distinctive broad forehead and the same plane on his cheekbones, and he had Jocelyn's eyes, so precisely that I had to remind myself that I didn't know him already.

"Are you the gravestone guy or the plumber?" he asked.

"The gravestone guy." His look said he would have preferred the plumber. "What do you need a plumber for?"

"Joshua flushed a tracking device down the toilet and it got stuck."

"A tracking device?"

"You know, like spies put on cars and stuff. A GPS transponder."

"You're kidding."

"He's trying to figure out where the poop goes."

"Joshua is your brother?" He nodded. "Older or younger?"

"He's eight." And, as I was obviously trying to reconcile that with so much ambitious high-tech sewer line analysis, he added, matter-of-factly, "He's an evil genius."

"Not too much of a genius, if his thing got stuck in the toilet."

The kid brightened. "That's what *I* said!"

"What's *your* name?"

"Billy."

William Junior, of course. I was still having a hard time adjusting to the unexpected intimacy of Jocelyn's eyes peering at me from the kid's face. I said, "I'm Eli."

"I know. You were my mother's boyfriend in high school."

"Who told you that?"

"Nobody," he said. "Little pitchers have big ears."

I laughed. "I'll keep that in mind. Are your parents around?"

They're upstairs. Mom's upset. Dad said to tell you he'd be down in a minute."

I considered pumping the big-eared little pitcher for more information on Jocelyn's condition, then felt the lowness of that.

"So, where's this toilet?" I asked.

* * *

Billy led me down the main hall and through a spacious sunny kitchen, then along a small hallway off the garage. The bathroom was to the right, a big guest thing complete with a shower. Beyond it, I could see the interior of the room under construction, the floors at the plywood stage, the walls still showing drywall, with some kind of paneling stacked in the center of the room.

Inside the bathroom, the evil genius Joshua was kneeling beside the toilet. He was smaller than his brother, with blonder hair, and Jocelyn's eyes in him had taken on some of the green from the Sherman side. He had a portable computer balanced on the trash can and was contemplating its screen like an air traffic controller during a thunderstorm with half a dozen planes running low on fuel.

I squatted beside the kid. The toilet was full right to the brim, the water mercifully clean. On the screen of the computer, I could see a grid map of the area, with a flashing red dot centered at the Sherman's house. The dot was definitely not moving.

Joshua barely glanced up as I entered, then returned his eyes to the screen.

"Has the toilet been draining at all?" I asked immediately, as he clearly was in no mood for small talk.

He shook his head. "It was draining slowly for a while, but I think the transponder shifted, and now there's nothing going

48

through."

"Did the thing have square edges or something?" He looked at me like I was an idiot. "Hey, you're the one whose GPS is stuck in a toilet pipe."

Joshua took a measured breath, clearly striving for patience. "It's ovate," he said.

"Ovate."

"Ellipsoidal. I put it inside an Easter egg. To facilitate the hydraulics. I'd calculated the diameter and the widest part of the egg should have had three millimeters of clearance at the narrowest point in the pipe."

"It must have gotten turned sideways, somehow."

"That's what I'm thinking too."

"So all we've got to do is bump it, right?"

"In theory," Joshua said. "But it's already past the U. I can't get at it, even with a bent fork."

I had already noted the fork, which looked like a Uri Geller botch. A sacrifice to science. I said, "Well, the first thing we need to do is bail some of this water out, to give us some room to work in."

Billy, who had been deferring to the main team since our arrival in the bathroom, promptly went off to the kitchen to fetch something suitable. While he was gone, Joshua and I considered the blinking red light on the computer screen again. Still not moving.

"Your brother said you're trying to find out where the poop goes?"

"Yeah," Joshua said. "I'm afraid it goes straight into the river."

I nodded, impressed. I'd never met an eight-year-old who worried about where his shit went, much less one prepared to flush a GPS transponder down a toilet to find out. "I'm pretty sure the sewage goes to a treatment plant somewhere first."

"That's what they said about the storm drains. But look at this—" Joshua tapped some keys and called up another map, on a larger scale. The blinking red light on this one was in the middle of the Chesapeake Bay. "That one started in the drain down the street last Friday."

"Yikes," I said.

"I get constipated just thinking about it," Joshua said.

* * *

By the time Bill Sherman came downstairs ten minutes later, Billy had returned from the kitchen with a Tupperware bowl and we had bailed out most of the water from the toilet, found a plumber's snake in the garage, and gently nudged the GPS egg into motion again. The flashing red light was on its way south under the front yard, moving slowly toward the main gravity line along the street, when the boys' father appeared in the doorway of the bathroom.

Sherman smiled at the sight of his sons and me huddled around the computer screen.

"It looks like we can tell the plumber not to come," he said.

Joshua gave me a look. "I thought *you* were the plumber."

"No, he's the gravestone guy," Billy said.

"Jack of all trades, master of none," I said. I stood up to go with their father, and said to Joshua, "Keep us updated, Mission Control."

"Roger that," he said.

"It's moving again?" Sherman asked, as we moved down the hall into the kitchen. We could hear the boys running the water in the bathtub, filling the Tupperware container and dumping the water down the toilet to help the egg along.

"Yeah. Away from the river, so far."

"I hope to God that thing ends up in a treatment plant," he said. "I've already blown my credibility with Josh on the storm drains. Did you know those damn things run straight into the river?"

"I was shocked."

"Me too." He paused at the refrigerator. "Can I get you something to drink? Coffee, orange juice? Scotch, with a splash of water?"

It complicated my already complex feelings for the man, that he had noted and remembered what I'd drunk the day before. The refrigerator door was crowded with family photographs held in place by magnets. My eyes went to a shot of Bill Sherman in a wading pool with his daughter. Ariel was wearing water wings on her arms and a pink polka dot bikini, her irrepressible curls barely impeded by the water. She was bright and laughing, carefree in the pool with Daddy, as happy as a human being can look. I thought again that there was no way my heart could stand this job.

"What are you drinking?" I said.

"Beer, I guess. The sun's over the yardarm, right?"

"By a good margin. I'll take a Bud."

I had meant to be low-maintenance, but he looked chagrined. I glanced into the open refrigerator and saw that there was nothing in there but German brews, something Danish, and something Czechoslovakian.

"I meant a Pilsner Urquell," I said.

Sherman laughed appreciatively and grabbed two. "I'm afraid I'm a bit of a beer snob," he offered apologetically as he opened them.

"Beer snobs don't say they're beer snobs," I said. "I think you probably just have good taste." It was too late to not like the guy, but with a little luck, I still had hopes that we could avoid being friends.

Sherman led us into the family room, which was rimmed with plastic bins full of toys, games, and stuffed animals. The coffee table was cluttered genially with airplanes and some race cars, and a big-screen TV loomed from the far corner. Above the fireplace hung a large framed photograph of the entire family, including Ariel, formally posed and painfully happy. The wall above the couch served as a sort of gallery for the kids' art and was crowded with finger-painted masterpieces and crayoned scenes. The boys' styles were quite distinct: Billy favored precise landscapes with animals, while Joshua already seemed to be designing nuclear reactors or something, and worked mostly in black and white. There were a number of mixed-media pieces involving macaroni and glitter. Ariel, I noted, had just started drawing stick people with balloons and big smiles on their faces, in exuberant colors.

Several of the toy bins were full of dolls, alphabet learning games, and things that made noises in complex ways pleasing to a three-year-old. I wondered briefly how Bill Sherman could stand it all; but I supposed his whole life was like that now.

Sherman sat down on the couch and I took the place beside him.

"What do I owe you for the plumbing work?" he asked.

I gave him a sharp glance, but he obviously didn't mean to insult me. It was just his way. I was an employee, and employees got paid for their services.

"No charge," I said. "I did it in the interests of science." And, as he hesitated, "Joshua would have figured out something soon enough anyway."

Sherman smiled at the truth of that. "He *is* amazing, isn't he?"

"He gets it from you, I'd guess."

"I don't know about that. Jocelyn's smart as a whip."

"It's all people-smarts, though." He looked vaguely troubled at this, resisting it, and I realized that I'd strayed into tricky territory somehow. Maybe it was the presumption that I might know his wife in some ways better than he did. Maybe he thought I was saying he and his kid were clueless wonks. I could have told him about the fifth-grade geometry class Jocelyn and I had been in together, in which the class project had been to make something illustrating geometric shapes. I had built a church out of empty match boxes and popsicle sticks, with every proportion dictated by the golden ratio of Φ, and Jocelyn had made a stained-glass window, simple as a jewel with leaded facets, nothing but color-drenched figures lit with inner light. She'd always gotten A's in our math and science classes but that was natural facility and a certain noblesse oblige; her real interests lay elsewhere. It seemed that some things that were obvious to me might best be left unnoted with Bill Sherman, however, and I shut up rather than getting myself in deeper.

We both reached for our beers, like tomcats coming face-to-face unexpectedly in an alley. Fortunately, the boys came through the room just then, carrying the computer.

"How's it going?" Sherman asked.

"It's still running along the main line, parallel to the street," Joshua said. "It's far enough away now that we'll get better reception upstairs."

The two of them moved briskly down the hall and clattered up the stairs. Bill Sherman said, "If that thing goes into the river, I'm going to have to buy a composting toilet or something."

"Me too. I'm sure Joshua could design a good one."

"He already has. It uses microwaves to speed up the process."

We sipped our beers again. The Pilsner was excellent, but I tried to ignore that. I couldn't afford to start preferring good beer.

"So, what have you got for us?" Sherman said, getting down to business.

Apparently Jocelyn would not be sitting in on the session. I rode past my uneasiness with that—mine not to reason why—and put my beer down. The coasters Bill Sherman had set out for us on the coffee table were glazed clay disks, hand painted in Rorschach swirls of child colors as vivid as a drunken Matisse. Ariel's work, I thought; everything in this house was a raw nerve. I rode past that, too, and put my beer down on one of coasters, then fetched my folders and schemata. We laid the papers out on the coffee table, making a space amid the airplanes and race cars, and bent over them together.

* * *

I have met with a lot of families over the years. These consultations with the survivors are close to the heart of what I do. Generally, in a way that may seem strange, I enjoy them. Grief makes people so much realer, most of the time. I love that moment when the usual defenses have dropped away and someone looks at you plainly in the light of whatever ultimates death has left them with. My grandfather dwelled in such awe, and it is precious.

But I was edgier than I had ever been. It wasn't just that Jocelyn's absence felt deeply wrong, or even that I was in love with this bereaved and wounded man's wounded and grieving wife. I had also taken some liberties with the material the Shermans had left with me the day before and was anxious about Bill Sherman's reaction. The original guardian cherubs sketched by their architect friend had been atrocious bits of cliché, and the lamb had been a joke, a caricature of innocence that would look silly immediately, turn ludicrous through the years, and might finally even come to seem like a sort of cosmic mockery. I had tried at first to just dilute the originals, on the off-chance that the architect friend would be present at the meeting and raise a fuss; then gave up and re-drew all the figures from scratch, slimming the angels down and aging them a bit, wiping the idiot grins from their faces, and generally trying to have them convey more compassion for the griefs of mortals.

The lamb had been easier: I had done it simple and straightforward, a realistic animal serenely unaware of its metaphoric burden. What I had really wanted to do was introduce a lion, but I figured the Isaiah imagery might be a bit too much. I knew right where I would put it, though, if the opportunity presented itself.

I also intended to make a case for a more enduring stone than marble for the figures: I'd seen too many marble lambs melt away over the years like butter in the sun, until they ended up looking vaguely like seals, and too many angels with their features eroded until their blankness itself seemed eerily complicit with death.

Bill Sherman's choice of an epitaph for his daughter's tombstone, lifted from Samuel Clemens's epitaph for his own child, had been pure heartbreak:

Warm summer sun shine kindly here;
Warm southern wind blow softly here.
Green sod above lie light, lie light
Good night, dear heart, good night, good night.

I had taken a long time finding a script that worked. Nothing Roman, rectilinear, or monumental in the least would do. The architect friend had lettered his in heedless Trajan and the thing looked like an emperor's edict. I had tried one version of something I had seen once in a rural graveyard in Suffolk, just handwritten letters etched with a nail in wet cement, with a couple of the words poignantly misspelled. It seemed perfect to me, but I knew it was too radical, and after many other drafts I had settled for a gentle variation on the Mistral hand lettering, which seemed to me to be about as conventionally informal as the situation could bear.

When we had run through the whole thing once, Bill Sherman was silent, staring at the epitaph, the lamb, and the angels in turn. I reached for my beer, but the bottle was empty; I had drunk it fast, out of nervousness.

"Do you want another one?" he asked, an alert host even in his pain.

"I'll get it myself, thanks," I said. "You want one too?"

"No, I'm good."

I went out to the kitchen and took one of the Danish beers this time. Bill Sherman hadn't budged, when I reentered the family room. I sat down beside him again and sipped at my beer, while he continued to stare at the sketches. The Danish beer appeared to be about 75% alcohol. I began to feel a little light-headed.

"This looks good," Sherman said at last. "Quieter."

I nodded carefully.

"The costs seem low."

"I'm giving you the family rate."

"There's no need to do that."

"Actually, I give everybody the family rate." He didn't smile. So much for the light touch. I said, as gently as I could, "Look, Bill, this isn't about money. For me, or for you."

"No," he said. "I guess it's not."

"So let's just get it right."

He hesitated, still resisting, and then something in him let go, and it was like a fog came off him. He looked at the plans again, but he wasn't seeing them now; he was somewhere else, someplace quiet and deep and real.

After a moment he stood up and crossed the room to stand in front of the sliding glass door that opened onto the back yard. On the patio outside, a barbeque grill stood covered with a tarp, near a round white table with its sun umbrella collapsed onto a central post, ringed by four white metal chairs and a high chair. The patio was ankle-deep in winter leaves, and bordered with flower beds brown with the debris of last year's plants, and the lawn beyond it looked like it hadn't been mowed yet this spring. Farther out in the yard, there was a sandbox littered with colored plastic pails and shovels, a slide, and a swing set with three swings set to different heights, like descending notes on a musical scale.

My grandfather made no bones about the nature of the work he taught me: You stand there, he said, in the glare of death and God and other people's deepest pains and hope— and God help you if you are not up to it.

"You're the third one we've tried to hire for this," Sherman said at last. "The first guy was someone from a company recommended by the funeral home, right after Ariel died." He shook his head, remembering. "We were still just going through the motions then. I mean, she died three days before *Christmas*. Her presents were wrapped already and hidden in the closet. They're still in there, we don't know what the hell to do with them. And this guy is trying to sell us some package deal monument straight out of a catalogue, one from column A and two from column B. It was pretty easy at that point to say no and just wait for a while. I mean, it was bad enough . . . picking out a casket."

His voice trailed off. I held my tongue and waited; there was nothing to do now but love the man.

"We tried again last February," Sherman said. "Right around Ariel's birthday. But it was still too soon. For Jocelyn more than for me, by then. But now. . . " He turned and looked at me. "I'm afraid to let this go any longer, is the thing. I mean, I can't stand it anymore. I go to the grave and there's nothing but grass and a pile of old flowers. I just can't handle that. It feels almost. . . like she never was, somehow. Like she's slipping away. I want something that says, Yes, this life happened. This child was born, and was loved. And is loved still. I'm ready for that. I need that, even." He took a breath, and added, with a note of appeal, almost of defensiveness, "And not just me. We all need to move on. As a family."

I nodded, and said nothing. It wasn't me he was arguing with.

CHAPTER SEVEN

After Bill Sherman had gone upstairs to show the memorial scheme to Jocelyn, I sat for a while on the couch trying to exercise the sort of serene and surrendered patience my grandfather was so good at, and failing. The Danish beer on the coffee table in front of me was only half-finished, but I was already at that point of drunkenness where everything was starting to mean a little more than my heart could bear. The Shermans' family room seemed unnaturally bright and clear, as if all the ordinary objects in it, the family photos and the children's art, the embroidered throw pillows and the toys, were on fire with the household's grief. "Take off your shoes, and come no closer," God told Moses on Mount Horeb, speaking from the bush that burned but was not consumed, "for the place where you are standing is holy ground." A big part of my job is not going insane on holy ground, in the country of awe.

I carried the bottle into the kitchen and dumped the rest of the beer down the sink. I really shouldn't drink on duty, and there is a sense in which I am always on duty. I found a glass in one of the cupboards, filled it with water from the tap, and went out through the sliding glass door into the backyard.

* * *

The afternoon was balmy, the best of a mild spring. A big apple tree in the far corner of the yard shimmered in a blizzard of white blossoms, and along the fence daffodils and irises had asserted themselves in the unweeded borders. There was a rose bush beneath the kitchen window that had been pruned so severely that it looked dead, a splayed bundle of thorny twigs.

I crossed the yard to the swing set, in the shade of the apple tree, and sat down on the left-most of the three swings, which I assumed was Billy Jr.'s, as the seat was set the highest off the ground. From here, the Shermans' house showed nothing but solidity, order, and suburban innocence. The windows of the second floor looked beyond the yard to the river. The bedroom on the upper right had boys' curtains of bright blue, and the room on the left, with cream-colored drapes, was probably the master bedroom. I lowered my eyes before the mystery of what was going on up there between Bill and Jocelyn Sherman, and lit a cigarette.

I started smoking the day my mother died, about five years ago. A ridiculous thing, a sort of cosmic tantrum. She had stomach cancer, diagnosed quite late, and it was not pretty at any point, but her final night was the worst. I was the one in her room that night, and it was like a storm at sea in a tiny boat where every wave swelled into swamping pain and every razor edge of wind slashed something else away and every thought of haven washed out beneath the waves, and by the end there was nothing left, no faith, no hope, no north, no south, no sky to steer by and no memories of landfall; and then the end went on, and on, and on still, beyond all meaning until time itself sank away and there was not even prayer, there was just a boiling sea of suffering without surface or depth, beginning or end, and a love that was everything, and was nothing but pain.

She died just before dawn, in a moment of quiet like the eye of a hurricane: a sad excuse for mercy, but as close as it got, by then. I saw her empty shell into its sack and went back to the house, where my siblings had gathered. My brother was on the porch with a cigarette and I took it out of his hand and breathed it in as deeply as I could, trying to find someplace inside me that was not already scorched and blackened by that night. My brother gaped at me in shock—I'd always been the smoke-averse one among us—and I just shook my head and took another drag. It was my intention never to speak English again; the Word could not unmake itself from flesh soon enough for me.

Half a decade later, the suicidal origins of the practice had receded, more or less; my smoking now was basically just a really bad habit, just like the Surgeon General says, and likely to be the thing that killed me. But it didn't matter much to me anymore how or when or where that black storm came, what shapes and patterns the waves made as they swamped the mortal boat. My mother had lived one of the healthiest lives I knew, and her gravestone was sitting in my shop with the face uncarved, because I hadn't found a way to raise a tool to it yet.

When I had finished the cigarette and ground it out, I looked around for someplace to put the butt. They say those things last thousands of years. The marble angels and the laborious etchings of faith and love on gravestones fade in the rain on a scale of decades, of centuries at best; the face of the Sphinx herself is sanded by the wind until the nose falls off and the savage enigma of her eyes recedes into blind vacuity; but the scorched filters of my Marlboros would be there, wherever I stashed them, for future archeologists. I am Ozymandias, and I died of emphysema. I finally stuck the butt in my pocket.

* * *

A moment later, the back door slid open and Jocelyn emerged. I had been expecting Bill, but I realized that I wasn't surprised. Some deeper part of me had been quietly waiting for this moment, while I went about my work. Some part of me had been waiting for this moment forever, and was waiting for it always.

I got off the swing as she crossed the yard toward me. She moved as I remembered her moving, like a dancer between routines. She was wearing off-white shorts and a light blue T-shirt that said, "GO, LADY MONARCHS," and she was barefoot. Her ankles were still impossibly thin, as delicate as spun glass. I would have thrown myself beneath the treads of a tank to protect those ankles.

Our eyes met as she reached me and her face shifted, one eyebrow cocking slightly, a corner of her mouth tucking back: a soft, sad feather of a smile, almost implicit, wafting over the moment's complexities.

"Hey there," she said.

I was happy, which was inexplicable. We might as well still have been on the bus in elementary school, with the backrow boys on the verge of mayhem immediately behind us and the girls all tittering in speculative amazement toward the front. I was where I wanted to be, with Jocelyn, and the complexities be damned. It really was that simple.

"Hey," I said.

"I'm sorry you had to wait."

I shrugged. A quarter of a century was nothing, as far as I was concerned, an eye blink; but then I realized she meant that afternoon. Or, knowing Jocelyn, maybe she didn't. I said, "It wasn't that long."

"Thank you for your work. The sketches are beautiful."

I heard the tone-setting note of formality with dismay. Like her husband, Jocelyn seemed determined to treat me, scrupulously, with all the civility due a hired hand. I couldn't blame her for that, much as it hurt. But I was not willing to go so quietly.

"It doesn't matter, does it?" I said. "You don't want a bunch of cherubs."

She gave me a glance, neither startled nor offended. It was more as if a child had said something unexpectedly apt and she was deciding how much weight to give it. Her eyes were as they had always been, Franciscan brown, steady and quiet and lit from within; and the grief in them was like an endless fall.

"No," she said quietly, at last. "I want my daughter to be alive."

My heart felt this like the thud of a dull chisel, but there was nothing to say. Work against the strength, my grandfather always said. It is the fundamental truth of working with stone: the weakest spot in a block, the part that is easiest to cleave away, is the stone that will betray you. You can spend days or weeks whittling a block down toward the essence of what you want from it and lose it all at the crucial moment by giving in to the temptation of the quick and easy stroke, the chip at the softer vein that splits unforeseeably and takes too much with it. The way to work with stone is the counterintuitive path of most resistance, the patient grinding at the stone's most unyielding core. It is the slowest way to work, but it is the only way to keep the truth in the stone and not leave it on the floor of the shop. I had waited for this moment with Jocelyn for more than twenty years; and I could only imagine that she had waited for it too, in her way; but there was nothing to do at this point but wait some more. Because the strength in this block of time, the adamantine heart of this moment, was Ariel Sherman.

Jocelyn held my gaze for a moment longer, and the fall went on, and on; and then, with an air almost of concession, as if I had passed some sort of test, she moved to sit on the middle swing, Joshua's swing, as I read it. I sat beside her, on Billy Jr.'s swing again, six inches higher up. The third swing, a foot lower still, gaped to our left, like a wound that might still bleed.

Jocelyn's feet, I noted, bore the faint traces of a fresh tan

line, as if she'd been to the beach once or twice this spring but had
not removed her sandals. Her toenails were unpainted, which I
took as one more disrupting effect of grief. She had always kept up
a lively pedicure of Whisper Pink or Cherry Bomb.

I caught a flash of movement within the house, at the
kitchen window: Bill Sherman, not necessarily monitoring us, just
moving around in there, but definitely making his presence felt.
The ghost of context, as if that empty swing beside us were not
sufficient for sobriety.

Jocelyn had apparently noticed her husband too, because
she said, with an air of dealing with certain necessary preliminaries,
"It really wasn't my idea to hire you, you know. I was against it,
actually."

"That's okay."

"Is it?" she said, frankly dubious.

"I just meant that I'm not insulted."

Jocelyn laughed, to my surprise.

"What?" I asked.

"Nothing. Just, it's impossible to insult you, I think. It
always has been."

I found *that* a little insulting. I said, "I'm perfectly capable
of taking offense." She gave me a look, amused and indulgent, that
said Bullshit. There had never been any fighting that look, and I cut
my losses. "You said at the shop that it was Bill's grandmother's
idea."

"That's right. She kept saying you'd be perfect."

"Well, I'm not," I said. "I have a clear conflict of interest
here. I should already have, um, . . . what's that thing judges do,
when they take themselves off a case?"

"Recused yourself?"

"Yeah. The gravestone carvers' ethics committee will have
my ass."

"They're strict that way, are they?"

"Rigorous." And, as Jocelyn smiled, "Anyway, I don't
think Marietta meant perfect for the job."

"No?"

I hesitated, but I was pretty sure I was on solid ground. Bill's grandmother and I had spent the better part of a week feeling our way toward getting her husband's epitaph right. On the day it finally clicked, we had taken a thermos of tea and some cucumber sandwiches and walked way down the beach south of Sandbridge, so far away from everything that we were stepping around wild pony droppings in the sand. We had found a spot at last near the Back Bay in the lee of a dune and settled in on a wool blanket with a tartan pattern in green and black and purple. We were the only ones in sight on a gray wintry day, and the gulls kept swooping close to check us out. Marietta was sipping Irish Breakfast from the red plastic thermos cup and nibbling on a finger sandwich as she read aloud from the collected poems of Yeats, and when she finally found the lines she wanted it seemed like the world had gone perfectly silent around us and that the breaking waves only made a ripple in the hush.

"Marietta's no fool," I said at last. "She's not talking about how well I can make chisel marks in a rock."

"Well, what, then?"

I hesitated again, but I had already gone out on the limb. "It's something that comes with working with stone, I suppose. You start to see it, because it won't go away: carve some truth in stone, however feeble or corny or seemingly inadequate it seems, and in twenty years or a hundred years it will read true, it will have been worth doing, no matter how you felt about it at the time. Carve something rote or ambitious or hollow, and in six months you'll squirm just to look at it. Carve something too soon—"

"What's your point, sweetheart?"

I blinked. "Did you just call me 'sweetheart'?"

Jocelyn smiled. "In a fond, but impatient sense. With a trace of sarcasm."

It was a touch of the Jocelyn I knew, easy and funny and smart. Which only made things harder, really.

"Darling," I said, "My point is: A gravestone can be a wall

or a window. Something you can't see past, or something that opens to the one you loved. I think what Marietta probably meant is just that I'm the perfect one to tell you that if you do this stone now, it's going to be a wall."

I suppose I had flattered myself that this would come as a revelation to her, but Jocelyn just smiled, gently and sadly. I felt her loneliness in the gesture. She wasn't resisting the truth; it was more as if she was disappointed that I should be so slow on the uptake as to bother to insist on it, as if she had expected better from me.

"It's not that simple," she said.

"No?"

"Bill has decided it's time we got our grieving over with. He's afraid it's going to kill the marriage if we don't get the memorial done soon."

"I know."

She gave me a sharp look. "What did he say?"

"Nothing about the marriage. But there was a note of . . . urgency, I guess. He needs something solid to hang onto right now."

"He needs a wall," Jocelyn said flatly. Her tone had an edge of something like bitterness, and of contempt. Bill Sherman was not wrong: his marriage was in deep trouble.

I said, carefully, "My grandfather would always quote I Corinthians 13 at times like this: 'Though I speak with the tongues of men and angels—'"

"And have not love, blah-blah," Jocelyn said. "But that's the point, don't you see? That's exactly the point. Sounding brass and tinkling cymbal—it's what everyone wants. It's what everyone *needs*."

"No," I said. "It's just what Bill thinks he needs, at this moment. I think what he probably really needs is some more time. Just like you."

She shook her head, almost wearily. "You never married, did you?"

I had never come close, but that wasn't what she was

asking. She was saying that I was naive. As if the misery of marriage were more educational somehow than the misery of solitude.

"No," I said. "I was engaged once, though."

Jocelyn gave me a startled glance. I met her eyes steadily. So much for professionalism, I thought, much less patience and humility. But she had been wrong, earlier: I was completely insultable.

"That doesn't count," she said at last.

"The hell it doesn't."

Jocelyn's eyes flashed, the first sign of her fire I had seen yet. But Bill Sherman's face appeared again just then at the kitchen window, frankly checking up on us this time, no doubt wondering what was complicating the transaction. It seemed worse to me, more intimate by far, to be caught arguing with his wife than to be caught making out with her or something.

Jocelyn seemed to think so too, because she stood up abruptly and said, "Let's walk down to the dock."

She was already moving before I got off the swing, and I never quite caught up with her on the path worn through the grass to the dock. It was the fourth grade fifty-yard dash all over again; apparently she could still outrun me any time she felt like it.

The lawn went over a slight rise and then sloped down to the river. Still a step-and-a-half behind, unwilling to break into the undignified trot it would have taken to actually catch her, I followed Jocelyn past two kayaks laid top-down on the grassy bank and onto the dock itself, which was relatively new and solidly built of weather-treated red cedar. The long main pier ran out to a shorter cross-tee. Jocelyn strode all the way to the far end and sat down without ceremony on the edge with her feet hanging over the water, where I finally caught up.

We sat for a time in silence. Across the water, I could see some of the real big-money estates, grand manors with broad manicured lawns sloping down to the shore. A motorboat labored somewhere around the bend, a low recreational drone.

"I really didn't want to see you again," Jocelyn said at last.

"Not now. Not like this."

I wanted to ask her how she *would* have liked to see me
again, but that wasn't her point. The woman's daughter had died,
her husband was pushing for a premature closure on her grief, and
her irrepressible sons, whose lives after all went on, were probably
at this very moment disrupting the sewer system of the Hampton
Roads area; and here she was faced, unwillingly, with an old lover
making his own mad implicit demand for God-knows-what
emotional impossibility on top of all that. Blessed are they that
mourn, for they shall be comforted, if they can find a moment's
respite from their loved ones.

I said, "I understand."

"I mean, for one thing, my hair is a mess."

I blinked, caught off guard, but that was Jocelyn. There
had never been anything to do with her but steer with the skid. I
said, "Yeah, well, if I'd known you were going to show up, I would
have been on a diet for the last year or two."

"Me too."

"Actually, you look great."

"Don't be ridiculous," she said.

"It's a little late for me to stop now."

She begrudged me a smile, conceding the point. We were
silent for a moment, watching the sunlight flash on the river,
listening to the cries of the cruising gulls. It was cooler here by the
water and, as a mild breeze stirred her hair, I caught a whiff of
something soft, a mild fruit essence, and saw the flesh on Jocelyn's
arms rise into goosebumps. Her skin had always been a
magnificently sensitive instrument.

Or maybe it had been a thought, because she said, "Do
you remember our old spot by the river?"

"Of course," I said, amazed that she would bring that up.
But apparently all I'd had to do for her to relax about our past was
to renounce any claim to it. And Jocelyn had always had more guts
than me in matters of the heart.

The place she was talking about was a sweet little stretch of sand beach beside the James River, in Surry County, not far beyond the cathedral on Hog Island. We used to drive out there a lot, especially during the warm weather when Virginia Beach got too crowded. The spot was wonderfully isolated and always felt like our private beach, though the looming chimney of the Surry County Nuclear Power Plant just to the east was definitely sobering. But even that specter, in those days before Three Mile Island, felt like part of the place's charm.

Given so much privacy and two teenagers in love, the issue of sex was inevitable. But Jocelyn and I had thought it through together; we were holding out for the solemnity of the wedding night, a high-minded position which added an acute erotic tension to those days on the beach.

We did make out, according to a strict Catholic code involving displacement of clothing but no actual removal. As soon as the days turned warm, we would drive out past the peanut fields and pork factories every Saturday and displace as much clothing as possible. During those lubricated days of baking on the sand, Jocelyn in her orange and gold bikini, with its overly firm bra structure and high waist, would make me crazy. She tanned exquisitely, like blond toast, just so; her shoulders and thighs grew smooth and brown in the sun. I oiled her devotedly, applying lotion to her back as she lay on her belly, her face resting on crossed arms. Her sun-bleached hair would be gathered up into an unassailable bun with a Mickey Mouse barrette and six hairpins; her breasts made sweet half-moon bulges on either side of her. Each time I reached the clasp of her bikini top in the course of my lubrications I would hesitate suggestively, then slide my hand beneath the strap, as was our custom. To unhook that clasp was one of the delights toward which I felt our patience and high-mindedness were moving us.

And truly, the sexual limits were no affliction. For me, just being with Jocelyn, anywhere, under any circumstances, was always joy enough. She was the world's best kisser, I worshiped her body, and the rest could wait as far as I was concerned.

And so we savored those warm languid days along the James. We ate ham sandwiches and talked about everything under the sun; we played gin rummy and drank iced tea from a thermos, through those purple straws with six twists in them that you buy on the boardwalk at Virginia Beach. To this day, watching liquid whirl upward through one of those straws remains a slightly dizzying sight for me. Once in the water Jocelyn's bikini top came off under my attentions and her wondrous pale breasts floated free and firm before me, but we both understood that this had occurred offshore and did not need to be confessed. I believe we may have been the only two Catholics in the country under the age of fifty who still went to Confession every Saturday afternoon, right before the evening mass.

I said now, "You smelled like apricots in those days. And coconut, of course."

"The apricot was my shampoo."

"Ah," I said vaguely. I had once begun to sob beside an apricot bin in a farmers' market in San Francisco, and I still choked up regularly in the produce aisles of supermarkets. It was hard to know how to feel about the fact that I had been emoting for more than twenty years over a shampoo.

"There was a little pomegranate in it too."

"Pomegranate!"

She shrugged. "It was a phase."

The breeze stirred again and I caught another whiff of the fragrance that had intrigued me earlier. I leaned a bit closer to Jocelyn's hair and sniffed, trying to be inconspicuous, but she caught me at it, of course, and smiled. Busted. I said, "What phase is this?"

"Asian pear and red tea," she said. "With a hint of freesia."

"You're kidding."

"I don't kid about shampoos."

It was a broad cue to smile, but I missed it. It had been a mistake to smell her hair. I was conscious suddenly of her physical presence, of the immediacy of her warmth, the arc of her cheekbones and the velvet fullness of her skin; and my breath stopped in my chest. Jocelyn's eyes had narrowed at the glitter on the waves, and I saw how the faint lines at their corners filled in. I wanted to touch those lines, to kiss them softly. I wanted to have seen them carved by time. But more than anything else, I wanted to get this conversation right, and I had no idea how to do that. It was clear to me by now that I should have said no to this job at the beginning.

The back door of the house slid open just then with a soft metallic whoosh, and Jocelyn and I both turned. Bill Sherman had emerged onto the patio. He paused for a beat, for delicacy's sake, letting his presence register, then frankly started toward us. Apparently his patience had run out.

I glanced at Jocelyn and found that she had already turned back to me. Her expression was scrupulously noncommittal, but I could read between the lines easily enough. This was her life, in the nutshell of this moment: she and I had only gotten as far as establishing what shampoo she was wearing twenty years ago, but in the time it took her husband to walk across their backyard and up the dock to us, the script called for us to have settled the issue of their daughter's gravestone.

I said, feeling ridiculous, "About the memorial—"

"I don't give a damn about the memorial, Eli. It's Bill's thing."

That was clear enough, at least. There's nothing like a deadline, even an artificial and misguided one, to precipitate the truth. I said, "I get that. It's too soon. That's pretty much my point."

Jocelyn just shook her head, but her eyes brightened as they filled. The tears began to spill over and slide quietly down her cheeks. My eyes filled too, an instant, visceral response, and I reached for her hand. It was cool and dry in mine, and felt almost weightless.

"Wait until you're ready," I said. "That's all I'm saying. Until both of you are ready."

"It's just not that simple, Eli."

"No. But you've still got to give love time to do its work."

"Like it did for us, you mean?"

I opened my mouth to reply, in the rhythm of conversation, but there was no reply, and my breath just came and went, once, and then again, a gulping futility, like a fish on a dock. There had been nothing of accusation in Jocelyn's words, and no heat: it was a flat truth, cold and glassy as the polished face of a slab of granite. If she had spoken with anger, I could have simply reeled and succumbed, as you would succumb to a superior assault. But this felt like being killed by a flashbulb going off: a burst of light without impact, that devastated. A flash, and I was posthumous.

Nothing had changed; the river sparkled in the sun and a gull glided by, soundless in the heart of the gentle breeze. Jocelyn's hand still rested in mine. I lifted my eyes and found her looking at me steadily. There was no satisfaction in her look, no pleasure in my devastation. It was more as if she herself had been there all along, waiting quietly in her own ruin, while I had bustled around in my fantasy of healing heroism. And now, for the first time, we were together. And we were nowhere.

The thud of footsteps on the planks behind us came as an actual surprise to me. Bill Sherman was striding up the dock. I had been wrong about that too, it seemed: there had been plenty of time, during his short walk across the back yard, for his wife and me to get to the heart of the matter.

I released Jocelyn's hand and stood up, automatically, to avoid the awkwardness of Sherman arriving upright with both of us seated and feeling like a third wheel in his own backyard. It amazed me, that I could stand. An emptiness, standing.

"You guys got everything worked out?" Bill said, as he reached us. His heartiness seemed like something from a different play, in a different century.

Jocelyn, who had remained seated, said nothing, rather spectacularly. And I had nothing to say. It struck me that I might never have had anything to say. The moment dragged on, moving from awkwardness toward pain. Bill Sherman was doing his best to maintain affability, looking from his wife to me like a man perfectly willing to laugh at a joke, if only someone would explain it to him. But it was clearly becoming a strain. I wondered how I was going to tell him that the job was a botch, that there'd been a flaw, not in the stone for his daughter's memorial, but in the guy he'd hired to do it.

Just when it seemed that the dock might collapse from the weight of the silence, Jocelyn stirred, and said, like a translator just doing her job, "Elijah was just telling me that he thinks we should wait for a while before we have the memorial done."

Bill Sherman looked at me and frowned. "Oh?"

I nodded helplessly. Sherman glanced back at Jocelyn, transparently suspicious, but she spread her hands in shared bafflement and shrugged, as if to say, It wasn't me, I did my best to talk some sense into him. I realized that Sherman was more aware of his wife's feelings about the timing of their daughter's gravestone than I had been giving him credit for. It had been unimaginable to me that he could know how she felt and still push on with the project. But he wasn't insensitive, it seemed; he was just determined.

Sherman turned back to me. "Well, that's really none of your business, is it?"

"No," I said. "Of course it's not."

"Are you saying we need to find somebody else to do the job?"

Jocelyn shifted just then, preparing to get up, and her husband immediately turned to her and offered his hand to help. Once she was on her feet, he kept her hand in his, and the two of them stood for a moment considering me, mutually offended by an uppity tradesman, and united in their grief. Jocelyn's abrupt transformation back into a wife was really quite impressive. She had been right earlier, of course: I was naive. The complexities of this marriage really were beyond me.

I said, "Forgive my presumption. I—I don't know. Maybe it would be best if you got somebody else to do it."

"Anyone you'd care to recommend?"

"You might give Joe Murphy a call. Murphy's Monuments, out in Chesapeake. He does good work."

"Okay," Sherman said. And then, "Well, thanks."

I was dismissed. The man conducted his business very briskly. I wondered if he fired lawyers this fast too. I said, "I'll get your money back to you, of course."

"Keep it," Sherman said. "I think we'll probably still use your sketches, if that's okay with you."

"That's what they're for."

"Good, then."

It was my cue to go, but I found myself unable to move. Sherman looked briefly troubled by the missed beat, but Jocelyn broke the impasse by saying, with pitch-perfect sincerity and a masterful trace of compassion for a befuddled old friend, "It was good to see you again, Elijah."

I looked at her, striving to keep my face appropriate, determined to get at least that much right. The strangest thing of all was that what I could only think of as her true self was still right there, her eyes steady and aware and acknowledging everything. "And you. I'm very sorry for your loss."

"Thank you. And thank you for all your help."

I was inclined to demur, on the value of my help. But I couldn't help suspecting that I had gotten the job done for her after all. It's a tricky business any way you look at it, dealing with grief.

"You're welcome," I said, and turned to make the long walk back up the dock.

* * *

Joe Murphy came by the shop three days later, just after noon. Joe is a short breathless man who always wears green—green jackets, green ties, clover cuff links, and belts like tanned grass snakes, as if in year-round observance of St. Patrick's Day. The Irish shtick wears a little thin sometimes, but Joe is okay. His first choice of career was high diving, but he hit his head on the edge of a ten-meter platform while trying to turn a back somersault with a twist, in his junior year of college, and has been subject to intermittent dizzy spells ever since. He still has the aspect sometimes of someone in mid-air. I find it endearing, actually, that even though Joe has pretty much lowered that ten-meter platform to ground level by now, he retains the habits of someone once familiar with heights. And to give him credit, Joe makes no distinctions when he gets down to business. He buries everyone with the same muted glee.

I was working on a special job when he came in, a stone for a dog. I seldom take on pet jobs, but this was for a little kid who had sidled in shyly the week before with about seven dollars in pennies, nickels, and dimes in a tin can. No quarters—apparently he spent his allowance quarters regularly on something else, video games maybe, and we were looking at the accumulated change. He was eight years old. The first thing he did was pour all his money out of the can onto my work bench. It made quite an impressive noise.

"My dog died," he said.

There was nothing to do but do it: I was giving him my $4.98 scrap granite special. I had tried to do it gratis, but it was important to him that it be a legitimate commissioned business transaction.

Joe took one look at the stone now and burst out laughing. "'Rowser,' eh?" he said.

"Beloved Mutt," I said. "Show a little respect, Joe." I was almost finished. The kid's conception had been simple: just the name, ROWSER, in straight Trajan caps. I liked that. There is a breathtaking absoluteness in undated stones. The kid had showed me the spot of the grave, a carefully heaped little mound under a maple tree in his back yard. Rowser, he said, had used to love to chase the little helicopter seed pods as they fell. The kid was going to plant irises around the stone.

I had promised the boy the stone would be ready that afternoon. Joe fidgeted a moment, watching me work, then said with discernible impatience, "You're a fine craftsman, Elijah."

"What's on your mind, Joe?" I asked, without looking up.

"I've been trying to call you all morning. All I get is some recording from the phone company. Did you know your phone's out of service?"

"Is that how they're saying it? 'Out of service'? How discreet."

"You knew, then?"

"I knew."

"You ought to get somebody on that right away. You're losing business, buddy."

"I suppose." I concentrated on the second R, thinking of those irises as I worked, and of the little maple seed pods twirling down in the autumn.

"Losing business," Joe repeated solemnly, weighting his words so frankly that I glanced up at him and set my tools aside.

"What is it, Joe?"

He bounced on his toes, flexing his knees. He'd picked up the mannerism in his diving days, I suppose: a little preparatory bounce, as if he were still at the edge of the ten-meter platform, taking one more deep breath before launching himself out into the void.

"This couple came in yesterday afternoon—" he said.

So that was it. "A lawyer-ish guy?" I asked. "And an elegant brunette?"

"Deep brown eyes to die for."

"Uh-huh," I said, noncommittally enough, though my heart panged. It was like Joe to notice such things.

"They were mad at you, Eli."

"And yet I remember them with such fondness."

"This is serious, man. You blew a big job."

"Did they give it to you?"

"Yeah." Joe looked at his feet.

"Well, then?" I picked up my mallet and chisel. School would be out soon and I didn't want that kid to show up and find Rowser's stone unfinished. I knew he had the memorial service scheduled for that afternoon.

"Why didn't you take the job, Eli? Is there something I'm not seeing in it?"

"What are you seeing in it?"

"Hell, it's their daughter. They want to do it proper. Big-time."

I shrugged. "Well there you go."

Joe was silent a moment, watching me work. That simple Roman R can be tricky, especially if you've already got another R on the stone. You don't want disproportionate or mismatched Rs: a little too much loop, and everyone who looks at the thing for the next few centuries will walk away with a slightly uneasy feeling.

At last Joe blurted, "Okay, so the woman's a little ambivalent about it, so what?"

It is at such moments that I can picture Joe's old diving days best: that sweet bold leap into space. I set the chisel down again. "Well, I did tell them that they might want to take a little time, before they do the thing."

"Is that our job, though?" Joe said. "Jesus, I'm not her psychiatrist. Or her priest, for that matter. And neither are you."

"True enough."

Joe swayed slightly. "*What*, then?"

"Nothing," I said. "I'm going to let this one pass, is all I'm saying."

"And spend your time doing little hundred dollar jobs for dogs?"

"$4.98. I'm having a special this week for mixed breeds."

"Let me at least sub some of the statuary for this one out to you. A few of the angels, maybe, I know how you love to do angels."

Joe actually has a film of the accident that ended his career.

I've watched it with him about twenty times. He'll get very drunk and then insist on seeing it. Even in slow motion it's hard to see the difference between the leap he makes then and any other leap of the hundreds he's got on tape. He'd hit that somersault a thousand times, it was his specialty dive, his bread and butter. In the one he screwed up, there is the same gathering of the thighs and thrust of the arms upward, the same soaring instant, the back curling into its tuck position, the knees coming up as the body rotates. But somehow he was out of alignment just that much. That's how he says it: out of alignment just that much.

I said, "Look, they basically fired me, Joe. I got in out of my depth, and they canned me. And I didn't feel that good about the thing to start with, to tell you the truth. I was only doing it because the woman was, uh, an old friend."

"Just do the angels," Joe persisted. "And the lamb—you know I can't do animals." And, as I picked up my chisel again and said nothing, "The husband is determined to do this thing, you know. Somebody's going to end up with this money. And nothing anyone can do is going to bring their daughter back to life."

I just kept working, concentrating on the curve of the last R. Joe and I did this every once in a while. He gave up and watched me work for a few minutes, and when I was sure he'd let it go, I said, "How about those Nationals this year? They've got the guns to take it all, don't you think?"

"No pitching," Joe replied sourly, which was true enough. He seemed relieved by now to leave it at that. We talked about driving up to D.C. to catch a game some Friday night and he took off.

I finished the Rowser stone in plenty of time, as it turned out, and had it ready when the kid came by. Throw in the complimentary iris bulbs, and I'd lost money on the job, but what the hell. Just thinking about all that purple and yellow around the undated stone the next spring was enough to make the world seem solid in its orbit. The kid set the granite reverently in the wheelbarrow he and his friends had brought to fetch it. They wheeled the stone off solemnly, taking turns pushing. They all wore armbands made of black construction paper.

Chapter Eight

The first job my grandfather gave me to do by myself was to take a block of hewn limestone, called a rough ashlar, and make a flat surface on it. It is a task that seems so simple that it is almost insulting. I approached it as a child approaches a piano, impatient to be on to the "real" work. The basic apprentice impulse is to go fast, to plunge straight into a sonata, your hands dancing across the keys, as you've seen the masters do it; and it is an added challenge, in working with stone, that a missed note often leads to bleeding. My grandfather used to smile as he applied the antiseptic and bandages, and say that it came with the job—that you wouldn't be a real mason until you'd taken enough skin off your hands to make a work apron.

The task took me forever, and I took enough skin off my

knuckles to get a decent start on that apron, but in the end I had it all worked true and clean and was just square-chiseling the margin to finish up the plane when a single light tap took off about six inches of the end. The entire corner split away, revealing a rusty streak in the block, where groundwater had seeped into it when the limestone was forming. A vein of weakness, thirty million years in the making and a moment in the undoing. It was lovely, really, a meandering whimsy of subtle russet. It's the kind of thing that gives a rock its character.

My grandfather, always alert to everything in the shop, came over as soon as he heard the chunk hit the floor, and we stood side by side looking at the ruined work.

"There was a flaw in the stone," I told him, defensively.

"There usually is," my grandfather agreed, amiably enough. "But it's your job to keep it there."

* * *

I had plenty of time, in the weeks following the fiasco with the Shermans, to think about that lesson anew. There are no excuses in working with stone; your mistakes are as plain as the break in the line of the block and there is no explaining them away. You may never know what it would have taken to keep the flaw in the stone, but you know exactly what you did to leave it on the floor of the shop.

It seemed to me that with the Shermans I had lost sight of the fundamental axiom of stone work: I had worked not against the strength of the situation, but along the easy line of my own weakness. The hard truth of the job had been two parents grieving the death of their three-year-old daughter, with their marriage knocked badly out of sync by the loss, and God knows what it would have taken to carve against the obdurate reality of that and do it right. But I had hammered away instead at the fissure of my private history with Jocelyn. I had convinced myself that I was offering service and comfort, but I saw now that the offer had been poisoned with ambition from the start—that I had secretly hoped to demonstrate the value of my absence in her life, in the hour of her need. As if all those squandered years had been not futility but a kind of training, preparing me to be a sort of wilderness guide on the river of grief: schooled by my own wanderings in the country of loss, I would guide Jocelyn through the rocks and rapids to healing, and so affirm our love and redeem the wasted time.

That fantasy of redemption had vanished in the weightless flash of truth on the dock. The real flaw had been in me all along, like a streak of old mud pressed into limestone by the weight of time. There was no wishing it away, there was only what I had never accomplished, which was finding the way to work that made that faultline part of the truth of the rock and not just the place where it broke.

* * *

The weeks after the fiasco with the Shermans passed painfully through bright slow days. Few jobs came in, and those that did were unremunerative, often spectacularly so. From May until the Fourth of July, I worked mostly for free. I managed to get the phone turned back on, but Mitchell, my landlord, was on my case almost daily, threatening to throw me out. For the first time since I had opened the shop I was four, and then five months behind on the rent. Thank God no one else wanted the place. But it was a tricky period.

With so little legitimate work coming in, I spent a lot of time working on the cathedral at Hog Island. It almost sounds glamorous to say it that way; you think of spires climbing toward heaven above an array of flying buttresses, of Gothic vaults tracing magnificent arcs, and intricate side chapels lit with candles, populated by the relics of saints. But all I was really doing on the cathedral at Awe was the grunt work that the unskilled day laborers of the Middle Ages did for a barely living wage, the sweat-and-dust stuff, heaving rocks from here to there, putting block on block in simple walls. I am barely competent at half a dozen tasks that in the past would have been overseen by half a dozen masters, and I miss those masters sorely.

The cathedral will survive my ineptitude and mistakes, though; it is one of the miracles of the form. Someone who shows up after me will do the finer things that weave my plodding efforts invisibly into the glorious whole, making arches soar from the pilings I set, and setting stained-glass windows into my rudimentary walls.

Or maybe not. Maybe the James River will rise with global warming, leaving an enigmatic, Atlantis-like ruin at the bottom of the Chesapeake Bay; or the next ice age will come and a glacier will grind through southeastern Virginia and churn the set stones into scattered rocks again. It really doesn't matter. I am at best an ant, collecting sand one grain at a time for a sand castle I will never see finished, and the tides are beyond my control.

In any case, the job seems to suit me. If you think anything but work done with love for its own sake is worth a damn, you're in for misery anyway.

* * *

On the first Sunday in August, I drove up to Shenandoah Springs for my grandfather's ninety-third birthday. During my childhood, my grandfather's birthdays had always been special occasions and even had a touch of seasonal pagan ritual to them. The family would gather and make a weekend of it, and on Saturday afternoon there would be a big cookout in the yard outside my grandfather's shop that lasted well into the night. With scores of people milling around amid the uncarved stones scattered through the yard, the scene looked like a party in a cemetery, but it never seemed to slow anyone down. The blackberries were always just coming ripe then and all the kids would be out in the brambles with buckets, and purple hands and mouths. At night, the Perseid meteor shower would add to the show, and it was years before I realized that those streaking stars had nothing to do with Ed Tremaine's birthday.

My grandfather himself suffered the celebrations with benign dignity and more than a trace of private amusement. To him, a birthday was mostly just the first date you carved on a gravestone. But he enjoyed the parties. He would find a congenial limestone block in a quiet corner of the yard and sit there sipping some Jameson's until he felt he had put in enough time, and then he would go to bed early.

The celebrations had grown smaller and quieter over the decades, as most of the family grew up and moved away, and since my grandfather had a series of strokes about three years before, the birthday parties had pretty much petered out. When I pulled into the circular driveway that looped past the shop and around to the house, the only other car present this year besides my grandfather's pickup truck, undriven since his last stroke, was my Aunt Terrie's battered Toyota. Terrie is a Bethanite nun, and it is my impression that all nuns drive Toyotas with at least 120,000 miles on them. She left her convent when my grandfather had his stroke, to come home and care for him and my grandmother, who had never learned to drive.

I crossed the big, unscreened front porch and slipped in through the front door to find my aunt in the living room, giving my grandfather his mid-afternoon snack through a tube. He can still get the occasional mouthful of food down, but he gets most of his nutrition through a port in his lower chest.

"Hey there, handsome," Terrie said.

"Hey gorgeous. Is this lunch?"

"High tea."

"I should have known from the crumpets."

"Look who's here, Pop, it's Eli," Terrie told my grandfather, but he had already registered my presence somehow and was beaming vaguely in my direction, like a blind person lifting his face toward sunlight. No one is sure anymore what he perceives of the world around him, or when, or how, it is all very hit-or-miss. Usually he is simply sunk into a drooly, musing place of his own. But he'll light up once in a while and I have learned to never count him out.

I went over to kiss him and he brightened a bit more, and gave me a three-tooth grin, though he couldn't find my eyes. This was pretty much as close as he came to lucidity lately and I was actually pleased to see him so responsive. There are days when he just feels like a big sad houseplant.

Terrie gave me a hug. She was wearing a simple dress of Bethanite brown, which is drabber than Franciscan brown. After two glasses of wine, Terrie calls it dog-shit brown, to my grandmother's dismay. She is a soft-spoken woman in her early sixties, mild as a dove and sly as a snake, with a fiendish and gleeful sense of humor. When I was a kid, she and her fellow nuns used to slide me down the banisters of the long curving stairway at their convent near Charlottesville. I still have occasional dreams of flying, in which I am surrounded by uproarious angels clad in dog-shit brown.

"I see that the cocktail hour has begun," I said, noting Terrie's glass of Merlot in progress amid the medical paraphernalia.

"I've got Budweiser in the fridge for you."

"You are a true woman of God."

"Want me to go grab one for you?"

"I'll get it myself. Is Grandma back there?"

"In spite of my best efforts to get her to sit down."

"Ooooghh," my grandfather said just then.

"What?" I said.

"It's all this alcohol talk," Terrie said. "I think he wants a Manhattan."

* * *

I found my grandmother in the kitchen, puttering around in her ceaseless slow-motion way, chopping some green beans with a knife so big it looked like she should be using two hands to wield it. She is a wren-like woman with a miraculous metabolism more or less untouched by the decades, and it is very hard to catch her sitting down. I gave her a hug and a kiss, then dodged the knife blade as she immediately resumed her chopping.

"So how's our boy been?" I asked.

She shrugged. "Pretty much the same. Good days and bad days."

"Seems like a good one today."

"He knows something special is up."

"It seems like it. He was asking for a Manhattan just now."

"The old drunk," my grandmother said fondly. "Your first beer is in the freezer, I wanted to make sure it was chilled."

"That's why you're my favorite bartender," I said. I gave her another kiss on top of her head and slipped past her to the refrigerator. My grandparents still have the same tiny gas stove they've had since the 50s, but their refrigerator is a state-of-the-art marvel complete with an icemaker built right into the door. They love those little crescent-moon ice cubes. But they don't entirely trust the technology yet, after thirty years, and still keep two back-up ice-cube trays in the freezer, ancient things made of galvanized tin with recalcitrant lever handles, whose blocky cubes I prefer for sentiment's sake.

My grandmother had laid the Budweiser neatly on top of the old ice cube trays. I grabbed the frosty bottle and closed the fridge, somehow managing to dislodge several of the papers that were held to the door by magnets. I bent to pick them up—a mass schedule for St. Martha's, a crayon picture of a bear eating a watermelon, which I had drawn in the first grade, a prescription for a blood thinner, and a small handwritten note. I looked at the note as I reattached the rest of the pages to the fridge door. It was an IOU for $1.85, from "JB," dated three years previously.

"JB," I knew, would be Father John Busby, a squat, bald badger of a man with whom my grandfather had fought quietly for the past forty years. Father Busby was the sort of priest who had memorized his sacred scripts during his seminary days and stuck to them unwaveringly, word for word, in any situation, for the rest of his life. I knew that my grandfather considered him a rigid man with a limited repertoire and, as much of my grandfather's own best work came down to subverting the prevailing rigidities at critical moments, the two had always had a tense relationship. Yet their paths had crossed inevitably on a lot of the deaths in the county for decades. As if this had not been sufficient opportunity to contemplate their differences, they had also, for as long as I had been around, gotten together for a particularly fierce game of rummy every Wednesday night. They played for a penny a point according to obscure rules that had gradually evolved to an intricacy beyond the reach of anyone else. They played even when, for one reason or another, they were not actually speaking to each other, a common condition between the two of them. My grandfather was often disgusted with the priest for bullying some poor mourner into a hasty orthodoxy; while Busby had frequently threatened my grandfather with excommunication for quasi-heretical or pagan inscriptions, and gnostic advice. This had always amused my grandfather, who was never one to worry much about his official status.

"Is this a rummy debt?" I asked my grandmother.

"Oh, that old thing," she said. "I suppose it is, from the last time they played. I should have thrown it out long ago."

"Did Busby ever pay up?"

"I'm sure he did, at some point."

"I'll bet he didn't, or it wouldn't still be up here."

My grandmother looked uneasy. She had never been comfortable with the fact that her husband fought with the parish priest and that he sometimes even accused Busby of cheating at cards. She was unfailingly good to everyone herself and preferred to believe that other people, especially priests, were good as well. This was ironic to me, not just because there was really no one with a sharper moral eye than my grandmother, but also because she herself had flashes of the most heterodox sort—gypsy-like stuff, witchy wisdom; old Druid echoes leaked out of her at the oddest moments. But she treated these as lapses or divine impositions.

"It's really not a big deal," she said.

"It would be to Grandpa. And to Busby, that cheapskate."

My grandmother's silence seemed an acknowledgment; but apparently it had only been a tactical pause to lull me into overconfidence because, after a beat, with a surprisingly swift movement, she snatched the IOU out of my hand and dropped it straight into the trash can.

"That's enough of *that*," she said.

I considered taking the note out of the trash again immediately, but I could see from the look on her face that that wouldn't fly. I hated to think of Father Busby coming out ahead with my grandfather, though, and when my grandmother turned back to her chopping, I quietly retrieved the IOU and stuck it in my pocket. She pretended not to notice, but I knew she had. Nothing gets by that woman.

* * *

My grandmother had saved the task of icing the birthday cake for me, a tradition that goes back to the days when I was drawing bears eating watermelons. It is a great job, as you can just wipe off your mistakes with your finger and eat them, which is not so with stone work.

I usually do something vaguely Celtic or floral, but this year for some reason I decided to get clever and did the icing in a mottled silver that looked like limestone, then lettered the birthday message in block Trajan script, complete with an angular shading on each of the caps that made them appear to have been chiseled into the cake. I was very pleased with myself and it was not until I had most of the work done that I realized that the net effect was to make my grandfather's birthday cake like exactly like a gravestone.

By then it was too late to rethink the concept. To make matters worse, I had messed up the D in "BIRTHDAY," letting

TIM FARRINGTON

the gravity of the downstroke on the bowl take the line back to the stem too soon, so that the inner space of the letter looked like a stepped-on potato. But the roast was out of the oven by then and there was nothing to do but get myself another beer and hope for the best.

When my grandmother carried the cake into the dining room after dinner, with the candles lit, it looked more like a tombstone than ever. As we sang "Happy Birthday To You," my grandfather stared at the cake in obvious disorientation. He may have been wondering whether he had already died and missed the event. But his eyes, I noted, settled quickly on the misshapen D.

I wasn't surprised by that: during the course of his various strokes, my grandfather could still work with stone right up until he couldn't hold the tools, and he was carving perfect letters long after he couldn't speak. I'm not sure what part of the brain is involved, but it appears to be indestructible. And I knew exactly what he was thinking now, looking at that D. He'd said it to me a thousand times: it's not the lines that make the space of a letter, it's the space that makes the lines. A line is a discovery, not an imposition. And so on.

After a long moment, my grandfather reached out toward the cake and stuck his finger right into the heart of the D. He came up with a fingerful of icing and looked at it with an expression of pure bewilderment. Carve against the strength, indeed. I think he was trying to figure out why the limestone was so soft. But my grandmother reached over and guided his finger to his mouth, and he blinked as he tasted the sweetness, and smiled his toothless smile.

I didn't know whether to laugh or cry, myself. But my aunt and my grandmother were laughing and I went with that.

* * *

After dinner, Terrie and my grandmother chased me out of the kitchen, which really wasn't big enough for three people, and I

88

sat in the living room with my grandfather while they did the dishes. At various points during his deterioration, it could be unnerving or painful to be with him, but you get used to pretty much anything after a while and I have come to love these quiet times alone with him.

I pulled in a chair from the dining room and sat beside him holding his hand. His calluses had softened and all the old scars and seams had aged into mildness, like an old battlefield where grass has regrown in all the shell holes. When he drooled, I wiped it off, and when he stopped breathing, as he did now sometimes, in capricious apneas that lasted for as long as a minute at a time, I held my own breath and waited, and the world seemed poised at the brink of mystery until he gave a shudder and a gasp, and his breath kicked in again. But mostly we just sat quietly together and from time to time whatever was going on within his depths would come to a point near the surface and I would feel a sudden answering firmness in his grip or see focus come into his eyes for a moment as his gaze sought mine. You could go a long time, waiting quietly for moments like that.

* * *

When the dishes were finished, Terrie and my grandmother joined us in the living room and we all watched the CBS Evening News, as we have since the days when Walter Cronkite was doing it in black-and-white. Then we got my grandfather into bed and I kissed my grandmother goodbye and headed out for my truck. Terrie walked me out into the driveway, as she always does.

"You seem a little down," she said.

It was like her to have noticed, of course. I considered confiding in her. But what could I say? My life had a Jocelyn-shaped hole in it. That had been true for twenty years, I just happened to have fallen into it again recently. I said, "It's that damned D on the cake. It looked like a goiter."

She hesitated, then decided to let me off the hook, and smiled. "He sure spotted it right away, didn't he?"

"'If the space is true, the line will be true,'" I said. "I think he was ready to recarve it right there on the spot. Thank God he didn't have a chisel."

"Well, the cake was beautiful, anyway."

"No, the whole concept was off. Next year I'm doing roses, no text, and a big yellow happy face for the sun."

"If he's here next year," Terrie said.

It's one of the things I love about Terrie: she never flinches. I said, "You'll call me right away, right? If it looks bad?"

"Of course. I just hope I can reach you. I called last month and the phone was disconnected."

"There was a little cash-flow problem for a while," I conceded.

"Do you need money?"

I laughed. She was so earnest. It was like she was ready to write me a check on the spot. I said, "You don't have any money, Aunt Terrie. You're a penniless servant of the Lord."

"Oh, right," she said.

* * *

It started to sprinkle that night just as I got back to Pungo, and I woke the next morning to a steady downpour, the first of a dry season. I hauled myself out of bed, made the necessary coffee, and drove to my shop. The place looked a bit forlorn as I pulled into the driveway, a sad little tin-roofed box, hunched against the rain. The soybean fields around it were churning like a green sea beneath the low sky. Through the rain's patter on my roof, I could hear my neighbor Mrs. Durka, the Armenian widow, playing her organ, a rousing cascade of insanely cheerful music that this morning more than ever made me want to weep.

Mrs. Durka had also left her usual plate of cookies out for me, probably the night before, and these had been scattered around the front of the shop by animals. A wet raccoon was nosing through the violated aluminum foil as I walked up. He lifted his head and looked at me. As I paused, he hesitated, ducked his head and snagged up the last of the cookies on the plate, and then walked off, working his jaw as if around a bite of peanut butter. Mrs. Durka's cookies were extremely dry.

I watched him go, then picked up the plate, unhooked the broken padlock on the shop's sliding front door, and heaved it open.

Inside, the roof was leaking in its usual six places and one new one. Little streams wound among the stones, meandering vaguely seaward. My shop is not so much a shelter from the elements as a slight modification of them. I began to set up buckets and bowls and barrels, and to rescue anything that seemed to need rescuing from the deluge.

I had gotten out of the habit of checking, but eventually I noticed that my answering machine's green light was flashing, once for each message received. I counted six, which in my business probably meant that six people had died. And yet that flashing unjustifiably cheered me. I am an appalling man, I suppose; but I was glad to have my work cut out for me.

CHAPTER NINE

In fact, only two people had died. The first three calls on the answering machine turned out to be someone with an 800 number who was sure that he could solve all my financial problems, a pitch for a different phone company, and someone named Waylene trying to sell me land in West Virginia. My state of the art answering machine can hold up to forty-five minutes of heartbreak and loss, and Waylene had taken up seven of these with her pitch.

The next two messages were briefer and more generally to the point. A high school senior had died of a heart attack in the middle of a preseason football practice, caught unawares by an unsuspected flaw in his aorta, while waiting for his turn on the tackling dummy. His graduating class had chipped in, and wanted a stone that people could sign, sort of like a yearbook page. It was the senior class secretary who had called, a gung-ho girl so full of her mission that her voice on the tape chilled me. I wondered what the kid's poor parents wanted, and how they felt about the autographed tombstone and the class project atmosphere that seemed to surround the thing. But I wrote down the chirpy girl's number.

The second of the deaths was mercifully without bitterness or even particular irony, a widow who wanted a double stone for herself and her husband of 57 years. He had just died—in bed, she noted frankly. She seemed quite proud, indeed, of the fact that he had died in their queen-size bed, and mentioned this twice. She even managed to imply that something enviably wild had been occurring: Herman Powell, it seemed, had died in action.

The last of the six messages was from Joe Murphy. He had called to tell me that the Shermans had decided not to do their daughter's monument after all. I was right to have passed on the job, he said. He didn't think those people knew what the hell they wanted.

My first impulse was to call him back immediately, to find out more, but on second and third thoughts, I decided that, on the whole, it was probably best to not know. Patience and humility, as my grandfather never tired of saying: the virtues stone demands of you must be made new every day. It had taken me more than twenty years of what I thought was patience to arrive at a working pretense of being over Jocelyn Page and that pretense had been blown in a few minutes with her. If it was going to take me another twenty years of humility to recover from that, I wanted to get to work on it as soon as possible.

* * *

One afternoon just after Labor Day, I was inking the letters on Herman Powell's straightforward stone. Margaret Powell had settled on a bit from the Song of Songs for the stone, a single epitaph for the two of them—

My beloved spake, and said unto me,
Rise up, my love, my fair one,
and come away. For, lo, the winter is past,
the rain is over and gone . . .

I was doing the script in Chancery italics, working from the full-size draft I had done on paper. My grandfather had studied lettering for a time in the late 1940s under John Howard Benson at the Rhode Island School of Design, and he had been an exacting stylist and an exacting teacher of calligraphic style—never harsh, but gently and relentlessly scrupulous about every detail of the lettering process, from the ritual cutting of reed pens from the stalks of sea oats to the intricacies of carving the subtly curved oblique planes of serifs in granite. There was an amazing liquid grace to my grandfather's script in stone and I had almost despaired, at times, of ever getting my lettering up to his standards. The learning process had been made even trickier by the fact that I am left-handed and had to translate a lot of the strokes into mirror-versions and find all my own angles. But in the long run I had worked my way into that exhilarating balance of structure and freedom that good calligraphy requires, and doing the fluid, elegant letters today was a pure and absorbing delight.

Etta James was singing "The Blues Is My Business (And Business is Good)" on my little boombox. It was a hot, still afternoon, the languid, effortless heat at the end of a long summer. The soybean crop had just come in and the fields around the shop were freshly plowed for the planting of winter wheat. When I heard the diesel engine on the dirt road between the fields, I barely registered the sound, assuming it was a farmer's truck, but then I heard the downshift and the changed tenor of the tires on my gravel driveway. I looked out through the open front of the shop and saw the Shermans' cream-colored Mercedes approaching.

Everything inside me went quiet, as if before a battle. But I was glad to see that car. For all my pep talks to myself about patience and surrender, it was obvious to me at once that I had been waiting, and even hoping, for something like this all along. Between grief and nothing, I'll take grief, as Faulkner said somewhere. As if that were ever really a choice.

I stuck my brush into the rinse water, wiped my inky hands on my pants, and went outside. The Mercedes pulled up in front as I got to the shop entrance and I saw that Bill Sherman was alone in the car. I felt no disappointment at Jocelyn's absence. Her husband seemed as much a part of my fate by now as Jocelyn herself.

Sherman turned off the engine and got out of the car. He was dressed in what looked to be his lawyer work clothes, a well-tailored dark gray suit, a patterned red tie like something from an English boarding school, and shoes that had probably cost the tithe on my annual income. In spite of this, he looked surprisingly unkempt: he was sporting about a week's worth of unshaved beard and it was in that twilight stage between a clean-shaven look and something you could trim. It was a look that made you feel he might ask you for a quarter, somewhere in the range of seediness or terrorist chic. I hadn't shaved in three days myself, of course, but I consider that a mason's perk.

I gave him a nod of welcome as he came around the car and showed him my inky hand apologetically to indicate that no handshake was necessary. Sherman stuck out his hand anyway, though, with an insistence that I already recognized as characteristic. I wiped my hand on my jeans again, twice, which probably did more harm than good, since my pants were pretty inked up as well; and sure enough Sherman's hand came away from the handshake with a smear of ink. But there really was no stopping the guy once he had an idea in his head.

"Sorry to barge in like this," Sherman said. Maybe it was a side effect of the scruffy facial hair, but he seemed unsure of himself, even tentative, despite the usual determined handshake. Very un-Bill-Shermanlike. I realized anew that I actually liked the man. How strange, given all the human complexities in the situation, that the sum of my feelings should come down to a pretty straightforward sympathy and affection.

"No problem," I said. I just hoped no one else had died.

* * *

We went into the shop to get out of the sun. Sherman accepted my offer of refreshments, but opted for water, and I went to grab a couple of bottles out of my little half-fridge. When I came back, he was standing beside the ink-lettered stone for Herman Powell.

"This is gorgeous," he said.

"Thanks. Chancery italics and the Song of Songs, it's hard to go wrong."

He accepted his water and we both twisted our caps off and took sips. Sherman looked around for a place to throw away the cap and I indicated the trash can. He stepped over to it and did a quick double-take as he disposed of the cap: the bin was full of beer bottles, like the aftermath of a frat party. I hadn't emptied it since Harriet Dumontane and I had killed a six-pack of Miller Lite in July, working out the details of her husband's epitaph.

"I thought you drank Bud," he said.

"Generally. But I'm an equal opportunity alcoholic."

He nodded, taking that in stride, and let his gaze wander around the shop, as if he were seeing the place for the first time. He seemed in no hurry to get to the point, and we both sipped our waters again. I would have liked to put him more at ease, but I couldn't think of anything to say—even at the small talk level— that didn't risk hitting a nerve. Something about the boys, maybe.

I was just working up to a question about Joshua's researches into the sewer system, when Sherman finally looked at me and said, "You really didn't have to give that money back, you know."

It actually took me a moment to realize what he was talking about. I had mailed the Shermans' thousand dollar deposit back to them as soon as my balky bank had released the funds, as a matter of course, and it really seemed like ancient history.

"Shit," I said. "I hope that's not why you came out here."

"No. But I was pretty pissed off about it for a while. I was going to send the check right back to you, torn in half. But Jocelyn wouldn't let me."

"A wise woman."

"What she actually said was that she was pretty sure you were an even bigger asshole than I am."

"It seems like a toss-up to me."

I had meant it as a humorous concession and a nod toward essential equality, but it came out sounding tougher than I had anticipated. We looked at each other for a moment, trying to decide how funny all of this actually was; then Sherman shook his head.

"It's probably pretty close, at that," he conceded. "Jocelyn likes to say that I am often wrong, but never uncertain. I didn't really understand the amount, though. I mean, how the hell did you arrive at $982.27?"

I had to smile; I had forgotten that part too. My account had been $17.73 in the red, of course, when I'd deposited the check; I'd sent back every penny I had. "Administrative fees. I've got my overhead to think about."

He gave a wry glance up, at my literal overhead of naked beams and tin roof, and this time we both smiled, thank God.

We took fresh sips of our water. The bottles were half-empty and I was already wishing we had beer. I had none at the shop, though, and I wondered if the 7-Eleven had any sufficiently high-grade foreign stuff. It seemed likely we would have to settle for Heineken. But any port in a storm.

"I suppose your friend told you that we decided not to go ahead with the memorial," Sherman said.

"He mentioned it."

"Did he say why?"

"I didn't ask. I figured it was none of my business."

He gave me an appreciative glance, acknowledging the fact that I was quoting him. "I'm sorry about that."

"No need to be. You were right. I was out of line."

"No. I should have listened to you."

"I'm not sure I said anything particularly coherent."

"You know what I mean."

I did, but it didn't seem like the point. "It really was none of my business. The main thing was for you and Jocelyn to work it through together. I'm glad to hear you did."

"We worked it through, all right, but not together," Sherman said. "I'm afraid that we've, uh, separated."

"What?!"

"Yeah. I've moved out of the house. A couple weeks ago."

"But . . . That's crazy. That's terrible."

"No shit," Sherman said. He raised the water to his lips and drank off the last of it like a shot, then tossed the bottle into the trash can on top of the bottles of Miller Lite, where it landed with a sharp plastic rattle. "Is there somewhere around here we could get a real drink?"

I was stunned, truly. I had assumed he was at the shop to ask me again to do his daughter's memorial, and I had been quietly preparing myself to tell him that, unfortunately, I was going into a monastery. Or something. That it was just too much for me. But apparently it was too much for all of us.

"Yeah," I said. "I know just the place."

CHAPTER TEN

The Tiger Cage was a gloriously ramshackle, driftwood-gray restaurant, halfway down the narrow strip of Sandbridge, that looked like something that happened to have remained after a particularly high tide. Beached precariously between two dunes on an unmarked and unpaved sand alley just off Sandpiper Road, it had a gorgeous view of the Back Bay from the rear tables, through structurally unlikely plate glass windows: it always looked like the next hurricane would take the whole place out. The interior decoration was strictly drunken fishermen on vacation, heavy on mounted tarpon, old buoys with seaweed stains, and group photos of sunburned guys on docks. There were large pictures of Ernest Hemingway, Jimmy Buffet, and Spinoza, the place's patron saints, behind the bar, and the tinny sound system always seemed to be playing "Margaritaville."

"Nice place," Bill Sherman noted, with a trace of amusement, not necessarily sarcastic, as the cute hostess in her Grateful Dead T-shirt and cut-off jean shorts led us to a table by the window. The place was almost empty at this time of the afternoon, with the lunch crowd gone and the happy hour crew yet to arrive, except for a couple guys at the main bar who appeared to have started their happy hours that morning.

"It's run by a former Navy fighter pilot," I said. "He got shot down over Haiphong in 1968, and hit his head on the canopy when he ejected. When he came to, he was lying in a pool of his own blood in a tiger cage, surrounded by angry North Vietnamese fishermen. And he had in his mind's eye the vision of a perfect margarita. He believes it was given to him by angels to see him through his captivity."

"You're kidding me," Sherman said.

"That's what he says, anyway," I said. "To tell you the truth, I think he uses too much lime. But most of the cooks here are former ARVN soldiers who got out on boats in 1975, or their kids, and they've got the best Vietnamese seafood this side of the Gulf of Tonkin."

"I'm surprised I haven't heard of the place before."

"They keep it as quiet as they can. Nick doesn't really like customers, per se."

We ordered the house margaritas, de rigueur, rocks and salt, and within minutes our drinks were brought out by a guy who looked like he might have slept on the beach the night before.

"Is that the owner?" Sherman asked.

"Yeah. Don't make any sudden moves. He's a little edgy."

"That's quite a limp."

"The fishermen had shark clubs."

"I should have known you'd lead the feds here eventually, Tremaine," Nick Landon said, as he came up to the table. Nick is a lanky amalgamation of bent bones; his right leg looks like a pipe cleaner that was worked on by a three-year-old, and his back has a permanent hunch. He keeps his iron gray hair just long enough to cover the patchwork of jagged scars on his skull. He has ten acres on Knott's Island and commutes to the bar three days a week by motorboat, always dressed in jeans and a pair of ancient cowboy boots worn soft with much service. The rest of the time the place is run by his main bartender, Nguyen Trinh, a former professor of literature at Saigon University who had been tortured for a year and a half by the new regime in the mid-seventies, apparently for his interest in early Sung poetry. It has been my contention for years that Trinh's margaritas are better than Nick's, angels notwithstanding. This pisses Nick off. Numerous blind tests have been conducted. I view it as a form of ongoing research.

"Bill's not a fed," I said. "He's just well-dressed."

Nick eyed Sherman, unplaced. "Sir, I'm afraid I'm going to have to ask you to remove that tie."

Sherman gave me a glance, to see whether Nick was kidding, and I indicated with my eyebrow that he probably wasn't. Sherman considered his options briefly, then turned back to Nick and said, "Bite me."

The stern lines in Nick's sun-leathery face deepened, then eased almost imperceptibly, his version of looking delighted.

"Nick, this is Bill Sherman," I said. "Bill, Nick Landon."

"Pleased to meet you," Sherman said tentatively.

Nick told him, "If you're going to waltz into a place like this dressed like that, you really should find a better person to vouch for you."

Sherman shrugged. "Sometimes you just have to make do."

"I hear that." Nick set the drinks down on the table and rotated them three times to make sure I couldn't tell which one he had made, and which was Trinh's. He lingered long enough to make a few more mildly insulting remarks about my character, then slapped Bill Sherman on the back, probably to let the wait staff and bouncer know that the tie was cleared, and left us to our drinks.

"An interesting guy," Sherman said.

"He's crazed," I said. "It's a miracle he's walking around upright. While he was in the Hanoi Hilton he memorized the entire *Theologico-Political Treatise* of Spinoza, unabridged, in the Elwes translation. If there's a long pause in a conversation, he'll sometimes begin to recite it. It was the only book on his cell block, except for something by Agatha Christie. I think he memorized Agatha Christie too."

We attended to our drinks. I had gotten the one made by Trinh; and I indicated this to Nick, who had been watching us from behind the bar. He confirmed my discrimination by raising his middle finger. Sherman sat back in his chair and looked out across the water.

"It feels like a nightmare," he said.

"This place has that effect on a lot of people. It usually passes by the second margarita."

"I meant my life right now."

I had known what he meant, of course. I held my tongue.

"I've got this pathetic little bachelor apartment in Ghent," Sherman said. "It's like I'm back in law school. I mean, I'm sleeping on a *futon*. I haven't had the heart to buy furniture. I'm afraid to do anything that might make this seem permanent. I'm eating Spaghetti-Os and microwave chicken pot pies. But I'm doing something wrong with the pot pies, because every time I cook them, they end up still frozen in the center with the edges too hot to eat." He reached for his drink and sipped. "Damn, these are good."

I said, carefully, "I take it the separation was Jocelyn's idea?"

"It sure as hell wasn't *mine*." Sherman shook his head. "I had no idea it had gone so far. I mean, I knew we hadn't been in the best of places. How could I not know? Our daughter died, for God's sake, we've been fucking miserable. But it still seemed like this came out of nowhere."

"What did she say?"

"She said she needed space. And time. I said, 'Fine. How

much space? How much time?' And she said, 'Long enough for you to stop asking questions like that.'"

I nodded. It was easy enough to picture the exchange. We were silent for a long moment, attending to our margaritas. Nick makes them in stemware the size of a small swimming pool, with no lifeguard on duty. Sherman took off his jacket and hung it on the back of his chair, then loosened his tie. He seemed to be responding well to the tequila.

"What setting are you using?" I asked at last.

"What?"

"What are you setting the microwave on? For the chicken pot pies."

"High," he said, a trifle defensively. "Just like it says on the package."

"Have you tried using 'Defrost' first?"

"The directions don't say anything about defrosting."

"Sometimes you've got to read between the lines."

Sherman looked dubious. He really wasn't the kind of guy who was comfortable reading between the lines. It seemed unlikely, in any case, that he had come to me seeking advice on how to microwave a chicken pot pie. I reached again for my drink, which was already down to the ice cubes.

"It's weird," Sherman said. "When I met Jocelyn, she was, well, . . . uncertain, I guess. Lost. It was pretty clear to me that she'd had some relationships that had really messed her up." He gave me a glance. "No offense."

I shrugged, unwillingly reminded of what Jocelyn had said about my insultability. She had been about half-right, I thought. Point for her, damn the luck. "None taken."

"It took her a long time to believe in me. To believe in us. To believe in herself, even. I mean, we'd go into a restaurant and she'd make me order for both of us."

This was almost impossible for me to imagine. Jocelyn's tastes had always been emphatic and specific, and were often complicated by a whimsical semi-vegetarianism. She would not eat things that had once been cute. I wanted to ask Sherman if he had ever ordered veal for the two of them. When I had known her, Jocelyn wouldn't even let me order veal, much less eat it herself. But I had to be humble here. During the period in question, I had been conducting random pharmaceutical research in northern California, with nothing to guide me but a guy who believed he knew which mushrooms would not kill you, and the Timothy Leary version of the Tibetan Book of the Dead. I certainly couldn't fault Jocelyn for letting Bill Sherman make her menu selections for her.

"She came into her own as a mother," Sherman said. "That was solid ground for her. But it's like we've come full circle, in some way, since Ariel died. I feel like she needs for me to order for us again. I mean, okay, maybe I pushed too hard, on the memorial. But I really thought it was what she wanted, deep down. What she needed, to move on."

I said nothing, with a conscious effort. I was thinking of that moment with Jocelyn on the dock, when she had undercut all my own notions of what she needed: that look in her eyes, the loneliness of ruin. I had felt shamed in that instant, exposed as a poseur, and it was almost impossible even now to think of it without cringing. But I knew that the truth of that moment had been much deeper than my chagrin. Jocelyn had not been throwing my failures in my face to shame me; she had been offering to share them. She had been saying, *See, here, now: for this instant you are undone too. Be here with me.*

I really didn't know what Bill Sherman expected of me. He was a decent man and it seemed to me that he probably had a friend or two who would sit with him in a bar while he rehearsed his version of why his marriage had fallen apart, who would nod sympathetically at all the right points in the story and tell him, Yeah, buddy, you did the best you could. Eventually, with the proper support, Sherman would even come to believe it, as completely as any human being believes the lies he tells himself.

Meanwhile, I knew exactly how much money I had with me, down to the penny, and I knew that if I put it all on the table right now, it would cover the first round of drinks, though the loose change on the tip would piss Nick Landon off. I could tell Bill Sherman, Yeah, you did your best, buddy. I could walk out of here clean. And I could tell myself what Sherman himself had told me once already, that it was none of my business, and that would be the lie I moved on with, as he moved on with his.

But apparently it was, somehow, my business, because here we were, he'd picked the wrong guy to have the drink with. My grandfather believed that love is the only courage, that simply to keep your heart open entailed every challenge a person could ever need to master. The pain inherent in caring for mortal beings was his professional meat and potatoes. But I was working more at the level of microwave chicken pot pies. I took a breath and waited one more beat, then said, distinctly, but with as little heat as possible, "Bullshit."

Sherman's nostrils flared: a man who was often wrong but never uncertain, brought up short. "What?"

"Bill, it was obvious from the moment you two first walked into my shop how Jocelyn felt about the memorial. She didn't want it. And I think you knew that perfectly well, at some level."

Sherman gave me a long, hard look, the anger playing through his features as he struggled with himself. It seemed like it could go either way, and I thought, If he hits me, he's paying for the drinks. But finally Sherman's face relaxed.

"Okay," he conceded. "Maybe it was just what I wanted. What I needed."

I began to breathe again. "Tell Jocelyn that, and you're probably back together."

He shook his head ruefully. "It's not that simple anymore. If it ever was."

Jocelyn had said the same thing to me herself, of course, at least twice. It was humbling. I took the hint and shut up, and we sat for a moment in silence. My drink had guttered and Sherman's was almost gone. It seemed likely to me that there wasn't enough tequila in the world to do us any good here, but I caught Trinh's eye and indicated that another round might be in order. He held up two fingers inquiringly and I nodded, then sat back, hoping I hadn't just ordered us doubles.

"The boys are taking this hard," Sherman said.

"What have you told them?"

"That Mommy and Daddy are taking some time off to sort some things out. That's it's just something married people do sometimes. But they know it's bad. Billy is doing his best to pretend it's all business as usual, but Joshua has set up a hot line."

"A hot line?"

"It's a special red telephone. He's got it in the living room. It doesn't have numbers on it, just one button, and if you press that, it calls my cell. And he's rigged our answering machine menu so that I can make my calls to the house go straight to the red phone."

"You mean, like, 'If this is Dad wanting to reconcile, press 3'?"

"Basically. All I have to do is press #."

"You should call it."

"I did. Jocelyn wouldn't answer it. I can understand that, she doesn't want to send me any mixed messages. But Joshua cried for two days."

The second round of margaritas arrived, along with some chips and salsa. Trinh gave me a wink, and hauled our empty glasses off. I tried the salsa, which was searing hot. I think the angels also gave Nick some recipes involving jalapeño peppers.

Sherman dabbed his tongue at the salty rim of the fresh drink and sipped.

"These really are fantastic," he said.

"Dangerously so."

"I believe they're affecting my perception of the space-time continuum."

"Uh-huh," I said, impressed. He sounded a little like Joshua.

We looked out at the Back Bay. An egret was hunting along the shoreline, standing perfectly still on one leg, its head cocked slightly as it waited for its moment. Beyond it, the water glittered ice blue in the September sun. The days were getting shorter, I noted; the afternoon, like the summer itself, was already winding down.

"Can I be honest with you?" Sherman asked.

"Only if we've exhausted the alternatives."

"I blame you for this, in a way."

I considered that for a moment, then said, "Let's give the alternatives one more chance."

Sherman smiled. "Maybe 'blame' is too strong a way to put it. But I can't help feeling that if it wasn't for you, this would be playing out differently. I think something deep got stirred up in Jocelyn, seeing you again, and that it made her readier to let things come to a crisis in the marriage."

I just looked at my drink. I could appreciate what it had taken for Sherman to raise the topic at all. Neither of us wanted to face this. But it seemed that I wanted to face it less.

"We could have gone to any of a dozen guys, for the memorial," Sherman persisted. "Marietta was telling us to try you, sure, but Jocelyn is no pushover. She could have steered us around you easily enough. But she didn't, she let it happen. Because at some level, she wanted to know. She needed to know." He looked at me. "The day we met, you said you believed in destiny. Do you remember that?"

"Yes. But I think I may have said it just to piss you off." And, as he smiled, "Besides, as a wise man once said, Destiny doesn't pay the rent, amigo."

"I just said that to piss *you* off," Sherman said. "There are more important things than rent. I think you represent something to Jocelyn—the road not taken, something like that. A self she didn't get to live out. I don't know what happened between you two, all those years ago. But I know she never got closure."

"Closure is overrated," I said. "A casket lid comes down, a

grave is filled with dirt. Is that closure? You and I both know it's not that simple. There is no closure in love, or in grief, there are only degrees of acceptance."

"Blah blah blah," Sherman said. "Are you really going to sit there and tell me that not once, since I told you about the separation, have you given at least a moment's consideration to what it might mean for you and Jocelyn?"

"Not once," I said.

"Bullshit."

I gave him an appreciative glance. It had just been a matter of time before that came back around, and in a way I was glad. It certainly balanced the scales. And he was right, of course. I reached for my margarita, then reconsidered, and pushed it away. On the wall near our table, neatly framed in Vietnamese teak, was a quote from Spinoza: *I determined, I say, to inquire whether I might discover the faculty of enjoying throughout eternity continual supreme happiness.* A worthy aspiration, I had always thought; or, given the context, a formula for alcoholism. It's tricky ground, inquiring after continual supreme happiness.

Nick came back over to us just then. The early dinner crowd was starting to drift in, and he wanted the table. It was the best table in the place and Nick was only willing to let me sit there during off hours.

"Everything okay here?" he said. I think it made him nervous that I hadn't finished my drink.

"Fine," I said.

"This is the best margarita I ever had," Sherman told him.

Nick smiled knowingly. "Best you ever will have, too."

"What's the secret?"

"I could tell you that," Nick said, and leaned closer, "but then I'd have to kill you."

Sherman laughed uncertainly.

"Name, rank, and serial number," Nick said. "'Nuff said."

"Actually, I switched the drinks," I said. "Bill has been drinking Trinh's."

Nick shot me a look, and I had a glimpse of what the North Vietnamese fishermen might have seen, prodding him in the tiger cage with their harpoons. Then he saw that I was kidding. He relaxed and shook his head.

"Someday you'll go too far, Tremaine," he said.

"I've already gone too far," I said. It had never seemed clearer to me.

"You got that right." Nick looked pointedly out at the imminent sunset. "Can I get you boys another round?"

"No, I think we're done here," Sherman said, showing remarkable Nick-savvy. He and I reached for our wallets at the same time, but he had two twenties out of his while I was still fumbling through my ones, and the incontestable simplicity of that prevailed. He and Nick shook hands like they were ancient friends who had been under fire together back in the day. I waved to Trinh and ducked Nick's last tender blow to the shoulder blades, then Sherman and I made our way outside and wove a rough line toward his car. I was grateful that he was the one driving. Two of those Tiger Cage margaritas will do me in, every time.

* * *

As we drove back to the shop, my head continued to spin. I knew it wasn't entirely the drinks. Sherman, for his part, was singing the University of Maryland fight song, something about turtles. His last exchange with Nick, and perhaps getting to say "bullshit" to me, had left him very cheerful.

The afternoon had disappeared into tequila and the sky to the west was orange and purple in the flare of the settling sun. I was so drunk that every curve on Sandbridge Road seemed apocalyptic to me and I concentrated on not throwing up. I was further chagrined to note how easily Sherman handled the driving. Jocelyn's husband was not only deeply principled, morally brave, and conscientious, but he could apparently hold his liquor better than me too.

109

Sherman turned south through Pungo, navigated between the ravaged soy bean fields without incident, and finally turned into the gravel drive and pulled up in front of my darkened shop. He turned the car off, and we sat in the sudden deep rural silence, listening to the collective drone of the crickets. It was a moment of peculiarly deep rapport. If Sherman had said to me, "You want to be with my wife, don't you?" I would have replied, "I can't remember a time when I didn't." Except, of course, for the only time when I actually could have been.

"I think I may have to throw up," I said.

Sherman nodded, waited for a truly heroic interval, and then said mildly, apparently resigned to stating the obvious, "I'd prefer you not do it in the car."

"Ah," I said. "Yes. Good point." I groped for the door handle, but the exquisitely engineered foreign exit mechanisms of the Mercedes would probably have baffled me even had I been sober and working in daylight, and finally Sherman leaned across and opened the door for me. I got out with as much dignity as possible—that is to say, none—and staggered as far as I could toward the far side of the shop before my stomach erupted.

When I returned, Sherman had gotten out of the car and was leaning against the front grill, looking south across the black vastness of the fresh-plowed fields.

"Are you okay?" he asked.

"Much better, thank you." I lit a cigarette and took a deep pull on it to change the taste in my mouth, then blew the smoke toward the darkening sky and settled against the car beside him.

"So, what do you think?" Sherman asked.

"I think I'm ready to begin a tequila-free diet. I think Nick Landon is a bad, bad man. I think Silver Patrón is the elixir of the devil and his minions."

"I meant about. . . well, you know."

I shook my head. The man really was relentless, when he had an angle. "I don't know shit, Bill."

"I think you should give Jocelyn a call."

"Yeah, right. I'll use the hotline."

"I'm serious."

He was, of course. I took another drag off the cigarette and looked away, across the fields, left a little at a loss by the irony of it all. In the southeastern sky, the first star glimmered through the expiring day's heat. I found it comforting; I find all the enduring things comforting.

At last I said, "I remember one summer night when I was five, my grandmother taught me how to make a wish on the night's first star. I was fascinated, of course, I thought it was a terrific deal. I remember I asked her all sorts of technical questions—I wanted to be sure I got it right."

"Uh-huh," Sherman said tentatively. I probably sounded pretty drunk; no doubt he wondered what I was getting at.

"Later on, when she had gone inside, my grandfather and I were still sitting out on the lawn. He hadn't said a word during the whole lesson. And I asked him what his wish had been. I assumed that everyone who knew about this star trick would be making wishes at every opportunity."

"Uh-huh," Sherman said again, still wary.

"And my grandfather said, 'I try not to make wishes anymore if I can help it, because it seems like I always wish for the wrong thing anyway.'" I looked at Sherman. "I didn't understand it at the time, of course. I was still wishing for a bicycle without training wheels, and a new football, and a big dog. But thirty years later I get a glimmer every now and then of what he was talking about."

Sherman smiled. "It sounds to me like I would have liked your grandfather."

"I don't know what to wish for, with Jocelyn, is all I'm saying," I said. "I actually do believe in destiny; I believe we're all in the hands of God here. But it's been more than twenty years since I thought I knew what my destiny with Jocelyn was. And those twenty years have taught me that whatever else destiny is, it's probably not a fairy tale with a happy ending. That's without even beginning to consider the mystery of what Jocelyn's destiny is. Or yours. Or the boys'. It's beyond me, it's all completely beyond me, and pretty much anything I can imagine doing at this point seems wrong to me. So I think I'll just leave it in the hands of God, where it belongs."

Sherman was silent for a long moment. I waited quietly, nursing the last of my cigarette, wondering how long I would be able to maintain this crazed level of equanimity.

"Okay, I can respect that," Sherman said at last. "But just for the record: If you change your mind and decide to get in touch with her, I want you to know you have my blessing."

"That's very . . . gracious, of you."

"Gracious, hell. More like realistic. She's got to run this thing out one way or another. Honestly, I would like to see her happy. And . . ."

"And?"

Bill Sherman met my eyes and gave me the thinnest smile.

"Well," he said. "Let's face it, it's not like it worked out that well the first time for you guys, is it?"

That was plain enough. And there was a comfort of sorts for me, in knowing he had thought it through.

Sherman reached into his pocket and rummaged for his car keys; he'd said his piece, it seemed. I dropped my dying butt on the gravel and ground it out beneath my boot toe.

"Thanks for the drinks," I said.

"My pleasure. I appreciate you taking the time."

"They're on me, next time."

"Fair enough," Sherman said. He shook my hand with his usual lack of ceremony once business was concluded, and got into his car. I watched the Mercedes's taillights until they disappeared, then turned and went into the shop.

Herman Powell's stone was sitting right where I had left it, the ink dry on its surface now. I looked at it for a long time, feeling all my failings keenly. I suppose that if I had completely believed a word of what I had said to Bill Sherman, I could have felt myself to be a decent man centered in the simple virtues. But as things stood, I felt defenseless against my sense of being a phony, a fool, and the worst sort of liar.

CHAPTER ELEVEN

To be patient is to suffer what must be suffered, with grace. There is even a point in the practice of patience where that practice is so sustained, where the suffering is seen to be so bottomless and seemingly endless, and endlessly embraced in ever-new surrender, that the practice of patience can come to seem complete. It can feel as if it is not work anymore, it is just how it is. Maybe that is what saints experience, an embrace of desire's perpetual defeat that has deepened beyond effort into a state of being. Patience has been cooked and cooled by time into compassion, like magma into granite; we wait for nothing anymore, truly. We are free of every scheme to cheat on our mortal dues and the touch that always had a grasping edge of need in it turns to a simple healing gift.

If so, I am no saint. I have a very simple mind, really: there is slow work, and there is stone. Slow work is the only way to work with stone without being destroyed by it in some way or another. This much, at least, is clear to me from years of trials and errors. I am in the business of eternity, but it is not the stone that is eternal. Stone is just very long-lived. It is born, in water or in fire, as the sediment accumulating on the floor of shallow seas that is compressed eventually into limestone and its kin, or as the molten rock from deep in the earth that rises as magma toward the surface and cools into the igneous rocks like granite. It lives, thrust up into mountains and carved down by rivers. And it dies the slow death of stone, worn away by wind and water, the play of temperature and the caress of rain.

In the life of a stone, I am essentially just one more fleeting incident in a long career: I am like a very specific kind of rain. A kind that occasionally uses dynamite, to be sure, and the occasional power sander and jackhammer, but nevertheless a slow, uneven process best seen as doing its work without thought or hope of a particular result on a scale of years and decades. And it is only in seeing myself as working like rain that I have been able to make any peace whatsoever with my own erratic weather.

It was humbling, then, after years of cultivating what I had thought was an atmosphere of patience, to realize how far from accepting the pace and method of rain and wind I actually was with Jocelyn. I was not a free man, and no amount of patience or humility could make me free in this case. I was what I had always been, a love accident waiting to happen.

* * *

The problem of meaning dawned on me abruptly in the spring of my senior year of high school. It happened unforeseeably, and without excessive resort to the mild hallucinogens a number of my friends were experimenting with by then. It was more like a virus, or like mumps or measles, for teenagers: a stage-of-life illness that usually runs its course without inflicting permanent damage. But apparently my immune system was deficient in some way, and the routine existential infirmity in my case turned virulent. I managed to fail every course my last semester of high school, including a study hall in which the only requirement was attendance. I quit the track team, dropped out of the chess club, and resigned from the honor society; and then flunked out of summer school as well. I stopped cutting my hair. If there had been a war that seemed worth fighting to me then, I might have gone off like my father to fight it. But the America my father had fought for was part of the problem for me by then. In any case, it was already too late for me, by the time I was eighteen, to be my father. Or my grandfather, for that matter. But unfortunately, in retrospect, it may have been too soon for me to be myself.

While I was sabotaging my standard-issue future, Jocelyn graduated third in our senior class that June, right on schedule. She had been accepted at Georgetown. Our plan for years by then had been to go off to college together. I would major in architecture and Jocelyn would major in English, or psychology, something that didn't involve differential equations, and we would get married and work hard and have kids and live happily ever after. There was already no going back to that vision for me, but Jocelyn was still the rock of my befuddled world. At that point she was the last thing left that made any sense to me at all. She loved me steadfastly even as I grew unkempt; she was as fearless about my soul's bewilderment as she had always been about snakes, bicycles, and bullies, and never insisted on a hasty reconfiguration. She took my frequently self-indulgent angst in stride, and even from time to time added perceptions of her own that indicated to me that her view of the world was at least as much a colored wound in the mundane gray grid, as mine. And yet she had an athlete's discipline of relevant movement: while I was often immobilized by an excess of meaning, Jocelyn, even at eighteen, could live with existence as a mystery on the most intimate and daily basis, and still get her homework done. When I was with her, I could still feel that life on the planet had some meaning, if only because of the continuity of her skin. But that didn't seem like enough to base a career on.

* * *

The night before Jocelyn left for Washington, D.C. to begin college at Georgetown, we drove out to Surry County with a bottle of excellent port that she had liberated from her father's bar, past the cathedral on Hog Island, to visit our usual river beach by the James one last time. We sat together on the bank as the sun went down, with the Quinta do Noval decanted into a couple of Slurpee cups. The moon, just past full, was coming up from behind the Hog Island nuclear power plant and bats whirled in the air above us in a nearly invisible frenzy marked only by the snap of their jaws on mosquitoes and the occasional flash of black on black, as if the darkness itself were quietly seething. I had not rinsed my Slurpee cup well enough and the aged tawny port had a hint of blue raspberry on the finish, but Jocelyn's kisses tasted like the wine itself. She smelled of apricot and pomegranate and I loved her so much that my skin seemed insufficient to convey it. All I really knew was that I would have crawled through fire to hear the music of her breath.

We sat on a blanket on the cooling sand. Jocelyn was wearing her basic summer outfit, shorts and a sleeveless tee-shirt. At the hollow of her throat hung the crucifix we had found on our first day at the cathedral. She had polished it to a fine sheen and attached it to a thin silver chain, and it glinted now in the moonlight.

This far away from the lights of suburban Hampton Roads, the stars were stunningly clear. In the fourth grade, Jocelyn and I had begun a project of renaming all the constellations, and we had gotten surprisingly far with it by then. To this day, I know certain constellations only by the names that Jocelyn and I came up with for them, in hours of lying on our backs in backyards and on beaches.

I remember my eyes going to the Big Dipper that night.
Jocelyn and I called it "the Drinking Gourd," from an old slave
song: escapees working along the Underground Railroad had
followed the Gourd to freedom. It had always been our favorite
constellation for that reason.

Jocelyn, tuned in to my attention as always, began to sing.
She had a marvelous voice, a natural alto softened and warmed by a
slight southern accent, and it always thrilled me to hear her. All the
elements of the world seemed to fall into a fresh and unforeseeable
order, as the twist of a kaleidoscope makes new beauty from a
jumble of color.

"Follow the Drinking Gourd, follow the Drinking Gourd—"
I usually chimed in and sang along, but that night I was
content to just listen. Across the river from the place where a
Dutch slave ship first sold twenty Africans into tobacco bondage in
1620, and on the verge of a long, uncertain journey ourselves, the
song had a special poignancy and edge.

"When the sun comes up and the first quail calls, follow the
Drinking Gourd—"
Jocelyn broke off abruptly and rummaged in her T-shirt. I
thought at first that she was going after a mosquito or something,
but after a moment she came up with the pewter crucifix. Its chain
had broken, for no apparent reason.

"Weird," she said. "I hope it's not an omen."
"Screw omens," I said. "We'll get another chain in D.C."
She hesitated a moment more, then shrugged it off and put
the cross in her pocket and began to sing again. Tears welled
unexpectedly in my eyes as I listened. I thought then that it was just
the poignancy of an era ending. I was feeling the port, and the
power of the moment, and I recognized the symptoms of an excess
of meaning coming on, the dissolution of comforting patterns into
flabbergasting Mystery. I remember taking Jocelyn's hand and
kissing it as she sang on, hauntingly. The question of our future lay
before us like the river itself, an uncrossable blackness, but the plan
at that point was still for me to accompany her the next morning to

D.C. and get a job bricklaying or something. It was the last time we thought we had forever.

"*For the Old Man is a-waitin' for to carry you to freedom, if you follow the Drinking Gourd.*"

* * *

I spent the week after Bill Sherman's visit applying myself assiduously to the task of not calling his wife. I didn't flatter myself that my barely-maintained restraint was some kind of moral triumph; the more I wrestled with the question, the clearer it was to me that I was holding off from contacting Jocelyn, not because it was wrong, wrong, wrong, but for reasons that were purely and frankly and basely tactical. The truth was, I would have called her in a second, but I couldn't see any way to do so that didn't end up looking like I was the vilest kind of scavenger, scuttling in from the shadows at the first opportunity, to raid the savaged remains of her marriage.

In this calculating frame of mind, it seemed likely to me that Bill Sherman had done the same math himself, and that him urging me to do the big obvious stupid thing as soon as possible was not as magnanimous as it had appeared at first, and might even have had an element of cunning. Clearly, Sherman felt that the image of the road not taken was unsettling Jocelyn, and disrupting a marriage already reeling from the loss of their daughter; and just as clearly, his sense was that the road not taken—me, that is—was a dead end. Therefore he was willing, and even a little eager, for Jocelyn to walk down that road far enough to realize that herself, and thus to get Closure. Pouring a couple of margaritas into me and egging me on to call his wife, in that light, was not a bad bet; it was in Sherman's interest, indeed, for the fiasco to occur as soon and as emphatically as possible. Purged of the fantasy alternative by the predictable disaster, Jocelyn would be free to turn back to the real work of finding the new ground the marriage needed.

I felt sympathy for Sherman's hopes and fears, and a

119

distinct sense of admiration for the courage and psychological sophistication of his approach. It was a kill-or-cure strategy with a high likelihood of succeeding. Especially, of course, if he was right and I was in some way a factor in Jocelyn's mind, and I followed the script and rushed in precipitously where angels feared to tread. But I did not intend to screw up with Jocelyn again.

* * *

On the morning of the autumn equinox, I got to my shop especially early, at about five A.M., intending to put the finishing touches on Herman Powell's stone, and found the answering machine's green light flashing—1-2-3-4, 1-2-3-4. Since the machine had been clear when I left the previous evening, I thought at first that a natural catastrophe must have occurred somewhere overnight, requiring a sad slew of emergency gravestones; but when I played the tape back, all four messages were from Jocelyn Page Sherman. She had called four times between nine and midnight the night before, as if she could will me to the shop after hours by sheer persistence.

From the first sound of her voice, everything within me began to seethe, an electric tumult, as if I had swallowed a live rattlesnake. Truly, I was terrified. It was precisely what I had wanted, of course, what I had hoped and longed for, but now that the moment had actually arrived, the unnerving reality of the situation began to hit me. It is a double-edged grace to be given a second life, under any circumstances; you are miraculously up and about, to be sure, but everything still tastes, inevitably, of ashes and dust. Lazarus, called back to life by Jesus after three days in the grave, stinking of decay, with his burial clothes hanging off him in tatters, must have wondered at times what he had let himself in for. I had felt that way often enough myself since the doctors got my heart beating again on that gurney in the emergency room at St. Francis: the taste of death's peace lingers with astonishing sweetness through your second life. It is why I am easier with the bereaved, I suppose, and why so much of my time is spent in the slow work of making stone speak for the dead. It is a job for Lazarus, commuting from the tomb. I know in my bones that the house of mourning is better than the house of mirth.

In the first message, Jocelyn said that she thought she was ready to do her daughter's stone at last. In the second message, apparently an immediate afterthought, she said she was by no means assuming I would do the job for free and named a price that was about three times too high even for Joe Murphy. The third message, about an hour and a half later according to my machine's automatic reckoning, showed what appeared to be the effects of some wine consumption, and told me to forget the whole thing, she wasn't ready to have her daughter's memorial done, who was she kidding anyway. It was heartbreaking.

But it was the last of the four messages, left just before midnight, that was the killer: "It's me again. I feel like an ass by now. Forget everything I've said. The truth is, I just need to talk with you. Can we talk? Soon?"

I would have called her back at once, at that point, but it was five in the morning and I had to assume that since she'd been up past midnight drinking wine and agonizing about things, Jocelyn probably needed her sleep. I took the necessity for delay as a sort of warning from God to not make any hasty decisions. But I was too jazzed up to get any work done, and in the end, I listened to the entire set of messages three times, then drove out to Little Island park at the end of Sandbridge and took a long walk on the beach.

* * *

As I headed south along the shore in the pre-dawn dark, the ocean's horizon to the east was just beginning to show the faintest softening into gray. The stars were still bright and clear. For a time after Jocelyn and I broke up, I had been unable even to look at the stars without crying, or getting nauseous, and the entire sky had seemed to me like a kind of primordial light soup, patternless and overwhelming. But time does heal. Time, and slow work. It is the truth that tears us open again.

As I walked, farther and farther south beside the gradually lightening expanse of the Atlantic, I did my best to convince myself that it would be wrong to call Jocelyn back. I mean, it was wrong, clearly wrong, wrong for so many reasons I could only begin to list them. It was unprofessional, unethical, immoral, insensitive, and poorly timed. It was unlikely, and unfruitful, and improper. It was dangerous. It was even a little crazy. When my grandfather insisted again and again that the only worthwhile work was done in love, this was not what he had meant. This, in fact, I thought, might well be catastrophically opposed to what he had meant: was probably selfish rather than selfless, likely greedy rather than humble, almost certainly grasping rather than surrendered. Certainly it was a far cry from simple attention to the original job at hand, which was the mete and proper memorialization of Ariel Sherman, the work of formulating her remembrance in the light of eternity.

I thought of Bill Sherman too, miserable in that cheap apartment in Ghent, with his sad futon and his touchingly misguided, by-the-book approach to frozen chicken pot pies, drinking me under the table at the Tiger Cage while urging me to hurry into a fiasco with his wife so that she could get me out of her head and get on with their marriage.

But none of that prevailed. In the end, it was Jocelyn. If Jocelyn offered me an apple, I would take it, no questions asked; I would take whatever fruit or vegetable she offered, indeed, anytime, anywhere, and I would gladly deal with whatever came with that. Most of life happens east of Eden; the Garden is still guarded by an angel with a fiery sword. But the state of the art, east of Eden, is that if you're with the one you love, the closest place to paradise you're going to find on earth is wherever you make the bed.

By the time I was five miles down the coast, the sun was just coming over the edge of the sea and it was clear to me that there was no way I was going to do anything but call Jocelyn back immediately. If God hadn't intended for me to call her, he shouldn't have created a world with telephones. And as for Bill Sherman . . . well, it seemed that he would get his fiasco after all.

I got back to the shop just after nine A.M. The phone was ringing as I came in. In my damn-the-torpedoes state of mind, I was sure it was Jocelyn and I picked it up serene in the anticipation of her rich strong voice, ready to embrace our fate. But it wasn't Jocelyn after all, it was my aunt Terrie, telling me in her quiet way that my grandfather was dead.

CHAPTER TWELVE

I had not expected to be dismayed by my grandfather's death. I had believed for years that I was fully and admirably prepared to welcome it as the completion of a rich life. So I was surprised, when it came to facing the actual event, that I fell down on the floor and could not move for at least an hour.

I kept thinking I would get up any minute, that this was nuts, but it went on and on. The same thing had happened, more or less, when my mother died. You would think that a decade of doing gravestones would have prepared me better to face that fact that people die, but obviously I still had a lot to learn. And I always did work very slow.

* * *

In the end, there was nothing left to do but stand up, brush the stone dust off myself, and get moving again. I shut down the shop, got into my truck, and drove north and then west. The radio seemed like so much noise and I gave up on it as a distraction almost immediately and just drove, smoking cigarette after cigarette. I was numb, unable to formulate a thought, and it was not until the highway passed out of the piedmont and into the foothills of the Appalachians that I began to have flashes of what lay ahead of me, and how different everything was going to be this time at the end of this drive I had made so many times through the years.

I stopped for a very late breakfast near Charlottesville. It was early afternoon by now and I'd been up since four, had walked ten miles on the beach, and hadn't eaten a thing. But when I finally sat down, I found that I wasn't the least bit hungry, I was just tired, as bone-weary as if I had been pushing the truck the whole way myself, and I dozed off over my eggs after the first bite. I woke from a grinding dream of sharpening a chisel that wouldn't hold an edge, a maddening mini-nightmare of inadequate tools, and stared at my barely-touched food as if a stranger had ordered it.

I gave up on the eating idea, drained my coffee, and left a twenty on the table. The waitress, for some reason, patted me on the shoulder as I left. I wondered if I had said something compromising in my sleep, but wrote it off to a theory I have nursed for years of mystical compassion among waitresses. It seemed obvious to me that everyone knew my grandfather had died, that it was written all over me, and that they were just being kind and giving me space.

As I started up the grade to the first mountain pass, about twenty minutes now from my grandparents' home, I could see Little Baldy Mountain to the southwest, its odd bare granite peak protruding above the blue-hazed trees. My grandfather used to take me up there for sunsets; he always said it was the best view on the back side of the Blue Ridge.

The panorama almost broke my heart; I don't think those mountains had ever seemed more beautiful to me. But I was damned if I was going to cry yet. It was not until I turned into my grandparents' driveway and pulled in beside my grandfather's truck, and my Aunt Terrie came out onto the porch, alerted by the sound of my tires on the gravel as she had been a hundred times before, that I lost it.

* * *

The funeral the next day drew a large, remarkably diverse crowd. I confess I was surprised by the number of people present. My grandfather had, after all, outlived most of his cronies and contemporaries. My memories of my own final visits with him while he was still active were all of silence and stillness in the bright peaceful shop, a lack of commerce that had passed relentlessly into serenity, and a vast privacy. I had assumed his worldly relations had more or less faded away. But the little stone church of St. Martha—which my grandfather had helped his father build, on weekends and holidays, during the Depression—was jammed to its dark oak beams for the funeral mass, and a still larger crowd had assembled outside to await the procession to the cemetery.

The funeral mass was said by Father John Busby, which was crazy, of course. All I could think of was how often he had told my grandfather that he was risking eternal damnation for various reasons, and that he owed my grandfather $1.85 from their last rummy game together. They really had done nothing but fight and play cards together, but now Busby was giving the sermon at the funeral mass, and my grandfather's official status was secure in spite of the best efforts of both of them.

The priest spoke eloquently and at length of my grandfather's piety and devotion, his eminence in the community, his virtues as a family man, his marvelous work. He had been, Busby said, "a cathedral mason of the old school, and a truly good man. A saintly man, even."

I glanced around the chapel as he talked on, to see if anyone but me appreciated the irony of all this. Beside me, my grandmother, tiny and radiant in black, was nodding along with the eulogy. I could see that it was music to her ears to hear my grandfather praised as saintly. No doubt it was also a great relief: my grandmother had always had a terror that Busby would follow through on his threats of excommunication, and I think my grandmother felt that Grandpa had gotten in under the wire.

On my left hand, my Aunt Terrie more straightforwardly simmered at what I knew she thought of as hypocrisy in the priest.

She had liked Busby as little as my grandfather had, but she had never shared the old man's sense of a working opposition. She caught my eye now, and rolled her eyes. Beyond her, the grief of my brothers and sisters appeared simple, and their attendance on the priest a little bored. My father, on the other side of my grandmother, had his face turned obligingly forward, but I knew his left eyebrow would be arching at this sermon. That eyebrow had always gotten him in trouble; it was absolutely ungovernable. He looked composed as he sat there in the pew, but I knew how hungover he must be. We had watched the Monday night Redskins game the previous evening at the bar in town, and the game had gone into overtime, which neither of us had figured on. We had ended up so drunk that the night had passed into a spontaneous wake. He had told me that he had loved his father and would miss him a lot, but that, frankly, he just couldn't get too worked up about the fact of death. He had seen too much of it professionally. He was dressed appropriately today in a crisp black suit, but I knew that he would loosen his tie at the first opportunity.

At last the mass ended. With the other pallbearers, I moved to the casket. It was closed now, for which I was grateful. The afternoon before, at the wake at the Chapel of the Oaks funeral home, it had been open to display the undertaker's embalming arts. It had not been a good moment when I approached the casket and saw my grandfather's body frozen there according to someone else's inadequate conception. It had been all I could do to keep myself from tipping the thing over, and generally laying waste to the Chapel of the Oaks, starting with the simpering organ music and working outward from there. If Father Busby's funeral oration had elements of deep irony, my grandfather's final passage through the Chapel of the Oaks approached farce. The Chapel, a large, standardized, all-purpose industrial-strength funeral home offering "the complete package of final accommodations for the dearly beloved," had displaced much of my grandfather's business since the late 70s. His low-key word-of-mouth style was no match for their aggressive marketing techniques and the hard-sell the Chapel salesmen employed like used car dealers. But of course my grandfather had never wavered in his own methods. He was aging himself by then, and unable to take on as many of the other kinds of heavy masonry jobs that had filled the gaps in his younger years. He would sit out in the yard in front of his shop reading Shakespeare, or passages from Isaiah, and waiting quietly.

And of course, in spite of all, the jobs had come in. Invariably, the people who wanted a certain kind of work done had found their way to my grandfather's obscure little place. They came from as far away as Pennsylvania, New York, and Kentucky, from Washington, D.C., and the Carolinas and Ohio. It was as if there was a secret understanding among a certain strain of people along the Appalachians and the Atlantic coast.

Now, however, the Chapel of the Oaks was handling my grandfather's remains. I had arrived too late to avert this; and in any case it was my grandmother's call, and basically none of my business. But as we bore the Deluxe Model Q Eternal Rest Casket toward the Chapel-supplied hearse, I was thinking of my father. The pleasure of watching his left eyebrow arch at all this nonsense was just about the only comfort I was able to find in it.

That, and, of course, the certain knowledge that my grandfather would have laughed and shrugged it off. He had never, as he used to say, worried too much about the shipping and handling.

* * *

At the graveyard there was still more nonsense. Father Busby spoke yet again. The mayor of Shenandoah Springs spoke. A Knight of Columbus spoke. I confess that I stewed. It appeared there was a serious movement to canonize someone who had nothing to do with my grandfather. The crowd was quite large; a lot of people had showed up to say good-bye to the old man.

At last it was over. The casket was lowered into the hole.

My father, and then my aunt stepped up and threw a shovel-full of dirt in after it; the mayor did the same, and then the other family members.

As I waited my turn with the other pallbearers, Father Busby came up to me. I was surprised by this. When I was a kid, I had served several years as an altar boy with him; but we had not spoken since I had left Virginia at eighteen, at which time I had told him in the James Dean way I was cultivating then that I preferred hell to the kind of heaven he and his gang ran. It was a typical statement of the time for me. I had cooled out some since then, of course, though I would never let on that I had to Busby.

"I was there when your grandfather died," he said. "His passing was very peaceful. I gave him the last rites."

His tone had a broad, practiced quality. I realized he was probably giving me the standard comfort-to-the-relatives remarks. But I was in no mood for it now. I said, "The last I heard, you owed him money."

The priest looked startled. "What?"

"There was an IOU from you on the refrigerator door. You owed him a dollar eighty-five. A rummy debt."

"I beat him as often as he beat me," Busby said a little testily, glancing around to be sure no one could hear us, but stout in his own defense. "He owed me money as often as I owed him."

"He was a dollar eighty-five to the good when he died," I said steadily. I had actually reconfirmed this with my grandmother, who had reluctantly acknowledged the situation, but had implored me not to pursue it. She had said my grandfather would have written it off, which was not true. I might have let it go anyway, if Busby had only given one sermon. But two had been too much.

"Well, that's true," Busby conceded. "A dollar eighty-five, that sounds right. I would have paid him sooner or later." And, as I said nothing, "I *would* have paid him."

"Of course you would have."

"Do you think I should pay Annie?"

Annie was my grandmother. "She wouldn't take it. She

took the IOU off the refrigerator and tossed it into the trash." And, as Busby looked relieved, I said, "I think you should pay *me*."

He met my gaze, then, and I saw what my grandfather had no doubt seen in him for four decades. His eyes were a strong firm brown, and very, very steady, unwavering.

At last he smiled, and reached for his wallet underneath his vestments. Somehow I had known, from everything my grandfather had said of him for years, that he would have his wallet with him.

"All I've got is a five," he said.

"I can make change." I rummaged in my own pocket, came up with three singles, and a quarter, and gave these to him.

"So I owe you a dime," he said.

"Call it even." I would have turned away; it was my turn to toss some dirt into the grave. But Busby touched my arm to stop me.

"He was a good man," he said. "A good, good man."

"A cathedral mason of the old school," I said, and did turn away then, before I hugged him or something.

* * *

It felt good to get the shovel in my hand. I threw a good load of dirt into the grave; and then another, and another. The wood handle against my rough palms was a comfort. I realized that one of the things that had bothered me the most about my grandfather's dolled-up corpse—aside from the lipstick, and the touch of rouge on his weathered cheeks—was that he had been given a posthumous manicure, and his hands subjected to lotions to allay the calluses.

I actually kept shoveling for a while, it felt so good to be working. I had tossed about six or eight shovels-full in before my father took my arm.

"Easy, there, sport."

"No, it's okay," I said, thinking he meant I was working

too hard, and I showed him the calluses on my own hands.

"No, let someone else take a turn," my father said. "There are people waiting."

I looked around, and realized how caught up I had gotten. "Yeah, yeah, of course, you're right," I said. "I'm sorry."

"A lot of people loved him," my father said, at which I began to cry. I surrendered the shovel to the next guy, a weathered sober man in clean overalls and a John Deere cap, and stepped aside to watch as the people approached and tossed their bit of dirt in. There were a scores of them; I had not realized there were so many.

A lot of them paused afterward to shake my hand, or embrace me, and to tell me how glad they were to have known my grandfather. Most of them mentioned a particular incident or piece of work he had done for them, a bit of timely wisdom or an act of charity; and most of them thanked me.

I was uncomfortable with the gratitude at first; I was dizzy in fact as it poured through me. I felt unworthy and misfit to the role until I realized that it really was him they were thanking, through me. I was a local convenience, and all I really had to do was to keep my mouth shut and stand in quietly for the presence that had brought them all there. Then I got less dizzy, and steadier on my feet; and at last I got quiet and calm and still, standing there in the sunshine in the expanse of green, amid the trees and stones, while the birds sang, seeing everyone as I supposed he must have seen them while he was alive, to cause such a crowd of love to come around.

* * *

The next day I went out to the Big Rabbit Quarry to pick out my grandfather's stone. The quarry is just inland from the fall line of the James River south of Richmond, where the more ancient bedrock of the western part of Virginia, the upsurge of igneous and metamorphic rock that made the Appalachians, meets the marine sediment of the tidewater region, and so you can find distinct strata of granite, slate, and limestone there. The quarry itself is one of the oldest working quarries in the country. My grandfather, like his forefathers, cut almost all of his own rock and some of the most vivid memories of my childhood were of the working trips I took with him to Big Rabbit.

The quarry in those days had been run by an old Quiyoughcohannock Indian named Jake Awahili, who was six-foot-six and had a majestic sweep of dark nose with two bends in it, one natural like the bend in a hawk's beak, and one acquired in a bar fight. The man who had put the second bend in his nose was dead, and Jake had spent eight years in prison for manslaughter, though he always maintained that if he'd known the guy was so fragile he would never have hit him so hard.

Jake did not actually think of himself as owning the land. He saw it rather that he was caretaking it for the spirit of the earth, but he would accept payment on that basis. I remember him and my grandfather sitting around with the tobacco my grandfather always brought. The two of them treated each other with elaborate respect. My grandfather wasn't a smoker by any means, but he would always take two ceremonial puffs from the pipe Jake provided, stifling his coughs politely. Even I would be given a ceremonial puff. It always made my head go light.

After they had smoked, Jake and my grandfather would go for a walk around the quarry, circling it once or twice or even in certain challenging cases three times, until my grandfather by broad means communicated to Jake what was required. Then Jake would stop at once and carefully tamp out the fire in the pipe, saving the remaining tobacco in a little possum pouch. He would stand for a moment absolutely still. He felt very keenly his role as mediator; it was more important to him even than his alcoholism. Jake always wanted to know what the stone was for—for a wall or a floor or what, or was it for a gravestone. If it was a gravestone, he wanted to know who had died. Then he would stand still for another moment, until the spirit led him to just the spot, a process that often took as much as an hour. Finally he would indicate to my grandfather the appropriate place from which to take his stone. Then he would go back to the house and smoke up the rest of the tobacco while my grandfather and I got to work. Jake Awahili had lived a great deal longer than his drinking habits and smoking might have indicated; his emphysema did not finally kill him until the mid-eighties. Though my grandfather never said so, I knew that he missed Jake Awahili's flamboyant mysticism more than a little. The old Quiyoughcohannock's peculiar blessing on a stone had meant something. What, God only knew, but a blessing was a blessing.

* * *

These days the Big Rabbit was run by Jake's nephew, Little Mike. I had known Mike Awahili since we both were ten and he was the premier centerfielder in the county Little League. He had played for the Sparrows, and I had played for the Oaks, and he had hit an awesome home run off my best fastball one night to knock us out of the regional playoffs. He had taken over the quarry from his uncle not long after I came back from California and got back into stone work myself, so our lives felt intertwined at that level too.

The Big Rabbit is set in some gentle hills southwest of Richmond, at the end of a one-and-a-half lane road rife with savage potholes from the big truck traffic. The quarry was quiet on the Sunday morning after my grandfather's funeral. Mike employs mostly cousins and tribesmen and the place has a pretty leisurely feel to it even during the week, though they can definitely crank things up for a big order. I knew the office would be closed down, so I drove past it and on to Mike's house, which is just far enough away from the quarry that the dynamite blasts don't break the windows.

Little Mike had heard me coming and he stepped out onto the porch as I drove up. He is even bigger than his huge uncle was, about 6'8", and shaped roughly like a limestone block himself, and as if that wasn't daunting enough, he had a twelve-gauge shotgun in one hand and a pipe in the other. Big Jake had always greeted my grandfather in the same way. They insist it is an old Quiyoucohannock custom, and I gather that the idea is that a visitor is being offered his choice of which way things can go. But you would have had to have been nuts to choose the shotgun with the Awahilis.

I knew Mike had heard about my grandfather, from the look on his face, and by how quickly he set the shotgun aside. We settled on the porch as always and stoked the corncob pipe, which was decorated in the ancient Quiyoughcohannock style, as Mike's bong is as well, and had a couple hits each while we caught up with each other. Then we ate several bowls of granola with raisins and bananas. It was pretty much the way things always went at the Big Rabbit. If you were in a hurry to get your limestone quarried, you went down the road to Eagle Rock in Botetourt County, where the noise never stopped.

Finally we went out into the quarry to pick out my grandfather's stone. Little Mike had stayed true to his uncle's old ceremonial way of choosing the blocks for a job, and we paused as we got down to the first ledge, waiting for the spirit to move.

The sky was threatening; after the sunny funeral the day before, a mountain rain coming. Little Mike was wearing a T-shirt that said, "MAYBE." Just that, no elaboration. I had wondered about it earlier, and I asked him about it now. He shrugged.

"My uncle gave it to me," he said. "I never understood it myself, until one day a few years ago, when your grandfather came by. We got stoned together—"

"Wait a minute. You got stoned with my *grandfather*?"

"Just that once. I think he might have thought it was a new kind of tobacco. He was trying to teach me how to roll the cigarettes with one hand, like my uncle used to do."

I could picture the scene perfectly. "So what happened?"

"Nothing," Little Mike said. "I never could learn that trick.

I still need two hands."

"No, I mean with my grandfather. Stoned."

"Oh, that. Well, he was cool. He was here to pick out a stone for some old guy who had died. And I was wearing this T-shirt. And he looked at it, we both looked at it, and then he said, 'So that's how your uncle did it.' Like it was a big revelation."

I looked at him. Mike had a nose like old Jake Awahili's, though it only had one natural bend in it, without the second violent angle. "I don't get it."

"It has to do with the nature of prayer," Mike said. "I mean, shit, we were blitzed. You sort of had to be there."

I shook my head. "I can't believe you got stoned with my grandfather."

We circled the quarry twice, and then a third time. Fat drops began to fall, intermittently at first and then in earnest. I had no intention of coming in out of that rain until I had picked out my grandfather's stone. Little Mike, for his part, acted like he stood out in the autumn rain all the time.

At last we stopped in front of a particularly old cut. It had last been quarried so long ago that natural erosion was evident again on the face, which was seamed beautifully in rose streaks. It seemed to me that the granite was ripe.

"How about here?" I said.

"Maybe," said Little Mike. He met my eyes, and after a moment we both began to laugh.

"Your grandfather was a hell of a guy," he said. "I'll miss him."

CHAPTER THIRTEEN

I spent another three days in Shenandoah Springs closing out my grandfather's shop, packing up his tools, and drinking too much with my Aunt Terrie. By the time I got back to my own shop, the hewn block of granite that Little Mike Awahili and I had picked out in the rain was sitting in a flimsy wooden crate in the front yard, with comic little red "Handle With Care" tags stuck all over it. There was a note from Mike on it. He had paid the shipping costs himself, and in lieu of an invoice for the stone had included a photograph of Big Jake Awahili and my grandfather in their late middle age, lounging on a ledge in the Big Rabbit quarry in twin black felt hats, both of them with devil-may-care grins on their faces, like old bandits. I recognized the hat my grandfather wore; I had taken it off the peg just inside his shop door the day before, and it was now sitting on the front seat of my truck, complete with its hummingbird feather.

I spent a few minutes trying to figure out where to put the unworked gravestone. The main work surface in my shop, a big oak tree stump, was already taken by Herman Powell's stone, and I couldn't really think of anywhere to put my grandfather's stone except in the back corner of the shop beside the granite block of my mother's untouched monument. There would have been a weird rightness to that—I really didn't know what to do with either of them—but it also seemed like a slippery slope of sorts. I could picture that part of the shop accumulating deferred griefs through time, littered with more and more unworked gravestones of people I loved, all my failures to make peace with loss sitting there as quite literal blocks. It would eventually become a sort of geological Bermuda Triangle; I would become known as the gravestone carver you went to if you really weren't ready for a memorial, and people with unresolved grief issues would regularly arrive at the shop, drink a six-pack of the beer of their choice with me, and then wander back there into the realm of the undone and never return.

I decided to just leave the stone where it was in the yard for the time being, and turned to unload the truck. But even here was emotional trickiness: the truck bed and passenger space were crowded with my grandfather's tools and all the accumulated sentimental odds-and-ends from his shop. My grandmother had insisted that I take everything, which made sense in its way, but it was unnerving to find myself the sole trustee of this treasure trove. My grandfather's life was here, and the lives of his father and those before him, all the way back to Jacob Tremaine; a centuries-spanning history of love and slow work was etched into the scars of every mallet and chisel. I felt completely unworthy to even be handling some of these tools, much less using them, and it was certainly impossible for me to see myself as owning them in any way.

There were hundreds of different tools: coffee cans and toolboxes crammed with dozens of chisels for limestone, marble, and granite; wooden mallets and steel hammers, air hammers, calipers, rasps, drills, straight edges, carpenter's squares, and various obliques. You really do need hundreds of tools for stone carving: I know guys who only use certain points for a single letter on a specific kind of stone: they have their Q point for marble and their S point for granite, and so on. But it is also true that most carvers have a few basic tools they use for most of their work.

My grandfather's main set of tools—a general pitching

tool, an air hammer, a quarter-inch chisel, several toothed chisels, a flat chisel, and a double-ended file—were in an exquisite old hand-crafted oaken toolbox made by his father, which I had set on the passenger seat of the truck and buckled in for the trip back from Shenandoah Springs. Beside that were several other items that had struck me with particular force: the hat with the hummingbird feather, the cherry wood mallet that Jacob Tremaine had brought over from Ireland in 1848, the sign that had hung over the entrance to my grandfather's shop, hand-carved on an oak plaque by Big Jake Awahili in 1955, that read, *"Except the Lord build the house, they labour in vain that build it;"* and my grandfather's second edition copy of John Howard Benson's translation and facsimile text of Arrighi's *Operina*, the first writing manual of the Chancery script. The book, purchased for $2.50 in 1955, was signed by the author, who had taught my grandfather calligraphy in the 1940s, and would probably have been worth a lot of money if it hadn't been almost comically beat-up from hard use. But it still struck me as priceless. And it seemed like as good a place as any to start: I laid it, along with the mallet, gently in the tool box, put the sign on top of that, placed the black felt hat on my head at a jaunty angle, and carried the armload into the shop.

Inside, my answering machine light was blinking faithfully—1-2-3-4-5, 1-2-3-4-5. I set the toolbox down on the counter and hit the PLAY button apprehensively. The first four calls were sympathy messages about my grandfather, from a sweet cross-spectrum of relatives and friends, including a call from Joe Murphy. His approach to helping me deal with my grief involved us getting very drunk together as soon as possible, which actually seemed like a good idea to me.

The final message was from Jocelyn. A daylight call, from the previous afternoon. She sounded determinedly sober and somewhat subdued, but my heart leaped anyway at the sweet music of her voice:

"Hey, it's me. I promised myself I would give you a week to call back, before I did anything else. But obviously I didn't make it the whole week and here I am. I hope all those semi-drunken messages didn't freak you out. I'm . . . sort of undone. But I'm not trying to guilt you into something and I understand completely if you don't want to call back. I mean, let's face it, it's probably the sensible thing." There was a long pause, and then she said, dryly, a pure Jocelyn touch, "It would be just like you to do the sensible thing now, for the only time in your life."

I had no intention of doing the sensible thing. I was undone too. And, after burying my grandfather, keenly conscious that life is much too short, even if you live into your nineties, to not return calls from your one true love. I picked up the receiver at once. The Shermans' home phone number had been written on my memo pad since I had copied it from their check, in a most professional fashion, the day of their first visit, and by now it had been circled so many times that it looked like a doodle of a supernova; but in any case I had long since memorized the number from all my non-calls over the previous months.

* * *

The phone at the Shermans' house rang four times and then the answering machine picked up. I don't know what I had expected. I suppose I had assumed that since I felt so firmly in the grip of destiny, in the perfect ripeness of the moment, Jocelyn herself would answer the phone on the first ring and the years and their complications would melt away like the last spring snow and flowers would bloom and birds would sing. We would speak truths of the heart, ancient and immediate, and all would be well and all manner of things would be well. But I was startled to hear Bill Sherman's voice on the answering machine, as firm, brisk, and in control of the situation as ever: "*Hello. You have reached the Shermans.* . . ."

There was no reason for Jocelyn to have changed the machine message, of course; it meant nothing, in itself, and changing it would no doubt have upset the boys and been too public an evidence of the separation. But it flustered me badly to hear Bill's voice. As he ran through the various options available to me, one for pager, two to leave a callback number, wait for the beep to leave a message, I considered just hanging up. I couldn't imagine saying anything into the machine that wouldn't sound like I was leaving a message for Bill saying that I wanted to sleep with his wife.

The greeting came to its end and, in the pregnant instant before the beep, I almost just cut my losses and hung up the phone. But at the last moment I hit the # button instead. Which was nuts, of course. If it was borderline wrong, and even felt craven, to leave a message, calling the hot line Joshua had set up for his father was simply despicable. But Jocelyn had been right, as always: it was just not in my nature to do the sensible thing.

The red phone in the living room rang once and Joshua picked up almost instantly. Of course. He'd probably rigged a beeper on his belt or something, to tell him when it was activated. "Dad?"

The hope and joy in his voice broke my heart. "Uh, no, sorry," I said. "This is Eli Tremaine."

"Who?"

"The gravestone guy, not the plumber."

"Oh, you." My heart sank further at his tone. Joshua was silent for a painful moment, and then he said, "How did you get this number?"

I would have liked to tell him it was a mistake of some kind, but it was hard to claim a wrong number on something so technically specific. "Your dad told me about it."

Another awkward silence followed. I was keenly conscious of not being his father. But it was several decades too late to do anything about that, and at last I said, to break the impasse, "How is your sewer research coming along?"

"The existing system seems adequate," Joshua conceded. "Sort of primitive. I submitted a proposal for some improvements, but I feel like they're just humoring me. There's a real institutional inertia."

"Bureaucracy."

"And money."

I was struck anew by how much work it took to remember that the kid was eight. I said, "I didn't say it to you that first day we met, but I am so sorry about your sister."

"She's in heaven now," Joshua said. I could hear the tentative note in his voice: still trying the notion out.

"Yes, she is."

"I wish there was some way to find out if she's all right there."

My heart panged. I had a brief image of his intricate brain at work on the problem, trying to come up with some equivalent of a GPS transponder for the soul, to trace his sister's course through the system. I said, "I think the whole point of heaven is that she's all right there."

"Still, you'd like to be sure."

"Yeah."

"Are you going to be working on her gravestone again?"

"I'm not sure."

"How do you do that?"

"What?"

"The stone. I mean, the lettering and all. Do you just start carving the letters or what?"

"I ink them on first," I said, wondering what he was getting at.

"And then use a chisel?"

"Or a point. Different tools for different kinds of stone."

"Have you ever thought of using a computer?"

I felt a sudden and unexpected sympathy for the sewer department officials, and a distinct touch of my own institutional inertia. "I honestly haven't. How would that work?"

"You could do your layout on the screen, and then use a computer-guided laser for the etching."

"Really?"

"Why not?"

"What about depth and shading?"

"I'd have to look into it," Joshua said. "But in principle it seems pretty straightforward."

"Uh-huh."

"A laser that could cut stone could double as a death ray."

"That could work out well," I said. "Then if business ever got slow, I could just switch the machine from script mode to death ray mode and make a few new customers."

Joshua laughed, and then, catching me off guard again, asked, "Are you going to start dating my mom?"

If I'm lucky, I thought, but I said, blandly enough, "That would be presumptuous." And, as he considered that blatant bit of obfuscation for chinks, "Is she around, by the way?"

"Yes," he conceded.

"May I speak with her?"

There was a pause; I suspected he was looking for some way to say no. But he finally said, grudgingly, "Sure."

The phone rattled on the table in the Shermans' living room, and a silence followed, during which I began, for the first time, to feel the vertigo and wonder what the hell I thought I was actually going to say.

* * *

The last time I had talked to Jocelyn on the telephone, I had called from a truck stop just north of Richmond on I-95, at 7 A.M. on the morning after our last night together by the James River. I called right about the time I was supposed to show up in her driveway for the drive up to Georgetown we had planned together. But I had awakened that morning at about four o'clock, from a dream in which I was playing golf with Jocelyn's father, Parker Page. We were on the last hole and I was two strokes up. I had tailed my drive into a fairway sand trap, but Parker hooked his into the woods, so I was in good shape. All I had to do was get out of the sand, hack it up the fairway onto the green, and three-putt, and I had him beaten. But in the dream the sand turned endless, a Saharan expanse. My mouth was parched, but not from the competitive pressure. The heat waves rippling off the dunes dissolved the world into an undulating haze, the baked sand stretched on and on, and I began to panic, not because I wasn't going to make bogey, or because I was going to lose yet another round of golf to Poppa Page, but because I was going to die there.

When I woke up, my entire body was jangling, as if I'd brushed a live wire. But I was weirdly, irrationally resolute. It turned out I had been mulling my course of action, invisibly, for quite some time. I dressed in jeans and shrugged on my backpack, which was already loaded for the trip to Georgetown with Jocelyn. I left my tools and books, my music and my extra clothes, in their boxes, left a note for my parents and an extra bowl of food for the dog, and walked out into the pre-dawn darkness. The suburban streets at that hour felt like a ghost town, but the stars were bright and clear beyond the streetlights. It was half a mile to the freeway ramp and I walked steadily, easy beneath the weight of the backpack, heading north and west, following the Drinking Gourd.

* * *

"Eli?" Jocelyn said, picking up the phone at the Shermans' house.

"Yeah. Hi."

"Did you call on this line?"

"Yeah."

"How—?"

"It's a long story."

"I'll bet it is. Obviously you've talked to Bill."

"Yeah."

"When?"

"I don't know. A month ago, maybe."

"He never mentioned it."

"It was a guy thing, I guess."

"I guess it was."

I couldn't read her tone, which was definitely overlaid with something. I had once spoken perfect Jocelyn, but my ear was rusty. I decided to just let it ride, and we were silent for a long moment. But at last Jocelyn got past whatever it was she was churning through and said, "Well, I'm glad you called. I was pretty sure you were scared off. Not that I could possibly blame you for that."

"I was going to call the morning I got your first messages. But my grandfather died that day."

"Oh, God. I'm sorry."

"I kept meaning to call anyway. But it was a little bit of a time warp kind of thing up there."

"I understand."

We were silent a moment, and then Jocelyn said, "Where are you now?"

"At the shop."

"Not at a truck stop?"

I was still fluent enough in Jocelyn-speak to understand that I was being gently twitted. It was actually a relief to hear the teasing note. The past might have been a minefield, but Jocelyn was willing to dance in it.

"Inbound, not outbound," I said. "I just got back, like, five minutes ago, with a truckload of my grandfather's tools."

"So you probably are going to need some time to—"

"No," I said. "I want to see you."

"Really? When?"

"Now?"

Jocelyn hesitated, and my heart sank, but it was a purely pragmatic pause, because after a moment she said, "I'll have to get a sitter for the boys, which may take a bit of doing. But I could meet you in an hour or so."

"Wonderful. Where?"

"How about at St. James the Apostle?" she said.

"Is that where—?"

"Yes. Is that okay?"

"Perfect," I said. "I'll see you in an hour."

CHAPTER FOURTEEN

The Church of St. James the Apostle was a wonderful old Virginia Beach institution, dating back to the 1630s. The first building was placed too close to the Lynnhaven River and it went under around 1690, at which point a second church was erected a bit more prudently inland. Most of the congregation had drifted west toward Kempsville over the decades, and then centuries, and the church stopped being used regularly around 1840. The original building burned in a forest fire in 1882, leaving nothing standing but a few shards of roofless brick walls and some scorched gravestones, but a local family continued to hold a service in the ruins once a year, to keep the site from reverting back to secular title. They finally started rebuilding the thing around the turn of the twentieth century and finished the "new" church just before World War I.

The true history of any place includes weirdness, and St. James was no exception. It was in the jail near the second church building that Grace Sherwood, known as "the Witch of Pungo," was held in 1706. Grace, it is said, was a beautiful and willful woman, and apparently an inconveniently independent one, and for years her neighbors had accused her of blighting their gardens, causing their livestock to die, exciting undue attention by their husbands, and other witch-like behaviors. It all came to a head in the summer of 1706, and on July 10 of that year, Grace was marched from the jail, trailed by the large and venal crowd that had come from all over the tidewater for the spectacle. They paraded her through the churchyard of St. James and down the dirt lane that is now called Witch Duck Road. At the point of land jutting out into what is now called Witch Duck Bay, she was ceremonially "tried by water": that is, tied up and tossed into the Lynnhaven River. If she had drowned, it would have proven her innocence, but Grace Sherwood managed to pull off a Houdini-like escape from her bindings. It is said that she lounged off-shore for quite a while, blowing spouts of water from her mouth, doing water-ballet-like moves, and generally taking advantage of the opportunity for a leisurely swim. When she did finally swim to shore, she was taken straight back to the jail, where she spent the next eight years awaiting a proper trial for witchcraft. In the end, the pack of petty women who had originally accused her relented, and Grace was finally released in 1714, and went back to her home on Muddy Creek Road in Pungo, where she lived into her eighties. The governor of Virginia actually issued a somewhat belated pardon for her just a few years ago. The spot of her house is a couple miles from my shop, and there is a decent bar nearby, right on the edge of the Back Bay National Wildlife Preserve, where I go from time to time to meditate on the vagaries of fate and beautiful women.

The Church of St. James these days is much more sedate, and less associated with jails: a squat, sturdy building of weathered brick cradled in the shade of centuries-old oaks and elms, with a modern wing of classrooms and offices to the west and the cemetery sprawling toward the river on the east. When I arrived that afternoon, Jocelyn was not there yet. The only person around was Charlie Fox, the cemetery sexton, whom I knew well from our professional entwining over the years. Charlie is a sweet potato of a man, lumpy and good-natured, with pale freckled skin that burns easily and hair the color of a fading carrot. As I came around the corner of the church, he was on his hands and knees, surrounded

by racks of plastic seedling cups, planting a bank of magenta
pansies along the shaded brick wall on the east side of the church.
The early-flowering masses of azaleas that illuminate St. James in
the spring had long since gone shabby, and even the July-blooming
crepe myrtles were spent by now; but Charlie loves his color, and
pansies planted in the autumn will bloom through most winters
here.

"Uh-oh," he said, glancing up as I approached. "Here's
trouble."

"Business is slow, I see," I said.

Charlie shrugged. "Weather's too nice. There won't be any
funerals until we get some bad weather. There's a hurricane just off
the coast of South Carolina right now. If it comes north, it's a
death sentence for at least three people."

It didn't appear that he was in any hurry to stand up, so I
squatted beside him companionably. Charlie is a truly good man,
with a slightly twisted sense of humor, which is typical of the
cemetery sextons I have known. He and I have dug, and filled, our
share of graves together, and Charlie loves to crank up his state-of-
the-art boombox while we work and blast out things like Queen's
"Another One Bites the Dust" and Oingo Boingo's version of
"Dead Man's Party," which is a real rocker. Today he seemed to be
in a bluesy mode, and Son House was singing "Death Letter" at a
reasonable volume.

"I got the letter this morning, what do you reckon it read? . . . "

Charlie also knows all the graveyard's ghosts. Grace
Sherwood is a regular visitor here and Charlie says she is still a little
pissed off about the whole witch-ducking thing. I remind him that
the sexton at St. James in 1706 was almost certainly involved in the
ducking, and that the Witch of Pungo's ghost is probably just
waiting for a ripe moment to kick his ass, but Charlie insists that
they have a good relationship. And he does work at it, I must
admit. The church grounds are redolent with a rich sprinkling of
rosemary bushes that Charlie has planted, grown from cuttings
from one of the original rosemary plants at Grace Sherwood's

Muddy Creek home.

"I got the letter this morning, what do you reckon it read? . . ."

Charlie sat back on his heels, brushed the dirt off his hands, and took out a pack of Camels. He offered me one, which I accepted, and we both lit up. A blue jay was squawking in a nearby oak tree, and a wren flitted across an expanse of grass, paused on the peak of a tilted old cruciform gravestone, then flicked away into the shade. Throughout the cemetery, half a dozen squirrels went about their business among the monuments, gathering the season's scattered acorns.

"You know it said hurry, hurry, 'acause the gal you love is dead."

"So what brings you out here?" Charlie asked.

"I'm meeting a friend."

"Ahh. A friend, eh?"

"It's not like that," I said. Though of course I hoped it would be. "It's an old friend from high school, whose daughter was buried here last December."

"Oh jeez," Charlie said. "Ariel Sherman?"

"Yeah."

"That was a bad one. Remember that freeze?" Charlie's first thought on any death is, perhaps inevitably, the weather. "I had to pour gasoline on the ground and light it, just to get the soil soft enough to get a shovel tip in. 'Bout burned my eyebrows off in the process. Small grave, though. A kid, I mean. Sad, sad, sad."

"Breaks your heart," I said.

We sat quietly for a moment. Son House gave way to Lightnin' Hopkins singing "Death Bells." Charlie is nothing if not consistent, when he's on a roll.

"Sounds like I can hear
death bells ringin' in my ear . . ."

"We had a funny one last week," Charlie said at last, more conversationally. "Guy ran a shipping business, pretty successful. Dies of a heart attack and it turns out he's requested a special casket—"

"Sounds like I can hear

death bells ringin' in my ear . . ."

"Uh-huh," I said. Charlie will tell his stories, it comes with the territory.

"So I thought I'd seen it all. But on the day of the funeral, lo and behold, a UPS truck is leading the funeral procession. Driving with its headlights on, right in front of the family's limo. Weird, right? Well, the whole convoy pulls in behind it, and sure enough, they take the casket out of the UPS van. And the casket is painted to look like a big wooden shipping crate, with 'RETURN TO SENDER' stamped on it in red letters. Can you believe it?"

"Yeah I knowed I was gon' leave on a chariot,
but I didn't know what kind o' chariot
gon' take me away from here."

"See what Brown can do for you," I said.

"Eight guys in brown uniforms as the pallbearers."

"I hope the widow didn't have to sign for it."

"Seems like a lot of trouble to go to," Charlie agreed. "It was amusing, though."

"A barrel of fun, I'm sure." I stubbed out my Camel and dropped the butt into one of the empty plastic planter six-packs. "Would you mind showing me the grave?"

"The UPS delivery? Not much to see, really. Joe Murphy's doing the stone, pretty standard, but it's not in yet."

"Ariel Sherman's."

"Oh." Charlie had the grace to look sheepish. "Yeah. Of course." He stood up with a sort of creak and a groan, but willingly enough, and led me through the cemetery, weaving among the monuments dating back to the seventeenth century deftly, like a cabbie in slow traffic.

"It's in a good neighborhood," Charlie remarked as we walked, and in fact I was a little surprised that we were going so far back in the cemetery. Plots at St. James are as precious as Manhattan real estate and Ariel Sherman's gravesite was in a prime location, in one of the older, shadier sections.

"It may be a little pricey for me," I said. "I was thinking

something more along the lines of a starter grave, in a decent neighborhood with good schools."

Charlie ignored me magnificently. "There are a bunch of Walkes right over there, and Kellams, and a couple Hoggards."

I just nodded. To me a grave means you are dead, and under ground, but Charlie delights in the finer social touches and community dynamics. And it was true that Ariel Sherman had been put to rest in a gorgeous spot.

We finally stopped in a grassy clearing that got sunlight even this late in the year, just beyond the big shade ring of a towering old oak tree. The grave itself was a simple patch of grass, stoneless, of course, but marked by a number of expiring bouquets in brass vases and a small rosebush. The bush had half a dozen buds forming, and one of them was just splitting open at the tip, showing a hint of gold.

"This is going to be beautiful," I said.

"The kid's favorite color was yellow," Charlie said. "They wanted a forsythia too, for the spring bloom, but I talked them down to this. It's totally against the rules, the lawn mower guy wants to kill me. But the husband slips me a twenty every time he's here, and he's here a lot. I'd take a bullet for this bush by now."

"Amazing that it wants to flower this late in the year."

"Good sun here," Charlie noted professionally. "But you're right, it really shouldn't be blooming until next summer. We put it in this March, at the parents' request, and of course they wanted flowers right away, but that's not realistic. I mean, don't get me wrong, it's a great strain, a Meilland hybrid tea rose, one of the hardiest types. Also know as 'Gloria Dei,' or the 'Peace' rose. And I've been giving it tons of this super-primo, semi-bionic, nuclear mutant plant food. The thing may stand up some day and take over the city. But it is sort of a miracle that it's budding already."

A movement back toward the church caught my eye. I glanced up and saw that Jocelyn had arrived. My heart leaped at the sight of her. My heart, it seemed, would always leap at the sight of her. She was dressed simply, in jeans and a gray sweatshirt. But she

151

looked wonderful to me.

Jocelyn spotted me and waved, and I waved back, self-conscious in front of Charlie.

"She doesn't get out here much," Charlie confided, in a lowered tone. "Not like the husband. I think this is the first time I've seen her here since last spring, in fact."

I felt a surge of furious adrenaline, at the apparent note of disapproval. "You're a gossipy old woman, Charlie."

He shrugged defensively, taken aback by my vehemence, but said mildly enough, "You say that like it's a bad thing." And, as Jocelyn approached, "Well, I guess I'll get back to work. Give me a holler if you need anything."

"Will do," I said, already regretting the snap.

Charlie ambled off back to his pansies, nodding politely to Jocelyn as they passed each other halfway. I stood on the grass in the sun, conscious of my heart in my chest. In the moment's welcome quiet, freed of the buzz of Charlie's brain, I was struck, for the first time, by the significance of the location Jocelyn had chosen for our first private encounter in twenty years. In high school, she and I would have seen a cemetery as a perfect place to make out and I would have been more or less entirely focused on getting to second base. But it was hard to generate much anticipatory lasciviousness standing here at her daughter's grave. Which was, I suspected, the point.

Jocelyn reached the clearing and stopped several steps away from me, about a foot beyond what I would have considered normal. I was ready to meet her eyes, but her gaze went first to the rose bush. It made sense: If Charlie was right, she hadn't seen the bush since it was planted, and no doubt it had filled out strikingly. But I still had to ride through a little wave of hurt at the neglect, and I felt a touch of unexpected sympathy for Bill Sherman, who had likely experienced hundreds of moments like this, as his wife's heart turned first and always to the place of grief.

Jocelyn looked at up me at last. Despite the extra physical step between us, there was nothing of distance in her eyes. It was the look I had seen on the dock that afternoon behind their house, ruined and defenseless, open to all pain, and without contrivance.

"Hey there," she said. Our old ritual greeting.

I said, "I see you found a new chain for that cross."

Jocelyn smiled and fingered the crucifix at her throat. "I didn't know if you would even notice."

"I noticed it the first day you came to the shop. It just seemed inappropriate at that point to start sobbing or something."

"That was the first time I'd worn it in twenty years," Jocelyn said. "Do you remember the night it broke?"

"Of course."

"You said, 'Screw omens.'"

The woman never forgot a thing. I said, "I think it's pretty well established by now that I am an idiot."

"I *did* get a new chain in D.C., as soon as I got there. I was still sure at that point that you'd show up again any day. But the new one broke too, and the one after that. It was like the thing had a curse on it or something—nothing would hold it. And, of course, no you. I wanted to throw it out, a dozen times, but I never had the heart. I finally just stuck it in my jewelry box."

Charlie cranked up his boombox volume just then, and the opening chords of Blind Willie Johnson singing "You Must Have That True Religion" blared out, a twanging plink of slide guitar, at a level just short of obnoxious. I realized that I had probably stung him after all, with that gossipy old woman crack. But I didn't want to hear anybody dishing dirt about Jocelyn.

"*Death is slow but death is sure, hallayloo. . .* "

Jocelyn smiled at the abrupt infusion of Delta moans. "Seems like we have a soundtrack."

"Charlie's usually pretty sensitive. I think I may have pissed him off."

She shrugged. "It's all right."

She meant that nothing much really mattered, in context. The silence of the grave at our feet could have drowned out a Metallica concert. I considered hollering at Charlie anyway, then decided she was probably right.

"Death is slow but death is sure, hallayloo.

Death is slow but death is sure, when death comes somebody must go.

Then you must have that true religion, hallayloo."

"I just wanted you to see this spot," Jocelyn said at last. "To get a feel for it."

"It's beautiful," I said, and wondered instantly whether that was inane. It was her child, after all, who lay here, beneath this sweet green grass and blue sky. But Jocelyn simply nodded.

We settled back into silence. It was a surprisingly easy, unstressed quiet, and I just went with it, waiting for Jocelyn to set the tone. She actually seemed serene, which I had not expected. At this point, I didn't know whether I should be courting her, crying with her, or urging her to reconcile with her husband. All I knew was that I was glad to be with her. The fear of the Lord is the beginning of wisdom, and twenty years without Jocelyn in my life had burned that fear into my bones. I would take what came with her now, whatever it was, as if it came from the hands of God.

Even Blind Willie Johnson's mournful tale of death and grief and faith seemed to fit the moment somehow. But the next song from Charlie's boombox was Sioux City Pete and the Beggars screaming out "Death Rattle." Heavy metal blues, edgy and raw, which is all very well if you're the only one in the cemetery and you're driving a backhoe, but in context it amounted to an assault. At least I didn't have to be uncertain about it any more: I had definitely made Charlie mad.

I drew in my breath to holler at him, because it really was too much, but Jocelyn stepped close and put her hand on my arm to stop me.

"It's okay," she smiled. "Let's go for a walk."

154

CHAPTER FIFTEEN

We walked out the north side of the cemetery, through the rusted iron gate, following a path through the third-growth trees that had reasserted themselves after the forest fire in the late nineteenth century, toward the Lynnhaven River. There was a palpable relief in being beyond the range of Charlie's boombox. I could hear a cardinal's deep-throated call, the chit-chit-twitter of sparrows, and the faint rustle of a mild breeze through the ancient oaks. A silence with texture: it felt healing, somehow.

We reached the river and paused. Somewhere not too far offshore here, the brick ruins of the original Church of St. Thomas rested beneath the water, doomed by a seventeenth-century farmer diverting the river for irrigation. Today, the Indian summer sky was crisp blue and gulls wheeled and cruised, going about their business.

There was a bike path along the shore and we followed it east toward the point, walking in that same, almost eerily serene silence. And yet I felt no discomfort. It had always been like this with Jocelyn, our silences were as easy as our talk, and in their own way as richly communicative. In our teenage birdwatching phase, we had used to sit in the woods for hours at likely spots, in a poised hush, waiting for some skittish bird or another to grow easy with our presence and show itself. I felt that way now: it was as if whatever Jocelyn herself had on her mind was the bird we were waiting for, and this silence was making a space of trust for it to emerge.

Meanwhile, my mundane mind chattered away. I wanted to ask Jocelyn whether there had been any paperwork filed on the divorce. I wanted to know how often she still saw Bill, what their conversations were like, whether they were still having sex. But such self-serving fine points and distractions were dismissed easily enough. I was overjoyed just to be walking with Jocelyn on this beautiful day. The rest would take care of itself.

We reached Witchduck Point and sat down on the bench that overlooked the bay where Grace Sherwood had slipped her bonds and frolicked. Across the river, the upscale homes with river views dominated the shore as far as you could see. The neighborhood had come a long way since everyone fled to Kempsville two hundred years ago.

"So—" Jocelyn said, "Did you ever find the gold?"

It was a typically sly, Jocelyn-shorthand way of cutting to the heart of our history. She was asking, with minimal preamble, if I had found anything of value, in abandoning our future to take off for California. I assayed her tone for bitterness and recrimination, but found none. She simply and truly wanted to know. It was a moment I had rehearsed in my mind for decades without finding an adequate answer.

I said, "I found Esau Tremaine's grave. My black sheep great-great-great-granduncle. It turns out he went out to California too, in 1848. My grandfather had never told me about him. All I ever heard about was Jacob, the good brother, the one who put down roots and did good work and never wavered."

Jocelyn was silent for a moment, and then, with a trace of dry humor, "Well, did your black sheep great-great-great-granduncle find gold, at least?"

"It didn't look like it. He was still up in the hills when he died. Jacob Tremaine had done the headstone, with Virginia

156

limestone."

She shook her head. "I've never known what you thought you were going to find, that we didn't already have."

I hesitated, still thinking about that original pair of Tremaine brothers, the mythic poles of my ancestry and inheritance, the one who arrived, and abided, and the one who never ceased from journeying. They were like tectonic plates in my soul, one stable as a continent, one always on the move, grinding, blindly, toward some unknown and probably unknowable end, and wreaking its inevitable havoc. I had come to see my life as something lived on the fault line between those implacable and conflicting realities, as the place where the tension of them crunching against each other accumulated relentlessly until it broke and the plates slipped and the earth trembled. What peace I've ever known is mostly post-earthquake peace, a conditional equilibrium born of periodic catastrophe. It seemed lame, and even base, to tell the woman I loved that she had probably done best, on the whole, to marry outside of the earthquake zone. But it was the closest I'd come to an angle on the riddle of myself in twenty-odd years of brooding.

I said, "I think I was shocked to discover that I wasn't my grandfather. That I had, as he once put it, 'a bit of the brother' in me. More than a bit."

Jocelyn shook her head, almost impatiently. "We all do, I think."

"My grandfather didn't. It was a complete mystery to him." I hesitated again. "It seems like Bill probably doesn't."

"No, he's got it," Jocelyn said matter-of-factly. "In moderation, of course." She smiled. "Enough to keep it interesting."

I felt a base pang at the fond acknowledgment of her husband's interestingness. It wasn't the sort of thing a woman intent on getting out of her marriage conceded. I realized that I had been fishing for some subtle diminishment of Bill. But that was Jocelyn: she called it as she saw it.

Jocelyn was silent for a moment, looking at the river.

"So what you're saying, essentially, is that you realized you were an actual living breathing complex human being," she said at last. "That you weren't going to be able to live up to some thoroughly unrealistic idealized image of mythic manhood, and you panicked and took off. That somehow you thought you had to be your grandfather to be with me."

"True love needs truth," I said. "I know it sounds pretty lame, at this point. I don't mean to seem flippant. I loved you, God knows. But my life then was a lie."

"So off you went to look for truth."

"Like I said, I know it sounds pretty lame at this point."

Jocelyn shrugged. "Anything you could have said would have sounded lame, frankly. I just wanted to get a sense of what particular lameness you were going with."

"Well, that's the state of the art."

"Eli, did it ever once occur to you, during this fit of tormented unworthiness over not being your grandfather, that I might not be your grandmother either? That I might not even have *wanted* you to be your grandfather? That I might, strange as it may sound, have wanted *you*? That we could have found some kind of truth together?"

"It did occur to me," I said. "But it took about fifteen years."

Jocelyn was silent for a long moment; and then, to my immense relief, she shook her head and laughed. "You goddamned idiot."

"I always did work slow," I conceded

"Don't I know it. I remember you getting thrown out of the fifth grade Christmas pageant because you felt like you hadn't had time to fully grasp your character and you kept freezing up at the Annunciation."

"It's no simple thing, being a shepherd. I still think the script had them taking that angel way too much in stride."

"You didn't even have any *lines*, Eli. All you had to do was

158

fall down on your knees."

"I realize that now."

"I actually loved you for that," Jocelyn said. "It was so sweet, and so . . . typical. So you."

"I loved you too. You were the best Mary that school ever saw."

"It was a stretch, playing a virgin, even in the fifth grade."

It was a chuckle line, and a gift of leavening humor in context, and I smiled on cue, but it wasn't really true. Jocelyn in fact and in spirit had still been a virgin at eighteen, when I took off. We had saved ourselves for a sacred wedding night that had never happened. It was ludicrous to be so pained by it, I suppose, so many decades later. But I would probably always wish I had been able to just fall to my knees in fifth grade, and in high school, and forever, and take that angel as it came.

Jocelyn felt my mood shift and sobered too. We were silent a moment, looking at the river. A flight of pelicans went by in a wavering vee; farther out, high above the water, an osprey floated on a thermal, vivid in black and white, poised for a hunting plunge.

"Did you ever try to find me, to get in touch again, during all that time?' Jocelyn asked at last.

"No."

"Why not?"

"I was ashamed. And . . . I don't know. It just seemed wrong. I'd made my choices, and left you to make yours. There was no going back."

She nodded. And, after another moment, "Were you ever in love with anyone else?"

"I suppose." Jocelyn looked dubious, "I mean, yes, in a way, a bunch of times. There was one woman in particular. A painter. She was beautiful, she had a sense of humor to die for, and she was smart as a whip. It was pretty damn good."

"And?"

I shrugged. "It sounds too stupid to say."

She smiled wryly. "And you're going to let that start

159

stopping you now?"

"She wasn't you, Jos." And, as she frowned and looked away, "And I wasn't me, not all the way. I'm only me with you, I think. That's just the way it is. When I let us go, I let the whole thing go. I wasn't ever really looking to replace you. That would have just been another lie."

"You goddamned idiot," she said again, quietly, and this time it wasn't a smile line.

We sat in silence once more. I felt thoroughly exposed, but also, in a deep way, weirdly at peace. It was out of my hands now. I had said what had to be said, for better or for worse. It felt like letting work dust settle, like a certain moment that comes in working on a figure in stone when it's time to sit back and see what's really been done.

At last, Jocelyn turned and met my eyes, and for the first time that day I felt the quiet rush of her true presence. She had been sitting in judgment, it seemed, as the moment demanded, and the judgment had been made.

"I want you to do the memorial, you know," she said, quietly. "Is that okay?"

"Of course."

"I'm ready."

I hesitated, then said, almost reluctantly, hating to mar the moment with inconvenient realities, "Is Bill?"

It was an inane question, on the face of it: Bill's eagerness to push the memorial through had been the main point of contention all along. But Jocelyn understood the scruple and nodded calmly.

"He's told me two or three times recently that I should call you, that he thought you were the right one for the job," she said. "He's sort of egging me on, actually."

I nodded. The guy had guts, I had to give him that. He was still betting the ranch on my unsuitability for his wife. He may even have been right about that, though I still intended to do my best to prove him wrong. But I felt a wrenching compassion for him anyway. Bill Sherman was focused on allowing Jocelyn to run free, all the way to the end of her crisis, and I knew it must be killing him to watch her go so far without him. But the truth was, his wife wasn't going anywhere, and never had been. All Sherman had ever really needed to do was stop chasing her toward a resolution, and abide with her in the country of grief. She was hiding right there in plain sight, going nowhere at all, and had been all along.

"So what's next?" Jocelyn asked.

"You still want to go with the design we settled on?" She nodded. "Getting the stone, then. I'll run up to Big Rabbit tomorrow and pick it out."

"Can I come?"

I looked at her in surprise. "To the quarry?"

"Yes. To help pick it out."

I looked down at the grass at our feet, rendered briefly inarticulate by a complex surge of emotions. There was no way to tell Jocelyn what I really felt about this memorial, what I had been feeling in waves since the Shermans had first told me of their daughter's death: that I wished it was our child—mine and Jocelyn's—who lay beneath this earth. That seemed monstrous to me: Thou shalt not covet thy neighbor's grief. But there it was.

I was also thinking, again, of Esau Tremaine's grave in California. It had felt like my own grave, then. And yet here I was, decades along now in a life that felt posthumous. It was clearer than ever to me that the ways of God are utterly inscrutable. I had made the choices that led me to that grave in the foothills of the Sierras, as Jocelyn had made the choices that led her to this one along the Lynnhaven River: nothing had changed in our essential destinies; we had both ridden our ships of fate down, on separate voyages over different seas. This reunion only sharpened that truth, and drew fresh blood. And yet, where there is blood, there is life. Somehow we were here together.

I said, "It's a helluva long bike ride. We'd have to leave early."

"I thought maybe we could take your truck, since we have

to bring back a thousand pound rock and all."

"Ah," I said. "Of course. Good idea." She'd always been the practical one.

CHAPTER SIXTEEN

The early stages of figure work are pretty straightforward: you start out with a pitching tool with a strong straight edge, and a heavy steel hammer, and just knock away chunks, the "fat" on the stone, the chips flying everywhere. The rock can surprise you during this stage, but it's unlikely to fool you so much that you ruin the job.

But there comes a moment when the points are all set and the fat of the rock is gone. It is time to move to the finer tools, the six- and eight-teeth points. You rough the figure out with the points, then use a smooth chisel to take away the tooth marks. And then comes the real grinding, using the rasps and files that bring out the finest features, working "dust by dust," as my grandfather used to say. And now you are taking away rock that really matters and there is no more margin for error. If you shave off something that was needed for the substance of a nose or a flower petal, that rock is gone for good.

Marble is the trickiest stone of all, touchy as glass, and as unforgiving. I once spent several days in my grandfather's shop getting a lily just right on a marble cross. I love doing flowers, and have always had a certain gift for them. I was proud of that one. But just at the end I got too ambitious and went one grain of dust too deep trying to finesse the stem and the marble split and the entire lily fell to the workshop floor.

My grandfather came right over as soon as he heard it hit. You couldn't splinter off a bad chip in that place without him hearing it. He picked up the flower and held it to his nose.

"I can almost smell it, it's so perfect," he said, and gave me a wry smile. "For all the good that's going to do you."

I still had that marble lily in my shop, and every once in a while at a critical point in a tricky job I will take a whiff of it, just to remind myself that it doesn't matter how much exquisite work you've done if you go one stroke too deep.

It seemed to me that in our talk by the river, Jocelyn and I had finally roughed out the face of our past together, to somewhere around the smooth chisel level. The specter of our teenage disaster was no longer a vague mystery submerged in a mass of historical rock. It had discernible features now, albeit raked with tooth-marks from the points. It wasn't a masterpiece yet, by any stretch; it was at best a decent start; but it was a work-in-progress at last, after twenty-some years. If those decades had taught me anything, it was that where there is work, there is hope. And I'd be damned if I was going to let this one end up on the floor of the shop.

* * *

That night, I dreamed of Jocelyn. In the dream, I was working on a stone walkway from Ariel Sherman's grave in the cemetery at the Church of St. James toward the river. I was aware that I was going to have to build a bridge or something when I got to the river, but I wasn't letting that worry me. I looked up from my knees, where I was contemplating a particularly knotty solution to the sidewalk's evolving pattern of slate slabs, and saw Jocelyn walk out of the church, which was not the actual church at all but something more like my grandfather's house in the Blue Ridge. She was wearing blue jeans and a red flannel shirt, endearingly large on her, and cowboy boots, for some reason, in which she had

managed to retain her usual dangerous angle. Her hair glinted in
the sun, showing a touch of red at the haloed fringes. I saw that she
had let it grow out, and fall straight.

I put my tools down and would have walked toward her,
but Jocelyn started toward me, gesturing for me to be still. I stood
and watched her come, and a trembling ran through me like a fire,
or electricity. Then it passed, and I was still, and still watching,
through the dream's deepening lucidity, as Jocelyn walked along the
sidewalk I had made. I was conscious of her heels, and her ankles
wobbling slightly, as the boots caught the cracks between the
bricks.

In the dream I remembered the moment I had, in essence,
died. It seemed that the churchyard air in which I stood was
suffused with the same radiance and tender irrepressible joy. The
oaks and maples reddened with the first color of autumn, the sky,
the river sound, and the Indian summer breeze stirring the nearby
oaks: everything was instantly vivid and precious, and seemingly
removed from time into some slow, kind, and eternal peace. *It was
always like this*, I thought, as I had thought when I left my body on
the table in the emergency room at St. Francis. *It was always like this,
and I just forgot.*

Jocelyn's eyes as she walked up had taken on the color of
the earth I had cleared for the walkway, and were quieter than I
remembered them. I took it as one more sign of how much I had
missed. As I felt no need to tell her anything but how beautiful she
was, I held my silly tongue, and smiled.

She smiled back; or perhaps she had been smiling first.
And she said something to me, or maybe she sang it. Even making
allowances for my strange ecstasy, I didn't know what to make of
that. I had a sense just then, in any case, that all sound might have
turned irretrievably to music.

Jocelyn took my hand and we began to dance, a kind of
easy graceful waltz, of the sort I had never been able to master in
the waking state, despite Jocelyn's best efforts to teach me. But
here we danced as if we had been dancing together for a thousand

years. I could feel her solid in my arms, warm and creamy-skinned, smelling of Asian pear and red tea, with a hint of freesia. There was a bird somewhere nearby whose song at that moment seemed to be the music accompanying us. It made me feel like kneeling, but Jocelyn was in my arms, we were moving together, and that was its own genuflection. The sky had never seemed more blue. Blue to give praise for, blue to make you lift up your hands.

* * *

When I had checked the radio reports the night before, Hurricane Marcella, the last, late storm of a relatively mild season, had been flirting with the coast of South Carolina. But it had not made landfall, and instead eased back out to sea overnight, moving northeast at a sprightly seventeen miles per hour. By the time I woke the next morning, it had gained some strength from the warm waters of the Gulf Stream and been upgraded to a category two storm, with maximum sustained winds of 120 mph. The radio weatherman placed it 150 miles east of Cape Fear and most projections had it continuing harmlessly northeast. Not that it mattered to me. The thing could have made landfall in the side yard of my shop while I was getting the truck warmed up and I still would have driven to Big Rabbit with Jocelyn. It wasn't every day I had a chance like that.

* * *

Jocelyn and I had arranged to meet at my shop early, at seven A.M., and leave from there. But I couldn't go back to sleep after I woke from my dream, and so I was out of bed, in and out of the shower, and at the shop by four-thirty. It felt like the first day of summer vacation to me. I made sandwiches and crammed an ice cooler full of soda and beer. I stopped at the Pungo 7-Eleven and bought candy bars for the road, Baby Ruths for me, Butterfingers for Jocelyn, the happy chocolates of our childhood. I spent half an hour sorting through the music in my truck, laying out a stack of cassettes for every possible range of mood on our journey, from Vivaldi through George Thoroughgood and the Destroyers, though with more Van Morrison than Charlie would have approved of. I had even shaved, despite the fact that it wasn't Thursday. It seemed unlikely that there would be kissing, given all the situation's complexities, but a man does like to feel prepared.

As the sun began to rise, the sky to the east turned livid, a volcanic crimson, as if streams of glowing lava were surging up from below the horizon and streaming over the heaped-up cumulus clouds into the ocean. I went out into the front yard of the shop with my Redskins travel mug of coffee and sat on the crate of my grandfather's uncarved stone, gazing seaward in awe. It was, I knew, a dangerous beauty: those flame-drenched masses of pent-up rain were merely the first hint, the whispered fringes of the tumult of Hurricane Marcella.

As I sat there, headlights showed on the dirt road between the spent fields of soybean rubble. I followed them as you might follow a particularly striking bird in flight, and a moment later Jocelyn turned into the driveway and pulled up in a silvery-blue Volvo SUV.

An upscale soccer mom vehicle, I thought with an unexpected pang. I realized that everything that reminded me of the Shermans' domestic life made me nervous, from Bill's solidly conventional lawyer's Mercedes to this thoroughly pragmatic Swedish armored personnel carrier for children. I would have preferred Bill to be roaring around in a midlife-crisis-red Porsche, and for Jocelyn to be on a Harley with a small traveling bag held down by a bungee cord, wearing don't-look-back leather. But both of them persisted in driving around like married people.

I hopped down off the crate as Jocelyn got out of the car, but she gestured for me to be still and walked toward me. I was reminded of my dream from the night before as she approached, though she was wearing jeans and sneakers and another ODU sweatshirt, and carrying an extra-large cup of 7-Eleven coffee. She was wearing the pewter Celtic cross again, cradled precisely in the sweet hollow of her throat.

As she drew near, Jocelyn's body language unexpectedly said *hug*. I leaned toward her, feeling a wave of vertigo as my arms opened, as if I were about to start flapping at the edge of a cliff. Jocelyn's mouth actually appeared to be heading for mine, and my heart surged, but at the last instant she veered off and lightly brushed her lips against my cheek. She had set her feet about six inches too far away for a proper hug as well, and used only her coffee-free arm. But our chests still bumped on the oblique embrace and my knees went mortifyingly weak. I caught a good whiff of her hair, it was Asian pear and red tea, just like in the dream, with a hint of freesia, a scent that apparently was going to affect me forever, the way that damn apricot-and-pomegranate had in high school. This was much worse than high school, though, when raging hormones had been my main problem in situations of physical proximity. Now it seemed like my heart would explode.

"You shaved," Jocelyn noted, amused. I suspected she understood that all too well.

"A momentary lapse," I said, hoping my voice didn't sound as shaky as I felt. "I try to shave once a week, whether I need to or not."

Jocelyn, mercifully, didn't pursue it. She turned and leaned back against the crated limestone to look east. The sky was growing more spectacular by the moment, as the magma-like red continued to infiltrate the masses of bruise-purple cloud.

"Incredible," she breathed.

"Red sky at morning, sailors take warning," I said. "It's Hurricane Marcella. But the guy on the radio said it was heading out to sea."

"Actually, I checked the Weather Channel just before I left, and the latest projections have it coming west. They're giving it a fifty percent chance of making landfall somewhere between the Outer Banks and Maryland by this afternoon."

Fifty-fifty sounded like money in the bank to me; I've

played nothing but astronomical long shots my entire life. But I said dutifully, "If you think it's too dicey, you don't really need to go. I mean, I can just run up there alone and get it done, whatever weather comes in. With a rock in the back, that truck of mine could drive through a tidal wave."

"No way," Jocelyn said. "I'm going. You couldn't stop me."

"I was hoping you would say that."

Jocelyn turned back to the sunrise and sipped her coffee. She appeared to be in no hurry, despite the approaching storm, so I picked up my own coffee as well, and hopped back onto the shipping crate, letting my legs dangle. Jocelyn glanced at me; our eyes met, and it was us, as simple as stone itself. In a moment, I was going to kiss her, violating several commandments and bringing down the wrath of God and society upon us. My grandmother would take back my grandfather's tools and stop sending me cider. My Aunt Terrie would have to start saying rosaries for my poor lost soul. Billy and Joshua would hate me. Only Bill Sherman would be pleased, because I would have blown it, more quickly than even he could have foreseen.

I said, "We should probably get going."

"Yeah," Jocelyn agreed, quickly enough that I was sure she had felt it too.

"Do you need to use the bathroom or anything?" I had already cleaned my bathroom twice that morning, on the off-chance that Jocelyn might go in there. I really am a ridiculous man.

"No, I'm good," she said.

"I've got a cooler, and candy bars for the road. Do you still like Butterfingers?"

She smiled. "Unfortunately. And they still go right to my ass."

"Nonsense. You've got an ass for the ages, you always have."

Jocelyn gave me a sharp glance. I realized that I had sounded much more fervent that I had intended. It was the kind of thing I would have said to her without a second thought in high school. My attitude toward Jocelyn's body, from every angle, had always essentially been one of awe and wonder. I was leaking adoration, badly.

"Butterfingers will be fine," Jocelyn said.

CHAPTER SEVENTEEN

I had put a truly preposterous amount of thought into music for the trip, but once we were actually driving I chickened out and just turned on the radio to a country music station. I was relying on God and synchronicity to supply the appropriate music, hopefully something sentimentally neutral, or at least just warm and wholesome; but it turned out that the station was in the middle of a big "Your Cheatin' Heart" countdown of the top forty infidelity songs of all time.

Jocelyn and I exchanged glances of rueful amusement as we twanged through several graphically cautionary tales of marital betrayal and moral catastrophe. By the third song, when a jealousy-crazed trucker plowed his rig into the hotel room where his wife and her lover were shacked up, killing them both— *"The desk clerk said it was all so clear: he never hit the brakes, and he was shiftin' gears"*—I was prepared to concede defeat, and I reached out and turned the radio off.

Jocelyn smiled. "'Momma's in the graveyard, Poppa's in the pen' isn't doing it for you today?"

"God is my DJ," I said. "But it seems He has a perverse sense of humor." I opened my tape box. "Okay, let's see, I've got Sioux City Pete and the Beggars . . ."

"How about Bruce Springsteen?"

I glanced at her and caught her smile. Our old road music. The girl had guts, that's all there was to it.

"Done," I said. I dug out the battered cassette of *Born to Run* and slipped it into the truck's tape deck. There was a brief grinding sound, a whir, a kind of hiccup, and finally the instrumental opening of "Thunder Road" kicked in.

"There are these new things called CDs," Jocelyn said, amused by the state of my technology. "They're amazing, really."

"I've been meaning to join the next century. Maybe I'll ask Joshua to digitalize everything for me."

"He'd do it for you, I'm sure. . . . He said to say hello to you, by the way."

Springsteen started singing just then. *"The screen door slams, Mary's dress waves./Like a vision she dances across the porch while the radio plays . . . "*

I said, "Joshua told you to say hello to me?"

"Well, you know, not in so many words, it was some typically cryptic Joshua thing."

"What did he actually say?"

"He said, 'Tell him I'm glad he doesn't want to be presumptuous.' I assumed you would know what he's talking about."

I nodded, thinking, Okay, Lord, I get it. And said, dissembling shamelessly, "He's got a scheme to computerize my stone carving."

Jocelyn laughed. "I'm sure he does."

"It makes me a little nervous, to tell you the truth."

"Joshua makes me nervous a lot," Jocelyn said. "That brain of his."

* * *

We drove for a while in a comfortable silence. It felt weirdly normal, being on the road with Jocelyn. We had done this

172

hundreds of times since the fourth grade, on foot and on bicycles, in home-made rafts courting drowning, in kayaks and canoes, and in high school cars that were always about to run out of gas or blow some crucial part. It was so easy that it was almost possible to forget for a while that we were on our way to quarry her daughter's gravestone.

The Adultery Jamboree had gotten us through most of Virginia Beach and Springsteen took us into Suffolk. Neither of us spoke again until the saxophone solo on "Born to Run."

"Wow, this brings a lot back," Jocelyn said.

"Yeah. I can still hear God in this riff."

"That's not God, that's Clarence Clemens. . . . Remember when we used to listen to this all the time at that old half-finished cathedral out on Hog Island?"

And every moment was holy, and the world was lit with perfect joy in the light from your face, I thought. The way the birds sang was my love for you, and the way the leaves moved in the breeze, and every stone in that place, and its history and future. But I was acutely aware of Jocelyn's tone, which was easy and even prosaic: a daylight tone of fond retrospect, without chiaroscuro. It seemed that whatever peace she had made with those days was shaded much less than mine, and I said, "I remember pouring peach schnapps into our Slurpees."

"When we couldn't get vodka."

"Eating Triscuits and Cheez Whiz."

"Trying to remember the difference between a great egret and a snowy egret."

"It's simple," I said. "One of them has yellow feet."

"Exactly. But which one?"

I smiled in concession: I still had no idea.

"Born to Run" gave way to "She's the One." It seemed that the subject might be done, but after a moment Jocelyn offered quietly, "I went up there once, about five years after you left."

I glanced at her, but she was looking out the window at the spent cotton fields. "To the cathedral?"

She nodded to the glass. "It was a sort of private pity party, I think. Or, like a ritual. I don't think I had really let you go, really given up on us, until that day." She turned then, and gave me a shy sidelong glance. "I sat up there on that ledge. Remember it? Where we sat that first day we found it?"

"Of course."

"And I cried and cried and cried. And I thought, This place is always going to be us, just like us, forever unfinished."

I could picture the scene easily enough. I had done the same thing myself, a dozen times. It hurt, to think of Jocelyn there like that. But it hurt in a good way somehow.

We silent for a long time after that, for miles, driving through the winding brown rivers and piney woods and peanut fields near Suffolk. But finally I said, feeling almost sheepish, as if I were confessing something lurid, "Actually, I've been doing a little work up there, the past few years."

Jocelyn looked at me. "At the cathedral?"

"Nothing spectacular, you'd hardly know it was happening from month to month. But steady, you know, one rock at a time. In about twenty years, I may have to find somebody who knows how to do stained-glass."

"My God," she said. "I'd love to see that."

"It really doesn't look that different, Jos."

"How far out of our way would it be?"

I laughed. "What, now, you mean? Like, from here?"

"It's north of here, right?"

"Yeah, more or less. But so is New York." I looked at her. "You're kidding, aren't you?"

"I don't kid about cathedrals, Eli."

"Or shampoos. I know. You're a very serious woman."

She smiled. "Exactly."

It was, in fact, a very Jocelyn-like impulse. I just wasn't sure my heart could stand it. I considered my options for a long moment, ranging from pleading navigational impossibilities, to sudden illness, to discovering a truck malfunction. There was the approaching storm, of course. But my sense was that Hurricane Marcella had nothing on Jocelyn, and at last I conceded, "It's probably about forty-five minutes out of our way. An hour if we stop at the Bacon's Castle Store and get Mountain Dews. Three hours if we stop at the Bacon's Castle Store and get beer."

"You've got beer in that cooler back there already, right?"

There really was no stopping the woman. I said, to cover all the bases, "Soda too."

Jocelyn smiled. "So let's skip the store and take an hour and a half."

CHAPTER EIGHTEEN

The thing is, you forget. The human brain can't hold it. Even when you remember, the memory is not it, it is just the best your brain can do. And then holiness, the enveloping hush of sacred presence, comes upon you anew, in the instant of grace, and you realize you never had a clue.

We came around the bend in the weather-battered asphalt road and cleared the last stand of loblolly pines. The cathedral loomed before us and it was as if I had never been to the place before, or as if I had always been there and everything else was a dream from which I was just waking up. In the sudden sharpness of the instant coming into focus, I could smell skunk cabbage in the charged air, and see the tiny ivory globes of the rattlesnake plantain flowering at the edge of the woods.

I stopped the truck and set the parking brake. Jocelyn and I sat for a long moment as the quiet settled like the surface of a pond after a rock has been tossed in. There was no hurry. I remembered that too. There was nowhere to go and nothing to do when I got there. It was here, it had always been here, while I was laboring to get somewhere else.

An egret disturbed by our arrival leaped from a nearby treetop, its spindly legs dangling, its vast wings flaring white against the cast iron sky. It floated breathtakingly for an instant, then drifted down and crossed in front of us, gliding right over the cathedral toward the creek. Its feet, I noted, were black.

We got out of the truck, I rummaged in the back for the cooler, and we approached the cathedral's triune entryway. I had grown a workman's nonchalance over the years here, like a callous, lugging my tools through the doorless openings, using the nave as a shortcut to my scaffolding, or ducking inside the arches to find some shade for a smoke break. But today I felt the doorways as what they were made to be, the *porta caeli*, the gates of heaven. The threshold of sacred space. And the fear of God came upon me. Not because we had just driven the wrong way down a hurricane evacuation route and out onto exposed tidal flats with a hurricane approaching; that was actually no big deal to me. I would have driven happily through the gates of hell with Jocelyn, even if we hadn't had an ice chest full of beer.

"It's so desolate," Jocelyn said quietly. "Clean. Like a desert."

"God and rock. It doesn't get much simpler."

"I could live here, I think, if it wasn't for the boys. The crazy old hermit lady of Awe, Virginia. Bathe in the river and let my hair go into dreads. Wear sackcloth. Speak to no one but the herons and the ducks."

"You'd look good in sackcloth," I said. "It would bring out your eyes."

"I'm serious, Eli."

"So you keep telling me."

A raindrop splashed on the stone flooring in front of us, a single fat splash. The air was still quiet, but it was a vivid reminder. I considered the possibility that we might have to ride out the hurricane here. When I first began working at the cathedral site, I thought the original builders were idiots and had built on sand, but when you rummage at the foundation it turns out that there is an underlying stratum of good Pleistocene granite beneath the tidal accumulations. Also, the cathedral was set on a slight rise on the lee side of the island, the better to shield it from storms and Spanish attacks. The spot is subject to the occasional floods—there are watermarks on the walls from the swelling James River during Hurricane Camille in 1969. But if it came down to it, we could always climb up to the clerestory level and hunker down. We had beer and candy bars. The thing was doable.

Jocelyn, apparently impervious to the developing weather, was still looking out into the nave. "It's amazing that this place is still here, isn't it?" she said. "You'd think that after three hundred years, someone would have found a way to put up a condo or a duck blind or something."

"Maybe it's zoned theological."

"I doubt anyone even knows it's here anymore. I think it just . . . stopped. It's a place where the world stopped." She looked at me. "You know how they always tell you, 'Life goes on' when someone dies? Like, 'A tragedy, such a tragedy. But remember, sweetheart, life goes on.'"

"That's what they say," I said carefully.

"Well, what if it doesn't? What if sometimes it just . . . *doesn't?*"

Her brown eyes were steady, and still, and fathomless. It was inevitable, I supposed, that her first thought even here—or perhaps especially here—would be of her daughter.

I felt a wave of that empathetic vertigo I can never get used to, and of its accompanying sense of helplessness. My grandmother could read tea leaves. She could read palms, and fortunes from the smear of gravy on a plate, and I knew that she could read someone's life in an instant in the way the steam came off their coffee or how they had buttoned their shirt that morning. But she refused to do it unless, as she said, the Lord seized her and rubbed her nose in it. She often said it was better not to know. But I have a weakness for knowing.

"Does that shock you?" Jocelyn said. "Such a morbid thought?"

"No. I actually think that morbid thought is true."

"So what do you do with that?"

"I don't think there is anything to do with that. Except keep loving, and keep working."

"Even when loving is as impossible as rock?"

"Rock is not impossible. It is just extremely hard."

Jocelyn looked at me for a long moment and then she smiled, a quiet smile, almost a weary one. "What a simple soul you are," she said. "Love, work, death. And then more love, and more work. A simple, simple soul."

"Not that damn simple," I said.

"I'm not complaining. It's actually a relief."

I laughed. "My simple-mindedness?"

"Yes. Bill is a very complicated man." Jocelyn gestured upward abruptly. "Is that your scaffolding up there?"

"Yes," I said, though I would rather have pursued the discussion of her husband and his complexities. It was something we needed to talk about. But I let that go for the moment. High on the south wall, I had begun setting the stones on the clerestory piers, and the twinned columns had progressed far enough that you could start to get a sense of the stained-glass window that would eventually fill them. It was tricky work. One of the main challenges in the construction of Gothic cathedrals is the fact that the higher you go—and thus, the less practical a free-standing ground-based pole scaffold becomes—the less structural support you have for scaffolding in the solidity of the building itself, because the cathedral walls are turning almost entirely into windows. The narrow plank platform I was working from at present was a jury-rigged thing, supported by a couple of angled struts slanting up from the triforium passageway to meet a set of horizontal ties passing through the window openings and secured on the outside wall. I had left out a couple of the window's sill blocks to keep a flat surface for the horizontal ties. The thing looked precarious, and it probably wouldn't have passed muster with a building inspector, but it was actually pretty stable.

I hadn't tried it during a hurricane yet, of course.

"Let's go up there," Jocelyn said, as I had known she would.

I considered all the reasons this was a terrible, even dangerous idea, then said, as I had known I would, "Okay."

* * *

From the scaffold you could see for miles. Our immediate neighborhood was all tidal creeks, marshes, and scraggly patches of sand-based trees. Due west was Chippokes Creek. It had shifted almost half a mile since the mid-1600s, as the tidal marshes silted up, but the cathedral's first builders had floated their limestone up it to a dock right beside the building site. The James River lay to the north, and from here you could see beyond the island to where it turned southeast at the nuclear power plant. The sky in that direction was getting seriously black by now, but the air was still quiet. There were no birds in sight and I realized that I couldn't hear the usual chorus of trills and squawks. The birds had already had sense enough to hunker down. But a quarter mile to the east I could see a small flock of about half a dozen Hog Island sheep, the feral descendants of escapees from the early settlers' flocks, grazing stolidly. They have had four hundred years to adjust to life on Hog Island and no doubt could handle a hurricane just fine. I was feeling a little poorly prepared, myself.

We sat down on the edge of the platform. I reached back for the cooler and took out a Bud Light for myself and, after a questioning glance at Jocelyn and a nod from her, a beer for her as well. We bumped our bottles together in a little toast and sipped. The beer was ice cold, the bottles streaming sweat immediately in the humid air. It was just after 8 A.M., a little early to be drinking even by sun-over-the-yardarm standards, but I felt that this qualified as special circumstances.

We sat for a time sipping the beers, our feet dangling over the precipitous drop down to floor of the nave. Jocelyn seemed in no hurry to get to any particular point.

And in truth, I was content just to be beside her, looking at her face. Jocelyn's features had showed up in the face of every angel I had carved for decades. I could have etched the lines of her cheekbones in the dark, by touch alone; my hands knew that arc, and the firmness of her jaw, and the breadth of her brow. My grandfather worked so slowly, I think, partly because every stone he chiseled had a person's features for him, and he loved to linger over them. Perhaps his kindness with the living came in seeing that same slow work in the future of every face he saw. But I had never been able to look at Jocelyn's face and believe she could be gone.

"You've really done an amazing amount of work here," Jocelyn said.

"I don't know about that. It will be a hundred years before this place needs a roof."

"It's not like the roof is the point, is it?"

I looked at her and smiled. "No," I said. "The roof is not the point."

"There's something so right, to me, in you working on this place. It's so completely . . . Oh, I don't know—"

"Futile?" I suggested.

"Devoted," she said. "Like a priest saying mass in an empty church. It actually helps me make sense of it all, in a weird way."

I shrugged uncomfortably. You get so used to working invisibly; it was actually disconcerting to feel seen in a generous light. I knew, too, that she was romanticizing the thing: the simple truth was, I had worked so hard, for so long, mostly to keep from going insane. God had seen fit to give me my life one rock at a time. I had no idea what it all meant, and every time I thought I did know, I got my ass handed to me. But that seemed extreme, and instead I said, "I'm no priest, I'm a day laborer. The pay's not much, but the benefits package is first-rate." And, as she looked resistant to that, "Plus, it's a great way to meet girls."

Jocelyn laughed. "Right."

"It got you up here, didn't it?"

181

"That, and a cooler full of cold Budweiser."

"Well, breakfast is the most important meal of the day." I hesitated, then said, "Jos, as far as I'm concerned, this place is a big pile of rocks. It doesn't mean shit. One second with you is worth every year of idiot labor I've spent on this place."

Jocelyn considered me for a moment, then set her beer down. She leaned over, took my face in her hand, and kissed me, very softly. It was like a butterfly landing on my lips.

A turkey vulture circled above us, black against the blackening sky, with twin slashes of white showing like scimitars across the underside of its big wings. The sun was quilted behind the mass of clouds to the east, and the thin light had a metallic feel. Thirty feet below us was the spot on the triforium level where Jocelyn and I had sat the first day we found the cathedral. I had carved our initials into one of the walls of the back passage down there, in the eleventh grade, just above a seventeenth-century mason's mark, in a blind niche where no one would ever see them but the church sexton and God.

"We're really going to do this, aren't we?" Jocelyn said.

She meant her daughter's gravestone, I was sure. Pretty sure, at least. In any case, my answer would have been the same. I said, "If you still want to."

Jocelyn was silent for a moment. At last she said, "Do you remember telling me that a gravestone can be a wall, or a window?"

"I remember you telling me it wasn't that simple."

"That was because Bill wanted a wall. And a window was unimaginable to me. I was just hanging on for dear life."

"And now?"

She shrugged. "He still wants a wall. He needs one, I think. And probably always will. It's a big part of why I married him: he's good with structure."

My heart sank. It was the crux of the same dilemma I had faced since the first day Jocelyn and her husband had walked into my shop. If I was going to be complicit in the ruin of her marriage, I wanted it to be for good old burn-in-hell adultery, and not because I had abetted her in letting her husband force a premature closure on their daughter's death. I said, "So what exactly is it that we're doing today, then?"

Jocelyn met my eyes, and surprised me with a smile. It made me realize, yet again, that there was no way I would ever completely understand her.

"Bill is finally getting his wall," she said. "But I'm getting my window."

CHAPTER NINETEEN

Everything was quiet when we arrived at the Big Rabbit Quarry. It had begun to rain, a gentle but steady rain, the weather flexing its muscles like a weightlifter doing a few warm-up stretches before starting to really heave things around. Little Mike had already closed the place down, secured the machinery, and sent his crews home in anticipation of the storm. But his truck was still parked in front of the office, and as I pulled into the graveled driveway, he came out onto the porch in his yellow rain gear.

"He's got a shotgun," Jocelyn said.

"Old Quiyoughcohannock custom. Not to worry. That's a peace pipe in his other hand."

Jocelyn frowned. "You didn't mention—"

"It's a ritual thing," I said. And, as she continued to look dubious, "Trust me. Mike's cool."

"I've clearly got a lot to learn about the monument industry," she said, and shrugged. "You guys work it out."

I got out of the truck and approached Mike.

"Big rain coming, white boy," he said.

"And me with a picnic planned."

"Big big rain. You can tell when the small animals take cover."

184

I laughed at that: Little Mike playing the nature sage. "The small animals on the weather channel, you mean."

Mike grinned in acknowledgment. "Who's our guest?"

"Do you remember Jocelyn Page?"

"Jostlin' Jocelyn Page?" Mike exclaimed. "Hell yes. Field hockey marauder. Best legs in Virginia, even with shin guards on." He gave me a glance. "Weren't you guys sort of an item, way back in the day?"

"Sort of. Her last name is Sherman now. The guy's a lawyer."

"And the legs?"

"Still the best in Virginia. She's wearing slacks now, though. No shin guards."

"I always wondered why you didn't stick with her."

"She and her husband came into the shop a while back," I said. "They want a stone for their daughter. A three-year-old."

"Ai yai yai," Mike said. He looked over at the truck and waved to Jocelyn, who waved back tentatively. "I can't say much for your timing," he muttered.

"It's not my call, Mike. She's been building up to this for almost a year."

Little Mike considered things for a moment, then allowed, "It might be better to get it done today at that, before the storm tears everything up. We didn't get some of the roads here cleared for two weeks after Bonnie. And we've worked in worse, I guess."

"Right after that ice storm last year."

"That was just stupid," Mike said. "At least this is for a damsel in distress. Let's smoke a little of the sacred weed and get to it."

I glanced at the sky. "You sure we shouldn't just skip the, uh, ritual element today?"

Mike just looked at me like I was nuts.

"This is no time to piss off the gods, man," he said.

* * *

In the quarry's single-room office, the weather channel was flickering on a battered RCA television. The set, with its rabbit-ears antenna doctored with dusty aluminum foil, dated back to the days of Big Jake, and the reception was shaky, but it was good enough for the basic information.

Jocelyn and I checked out the latest storm reports while Little Mike fiddled with his pipe. Hurricane Marcella was fifty miles off the coast, near the Virginia/North Carolina border, grinding toward a projected landfall in four hours somewhere around the Back Bay. It had swollen into a Category 3 storm by now, with the winds topping out at close to 130 miles per hour. The weather guy looked duly grave, but this was his big moment and he could barely contain his glee when he speculated that Marcella might even make it up to Category 4 before it hit the coast.

"You can kill the tube, Eli," Mike said. He had dug out his best pipe, a Quiyoughcohannock masterpiece made out of clay and jointed with copper by somebody long before Big Jake's time. It was about a foot and a half long and quite substantial; Little Mike had once told me that the Quiyoughcohannocks, in their pragmatic fashion, preferred a peace pipe that could also serve as a club if the peace thing didn't work out.

I clicked the television off and Jocelyn and I joined Mike at the work table by the west window. He had cleared it for the occasion and set up a candle at the center, around which he had laid out a squash gourd rattle, a sash of polished purple conch beads, a pouch of ground maize, and some dried persimmons.

Mike picked up a box of big kitchen matches, took one out, and drew the match along the box flint. In the sharp silence after the squelching of the TV you could hear the scrape of the match head and the hushed flare of the flame.

"What is your daughter's name?" he asked Jocelyn.

She blinked, caught off guard, then said a little shakily, "Ariel. Ariel Marie."

Mike nodded. He touched the match's flame to the candlewick and it caught there, and suddenly Ariel was with us.

My arms rose into gooseflesh. I had seen Mike do this before, but it always took me by surprise. Even if you could get past his sheer imposing size and fundamental surliness, and the shotgun, and his bad haircut and the dope, it was still impossible to see it coming. The guy was *kwiokosuk*, a priest of his tribe.

"We will meet her spirit today and give it a home," Mike said. He picked up the sash of conch beads and handed it to Jocelyn. "And this belt will remember our words."

CHAPTER TWENTY

Outside, the rain was beginning to gust in sheets. Mike tsk-tsked at Jocelyn's inadequate raincoat and dug up some serious rain gear for her, a huge yellow jacket, rubber trousers, and knee-high boots. I was wearing my grandfather's fedora, which made a nifty rain hat, and a Marine Corps surplus poncho to leave my arms some range of motion for hammering. We took both Mike's truck, which had a good set of basic quarrying tools, and mine, which had a jib crane bolted to the bed for loading the rock. Mike led the way, with Jocelyn riding beside him, and I could see their heads bent together in conversation as I followed them along the ridge road toward the eastern end of the quarry.

The Big Rabbit's sprawling 800+ acres are part of what geologists call a mesozoic basin, a giant puddle left behind when the African and European plates of what was at that point one huge continent pulled away from North America about 250 million years ago. The main limestone deposit, called simply Awahili Pit One, is settled in the bottom of the basin like coffee slopped into a saucer, its rock calcified from sediment left in a shallow sea during the age of the dinosaurs and then compacted over tens of millions of years by heavier debris eroded from the Appalachians to the west. The hills along the western rim of the saucer are the worn-down remnants of that once-imposing chain, with bedrock a billion years old or more, but the hills to the east were formed by a more recent intrusion of granite, and the stone in Awahili Pit Number Three, where Mike was leading us, is subtly different stuff. Not just technically younger, but *rawer*, fresher, even vivacious. I suppose it takes a certain kind of mind to find much wildness in rock; but I had always thrilled to this adolescent stone. It couldn't have been more than a couple hundred million years old, it had cooled out of deep magma so recently, geologically speaking, that it was practically still warm.

I clicked the windshield wipers on the truck up to the second setting as we turned off the main road along the ridge and started down the switchbacks into the quarry pit. Even in the palpably worsening rain, it was a lovely drive through some second-growth pine and oak forest; parts of the Big Rabbit are actually a nature preserve.

We cleared the trees and the quarry pit opened out below us, a descending staircase of squared-off tiers, eerily monumental, like a Mayan pyramid frozen in mid-birth from the hillside. I had figured that Mike would drive all the way down to the lowest ledge, which was the most recent exposure, and thus the rock least likely to have been damaged by blasting or the accidents of excavation, but his truck's brake lights flared red in the middle of the first switchback turn. He stopped right next to the spot where he and I had quarried the granite for my grandfather's stone the week before.

I pulled in behind him and turned the engine off. Off to the right was the oldest section of the quarry; you could see up to the ridge from here, where the original outcrop of boulders, exposed by erosion centuries before, still jutted, balcony-like, over the first of the worked ledges that had hollowed out the hillside below. The granite here was classic Big Rabbit granite, the very fine-grained, silvery gray rock suffused with a subtle rose hue and streaked with lavender, that I had recognized instantly at the grave of my ancestor Esau Tremaine in California.

Jocelyn was out of Mike's truck almost before it stopped
rolling, walking purposefully, not toward the quarried ledges to our
right, but toward the more or less unworked landscape on the
other side of the road. There wasn't even granite over there, as far
as I knew. All I could think was that she should have used the
bathroom back at the office, but I saw that Mike had gotten out of
the truck too and was unloading a hand-held Rockwell 330 drill
from the back. I set my parking brake firmly against the grade, and
got out to join him in the rain.

"She spotted the old cut over there," he said as I walked
up.

"I didn't know there *was* an old cut over there."

"It's quartzite. Nobody's worked it for a hundred years."

"Does she know that?"

"You can try telling her too," Mike said. "I just work
here."

I almost smiled, picturing the exchange. Trying to tell
Jocelyn something she didn't want to hear was like working granite
with limestone tools; something always gave, and it wasn't the rock.

Mike was still struggling with the big manual drill and I
stepped in to help. Together we heaved the thing off the truck bed
to the ground. Mike drew out several three-foot drill rods and set
them beside the drill, then began to hook up the air hose to the
compressor.

"So what's the story with the husband?" he said.

"Did she say anything?"

"She said they've separated."

"Then I guess that's the story."

"She showed me this sketch he'd had done of the
memorial. Marble lamb, dwarf cherry tree. The works."

"And?"

Mike looked at me. "And then she tore it up."

"Really?"

"Down the middle, and then across, and across again."

I mulled that. The rain streaming off the fedora's brim was

pouring into my poncho and down my back. I turned the back brim up and the water started going past my nose, and down my front.

"They haven't exactly been on the same page with this thing, from the start," I allowed.

"Well, there ain't no page now," Mike said. "It's confetti." He got the hose attached, opened the choke on the compressor, and yanked the cord. The engine gurgled once and died.

"This is going to be a bitch in this rain," he said. "Why don't you take the drill over there, and I'll run the hose to it, and bring a plug and feather set, when I get this fucker going."

I hesitated, then said, "That was something, back there at the office, Mike. I never saw you do anything quite like that before. With the belt and all."

He shrugged. "There's a lot you haven't seen, amigo."

"Did you make that up on the spot?"

"Some of it. I saw my uncle do something like that once, more or less."

"It was good for her, I think," I said. "Healing."

"Blah blah blah," Mike said, and yanked the cord again on the compressor. It was pretty obvious to me, sacred considerations aside, that he just wanted to get this thing done and get out of the rain before the damned pit flooded and the roads all washed out.

* * *

While Mike was wrestling with the balky compressor, I duck-walked the drill over to Jocelyn, who was standing on a narrow ledge at the foot of a twenty-foot tall outcrop of quartzite, holding the wampum sash as if it were a live egg. Above her, the rounded top of the mini-monadnock was swirled in the characteristic erosion patterns of quartzite, a mosaic of fitful curves, like the fingerpainting of a giant four-year-old, and the exposed face of the cliff was broken into the horizontal bedding planes characteristic of sedimentary rock. Quartzite begins as sandstone; this lode had once been simple compacted silt, from a Paleozoic river bed perhaps, as limestone is compacted calcium. But sometime during its history, probably when the neighboring granite's magma had surged its fiery way toward the surface, the original rock had been alchemized by the heat into its present crystalline form.

Jocelyn gave me a smile as I waddled up and plunked the drill down on the ledge. I was struck by her air of quiet certainty. On this naked ledge of slippery rock, with the wind whipping sheets of rain across our faces, she seemed serene in a way I had not seen since she had walked into my shop the previous spring.

"Mike said you tore up the sketch," I said.

Jocelyn nodded and reached into the deep pocket of her raincoat to draw out a handful of paper shreds. Mike had not exaggerated: the thing was confetti. Jocelyn raised her hand and opened her fist to the wind, and the fragments scattered in a gust of raindrops and were gone.

"So much for Plan A," she said.

The compressor motor roared just then as Mike finally got it running. It sputtered once as he eased off the choke, and then settled in to a steady drone.

I said, when the noise had eased, "Is there a Plan B?"

"Right here," Jocelyn said, and patted the boulder beside her.

I considered the thing, trying to not look dubious. The quartzite here had a dull reddish hue, probably from manganese, and Jocelyn's boulder looked like a rotten pomegranate that had been dropped and then whacked with a machete. Its inside face was roughly planed in the corduroy pattern of the old-style drill rods, where neighboring rock had been removed, and it was pocked with divots and pick marks from someone sampling it. The rock was a remnant of the original outcropping, the exposed stone that had drawn the quarrymen in the first place, and beyond it was a sheer drop of a hundred feet or more. Quartzite is actually very durable stuff—around 7 on the Mohs scale of mineral hardness, the same as granite. The Quiyoughcohannocks used it for arrowheads, and it makes a lovely fireplace or exterior wall. But you don't see many quartzite gravestones. It polishes up like a gemstone and tends to be a bit too vivid.

Mike came up to us, dragging the compressor hose and lugging a plug and feather set. He set the tools down, adjusted his hood against the wind, and said, "So, what's up?"

Jocelyn gave him a smile and patted the boulder again. Mike took it in at a glance, then looked at me. He was thinking exactly what I was thinking. Jocelyn's boulder was wild rock, battered, irregular, and useless for anything except railroad bed fill, which was why it was still here. There were two old drill holes toward its back side, where someone had made a half-hearted attempt to start the ledge with it, then decided it wasn't worth the trouble and moved farther into the hillside.

The wind surged, flinging a solid sheet of rain across our faces. I staggered, and grabbed the fedora to hold it on my head.

"It's in a tricky spot," Mike ventured, when the gust had passed. "I'm not sure we could even get it loose without the damn thing rolling down the hill."

"I'm sure you guys can figure something out," Jocelyn said placidly. Her hood had blown down in the wind, but she made no move to replace it.

Mike opened his mouth to try again, then closed it and looked at me. My turn.

I said, as mildly as possible, "Jos, I'm having a hard time picturing this. I mean, by the time I knock all the projections off and get this thing squared up, there's not going to be much left of it."

"I don't want you to square it up. I want to use it just the way it is."

"The way it is. You mean, polish the—"

"No polishing," Jocelyn said. "No cleaning it up at all. I want it raw. Just like this. Take it off the mountain and put it on the grave."

I met her eyes. With her hood down, the rain pelting her face looked eerily like the lines of tears, but Jocelyn's expression was unstrained. I felt the deeper reality of her purpose like a different kind of air, a sudden quiet place that made the storm transparent. It was humbling. It is so easy to forget, sometimes, that grief is the beginning, not the end of work.

I said, "The stone the builders rejected. . . "

Jocelyn's eyes deepened at the corners, but all she said was, "Will you do it?"

"Of course."

She smiled at last. "Good. I'd hate to have to get Joe Murphy up here."

"We'll do it," I said, and glanced for confirmation at Mike, who hesitated a moment, then shrugged.

"We're here to serve," he said. "But it's going to be a bitch getting the truck out on this ledge."

CHAPTER TWENTY-ONE

Mike and I got right to work, and it was in fact a bitch getting my truck out there. The rock here had last been quarried before the advent of the internal combustion engine and I suppose the ledge was wide enough to leave working room around a horse-drawn wagon, but there was a real question as to whether my one-ton would even fit into the space. We backed it in there anyway, taking it inch by inch, with me at the wheel praying over my lowest reverse gear and the rain pouring through the windows, wide open so that I could hear Mike hollering directions from the back of the ledge. I had removed the cooler from the truck before we started the operation, so that if I rolled off down the hillside, at least the survivors could have a beer and toast my memory.

I knocked the mirror off the right side, scraping the cliff on the way in, and when we finally got the truck in place, most of the outside tire of the dual set at the left rear was sticking out into space. I climbed out of the cab through the passenger door as there was nothing on the driver's side but a hundred-foot drop.

"Whew," Mike said, when I got my feet back on the ground. "All I could think was that your grandmother was going to kill me when I had to tell her I let you back off a mountain while we were working in a hurricane."

"Nothing to it," I said, trying to keep the quaver out of my voice. "If you've got a quarter for the parking meter, we're good to go."

"Let them try to tow you," Mike said.

* * *

The rest of the job went more easily. Mike and I had always worked well together and we were both motivated to just get it done and get out of the rain. We shooed Jocelyn into some shelter beneath an overhanging ledge of squared-off quartzite, left the cooler in her care, and got to it. While I drilled a series of holes along the back side of the boulder, Mike used a diamond-bit chain saw to make a deep horizontal cut along the front base. We had two good angles on the rock and it really wasn't going to be a big deal getting it out.

The rain was coming down more or less sideways now, the wind blasting so hard that you had to set your feet against it. My poncho kept flipping up around my face and my hat wouldn't stay on my head. I finally gave up and took both of them off and stashed the poncho in the truck cab. I was going to leave the hat there with it, then thought the better of that: if the truck rolled off the cliff, with or without me, I didn't want the hat to go too. So I took the fedora over to Jocelyn.

The recess she had hunkered down in was about two gravestones deep and three high; or, more realistically, two loads of railroad bed fill. Sitting in the driest corner with her back against the wall, Jocelyn looked remarkably at ease. She had availed herself of the cooler and was sipping a beer.

"How's it going out there?" she asked.

"Just the same old wind-whipped work on the edge of a cliff in a driving rain kind of stuff."

"Admit it, Eli, you're having a blast."

"It's not bad for a first date," I said, and put the hat on her head.

196

Jocelyn smiled and tilted the sodden fedora to a jaunty
angle. She looked adorable in it, of course.

"This is crazy, isn't it?" she said; and then, grinning, as I
hesitated, "Come on, Eli, admit it. It's nuts."

"Well, the Lord works in mysterious ways."

"I'll take that as a 'Yes.'"

"The Lord may be a little crazy," I conceded.

She seemed satisfied with that, and held out the beer to
offer me some. I accepted the bottle and took a polite sip. If I did
end up driving the truck off the cliff, I didn't want to get busted for
a DUI when they recovered my shattered body.

Jocelyn looked out at the ledge, where Mike had finished
his deep cut and was rigging a pneumatic block pusher. I already
had the plug-and-feathers in place in the line of holes I had drilled
along the back edge. "How much longer, do you think?"

"We're just about ready to pop it out of there. If we can
manage to load it without knocking the truck over the edge, we'll
be out of here in fifteen minutes."

"And then?"

I looked at her, not sure what she was getting at. "Well,
then we drive home straight into a hurricane, I guess, and hope for
the best."

"Will that be safe?"

I had to laugh; it seemed a little late to start worrying about
safety now, with the truck hanging off a wet cliff in a gale.
"Compared to what?"

"I was just thinking we might want to stop somewhere. To
ride it out."

"You mean, like, a motel or something?"

Jocelyn smiled. "I believe that is the accepted practice for
stranded travelers."

I met her eyes. She seemed to know exactly what she was
saying. She always did. But I had to be sure. "One room or two?"

"One."

A wind shift blew a fresh wave of rain into the recess just

then, but neither of us flinched. Jocelyn was dressed for it, and I was so wet and chilled by now in my soaked T-shirt that the drops felt warm.

When the gust had passed, I said, "I'm not sure that would be prudent, Jos."

"It would be more prudent to drive through a hurricane?"

"That's not a rhetorical question, and you know it." And, as Jocelyn simply held my gaze, I said, "One bed or two?"

"One, silly."

"Definitely imprudent."

"There are no prudent options here, Elijah. You're on a mountain in a hurricane with a married woman. It's the devil or the deep blue sea."

The woman did have a way of putting things. I heard the air compressor rev up again, which meant that Mike had the pneumatic bag set up and was basically ready to go.

I said, "When Joshua told me not to be presumptuous, I'm pretty sure this is what he meant."

"Well, you guys will have to work that out, then, won't you?"

"Yo, Tremaine!" Mike hollered. "It's raining out here."

"Yeah, I'm coming," I called. I turned back to Jocelyn, and was struck anew by the calm and lightness of her manner since she'd picked out the stone. In the soggy fedora, with the sleeves of the yellow rain jacket drooping past her hands, and the rubber boots engulfing her legs, she looked like a carefree nine-year-old on a pretend whaling expedition. She looked like the girl I had fallen in love with in fourth grade.

I said, "You're sure about this?"

Jocelyn smiled. "I suppose it could be the beer talking."

"Then save some beer for me," I said, and went out into the storm.

* * *

"Slacker," Mike said, when I got back to the work ledge.

"Sorry about that."

"I hope you guys got it all worked out."

"We barely scratched the surface," I said. "So what's the plan here?"

"You get up there and tap the plug line til we've got good tension on it, then I'll pop the bag, and we'll see what cracks."

"Sounds good," I said, and grabbed the sledge and some safety goggles. It is very important to wear protective lenses during quarrying work, so that when you get hit in the face by a hurtling chunk of rock, the doctors can figure out where your nose used to be.

I clambered up behind the boulder. The plugs in the line of holes I'd drilled were rigged in series and connected with a tungsten master bar, so that I could drive all of them at the same time. I set my feet and glanced at Mike, who gave me a thumb's-up; I swung the sledge and whacked the head of the master rod, and then again.

At the third hit, the rock gave a little creak as the plugs began to spread the feathers deep in the rock, and I stepped back while Mike started up the Pneumopillow. Pneumatic block pushers are wondrous tools, especially if you've ever done any quarrying without them. They are skinny, unimposing-looking little things that look like seat cushions or yoga mats, thin enough to slip into a chain saw cut in a rock, but they work miracles. Once the pillow is in place, you inflate it, with either water or air, and the expanding bag generates a tremendous amount of thrust and, hopefully, shifts the entire bank of stone.

Mike revved the compressor and fired up the bag. The boulder shuddered, then gave a satisfying crack as it broke cleanly along the base. Just like that. I stepped in and hit the master rod again, hard, and the back split too.

"Bingo!" Mike hollered. He kept the bag inflated while I slid down from behind the boulder and climbed up onto the truck to swing the crane around.

The wind was much worse on the truck bed, since it was clear of the slight lee of the cliff; working the crane felt like trying to rig a sail during a typhoon at sea. I had taken off the safety goggles by now, because I couldn't see a damn thing with them on. I got the jib centered over the boulder, jumped down to help Mike rig the harness, then climbed back up into the gale. I put the winch into its lowest gear and cranked it up until the boom creaked and the cable went taut.

"I'm gonna let the air bag go," Mike yelled over the roar of the compressor and the rain. "Do you want to get off the truck?"

He meant, of course, that he thought the weight shift might send the truck over the edge. But leaving the crane unmanned might do that too. I said, "If anything happens, I'll probably have time to jump off, right?"

"Probably," Mike said dubiously.

"So let's just do it, and get out of the rain."

Mike gave me a moment to change my mind, then shrugged and turned to deflate the air bag. The boulder sank half an inch and the crane groaned as it took the full weight, but everything held.

"Good to go," I said.

"Watch that projection on the way up. You've haven't got a whole lot of room there. . . . And Eli?"

"Yeah?"

"If it does go, remember to jump toward the hill."

"Thanks, Mikey," I said, and put the crane into second gear. The boulder lifted easily until it was almost level with the truck bed, then snagged on the outcropping Mike had noted. I gave it more power; the crane's motor whined and the boom arched a little, but the rock stayed stuck. What I should have done then was back off and take it more slowly, maybe with Mike going up behind the boulder with a crowbar to try to lever it past the snag, but I was cold and wet and tired and I downshifted and gave the crane a tad more power still. The boom tensed like the string on a bow and the winch motor began to scream.

"Ease off! Ease off!" Mike yelled, just as the outcropping crumbled and the boulder popped loose.

The boom jerked upward, yanking the boulder toward the truck like a yo-yo in a botched trick. When the rock reached the end of the boom's play, the gears in the jib's pivot all stripped and the rock just kept coming. I ducked as it hurtled past and smashed the back window of the truck, then swung back.

For a long instant the two thousand pounds of quartzite hung over me with the straps and pulleys creaking. I had time to note that I was out of the rain and wind at last, to be amused by the irony of that, and to feel a peace so deep and rich and immediate that it made every fear irrelevant. I did hope that Jocelyn wasn't watching, though. It seemed like such a silly damned way to die.

But the rigging held. The rock settled at the limit of the drooping jib, with inches to spare above me.

I glanced out from under the boulder and saw Mike's face peering at me over the edge of the truck bed. His eyes were a bit wide.

"Oops," I said.

Mike just shook his head and held out his hand to help me out from under the rock.

"There must have been a better way to do that," he said.

CHAPTER TWENTY-TWO

We took a quick break while I smoked a cigarette and got my heart rate down, then managed to coax the broken crane into settling the boulder the last couple feet down onto the truck bed without destroying anything else. The one-ton sank on its shocks at the load, but it looked like the suspension would hold if I took it slow. It turned out that Jocelyn had not witnessed the fiasco with the boulder; she just assumed that the wind had made it tricky, and Mike and I were content to leave her sense of the loading of her daughter's gravestone at that. I suppose we both felt stupid enough already.

We secured the boulder on the truck bed, and then Mike went up to the sheltered nook to have a beer with Jocelyn while I cleared the broken glass out of the truck's cab and rigged a tarpaulin across the gaping back window to keep the rain out. It actually felt good to clean up my mess a little, like a small penance. A smashed window and a busted crane were nothing, of course, compared to the mess that was coming if Jocelyn and I actually stopped at a motel. But I decided to not worry about that yet.

* * *

Jocelyn waited in Mike's truck while he and I eased my truck back off the ledge. It was pretty straightforward on the way out; I didn't even scrape the cliff this time, since I had already knocked the right-side mirror off on the way in.

Jocelyn had given Mike back his rain gear and was once again wearing her hilariously inadequate but very stylish London Fog raincoat. She gave Mike a big kiss and asked him how much she owed him, and he just laughed and helped her up into my truck.

"You guys aren't going to try to drive back in this are you?" he said. "You're welcome to stay here. You can just—"

"We might stop somewhere if it gets too bad," Jocelyn said.

Mike blinked.

"Ah," he said. "Well, sure. That would be, uh—" And he looked at me for help.

"Prudent?" I suggested.

"Yeah," Mike said. "Prudent." He closed the passenger door for Jocelyn and came around to me.

"Be careful out there, buddy," he said quietly.

"I'm just going to take it slow and try to stay between the navigational buoys."

"I didn't mean driving."

I met his eyes, which were obsidian black and usually inscrutable. But not now. Little Mike was really worried.

"Neither did I," I said.

* * *

We followed Mike's truck up and over the hill and then down to the turn-off to the quarry office. Mike flashed his lights and honked his horn in farewell as he went left, and we waved and drove on. Even at fifteen miles an hour, the rain was drowning out the windshield wipers, but on the quarry roads you could pretty much feel your way from pothole to pothole. The truck was handling weirdly, not just because of the wind, but because the boulder in the bed was off-center; we'd had to set it down where the broken crane would let us. But by then we'd just been glad that I wasn't under it.

We made the turn southeast onto the county road and I tried taking the truck up to twenty miles per hour, but the world just disappeared into a wall of gray. I eased back down to fifteen, so that I could at least glimpse the road on the wipers' downstroke. It was a two-lane highway with no divider and I hoped that anyone coming in the opposite direction was going fifteen too. But for the moment it looked like we were the only maniacs out here.

Jocelyn's cell phone rang just then in her pocketbook. I was struck by her ring tone, which was very non-standard, a clutch of horns playing "Nice Work If You Can Get It."

"That's probably Bill, checking in," Jocelyn said. "He's got the boys today." She took take the phone out of her purse and glanced at the screen. "Yeah. Bill's cell."

"You should get it. He'll be worried."

"He'll be way more worried if I talk to him."

A semi was approaching on the other side of the road. Some wacko determined that not even a hurricane would interrupt the supply of corn flakes to central Virginia. Of course, he was probably thinking the same thing about me and my rock.

I said, "I think you should talk to your husband."

"And tell him what?"

"Well, the truth, I suppose."

Jocelyn just looked at me. The truck roared by, flinging up a solid wall of spray. For two beats of the wipers there was nothing visible but water. When I could see again, I added, "Or a shameless lie that will come back around eventually to haunt us all."

Jocelyn laughed. "That helps a lot."

"It's your call, Jos."

She held off for another chorus of "Nice Work If You Can Get It," then shrugged and punched "TALK."

"Hey," she said. ". . . No, we got it. It was, um—" She

floundered, apparently at a loss to characterize the scene at the quarry.

"No sweat," I supplied.

"—pretty easy, all things considered," Jocelyn said, rolling her eyes at me. "The quarry guy, Mike, was awesome, a real sweetheart. . . . Yeah. So, how are the boys?" Jocelyn laughed. "Typical." She covered the mouthpiece and said, "Billy and Josh want to go out in their boat. Joshua apparently thinks that the middle of a hurricane is a perfect time to take some water samples for his sewage dispersion study."

"Joshua is doing a sewage dispersion study?"

"He feels that the EPA monitoring mechanisms are inadequate." Jocelyn turned her attention back to the phone. "You told them what they could do with that idea, I hope. . . . Good man. What's it like there? . . . Uh-huh. Wow. . . . Well, there's our firewood for the winter, I guess. . . . No, actually, we've left the quarry, we're already on our way back."

I could hear the rise in Bill Sherman's voice even over the din of the storm, the tarp flapping around the back window, and the low-gear roar of the truck. Jocelyn gave me an inscrutable glance as she listened to what was clearly an earful. "About fifteen miles an hour. . . . It's all right, Bill. Really. . . . Yeah, I know. . . . No, no, of course not." She listened a moment more, then turned to at me again. "He wants to talk to you."

"No way," I said, but she had already handed me the phone.

"When I said you had my blessing, I didn't mean to take her out in a hurricane," Bill Sherman said.

"Actually, we're on a hurricane evacuation route."

"Driving the wrong way."

"Bill, when was the last time you got Jocelyn to change her mind when she was hell-bent on doing something?"

Sherman was silent for a moment, conceding the point. I could hear the roar of wind in his background, over all the noise in the truck. When he did speak, it was in a more conversational tone.

"She said you guys managed to get the stone quarried before it got too bad."

"Yeah."

"How does it look?"

I had a flash of the confetti of his vision of his daughter's gravestone flickering away in the wind. "All rocks look pretty much the same at this point in the process. Like a badly pulled tooth." And, to change the subject, "What's it like there?"

"It's wild. We're right in the fucking middle of it. The power's been out for hours, the river's breaking over the dock, and we've got two trees down in the back yard."

"Not that apple tree, I hope."

"No, that's still up. For the moment." Sherman caught himself and said, "I can't believe we're having this conversation. We can do the goddamned storm damage report some other time. All I wanted to tell you was to get off the road, for Christ's sake. Find yourself a motel somewhere."

I didn't want to be having this conversation either; but I couldn't see any way to avoid it, much less address the real issue. I certainly wasn't ready to ask Bill Sherman whether he was thinking of one motel room or two. "Look, we're probably safer than you are, at this point."

"Just get off the fucking highway, man. Pull in somewhere and sit it out. I mean it."

I glanced at Jocelyn, who raised her eyebrows as if to say, You guys are on your own. I said, "We'll certainly take that under advisement."

"Goddammit, man"

The truck shuddered as we hit a patch of standing water; the highway was beginning to flood in the low spots. I took it down to second gear and said, "You're breaking up, Bill. What did you say?"

"I said—"

I clicked END CALL, and turned off the power for good measure.

"Lost him," I told Jocelyn, handing the phone back to her. "Must be the storm."

She glanced at the screen, noted the power situation, then closed the phone and put it back in her purse without comment.

"He *wants* us to stop," she said.

"That was my impression."

"I guess that makes it easy."

It didn't, though, and we both felt it. The phone call had been a marvelous reality check. I could feel the lineaments of all the ties that bind, the children raised together, the years of shared history, a thousand flimsy strands webbed by the decades into sinew. Jocelyn had been right, that day at her house: there were things an unmarried person simply could never understand. The only one surprised by the power of all this stuff was me.

* * *

We drove in silence for a time. The standing water on the road was more or less constant now in the low spots, and the whole highway was becoming a low spot. One of the corners of the tarp over the back window began to flap, and then flail, working loose in the wind.

A sign loomed out of the deluge just ahead of us and I squinted through the streaming water on the windshield to make it out: REDUCE SPEED AHEAD. It was either God's perverse sense of humor, or we were approaching a town. I took it down to ten miles an hour, in case it was some kind of speed trap.

"There's a motel up there," Jocelyn said. "Just after the gas station, on the left."

"Yeah," I said. It was a typical semi-rural lodge on a minor highway, two rows of first-floor rooms and a gravel parking lot. The hunters probably used it once in a while, but the red VACANCY sign looked like it had been burning since the dawn of time. I drove past it.

"If you're waiting for something better, you're dreaming,"

Jocelyn said.

"We need to talk about Bill. And the kids."

"It's a little late for that, isn't it?"

"Better late than never."

"I'm not sure there's anything to say."

I just looked at her. Denial had never been Jocelyn's style.

"I don't even know where to start," she said.

"That's sort of my point."

We cruised the main drag of the small town, leaving a wake in the streaming street. There were lights on at the Qwik-Mart, the hardware store, and the Shell station, but everything else seemed shut down for the storm. At the end of the run of buildings, another motel loomed, the Prince George Suites, looking decidedly unregal. I drove past that too.

"You can't just keep driving in this, Eli," Jocelyn said.

"Actually, I can."

She considered me for a moment, then put up the collar of her coat, as rain was starting to come through the widening gap in the tarp's coverage of the back window. We approached another small town, and passed another motel. This town even had a stoplight, thrashing in the wind but discernibly red when we reached it. I stopped in the middle of a small pond and we waited, absurdly, the only vehicle in sight, for the light to change. The trees even along the relatively sheltered main drag were bending nearly parallel to the ground now. I took the opportunity to try to secure the tarp, but succeeded only in making it slightly worse by the time the light turned green.

"I think Bill and I probably would have made it, if Ariel hadn't died," Jocelyn said.

I tried taking the truck up to third gear. Twenty miles an hour felt like breakneck speed by now, but for a moment I could still see, and I began to recalculate how long it was going to take to get home. But we had been in the lee of some buildings; when we cleared them the windshield turned opaque with water again, and I downshifted.

"He told me that when you guys first met, he used to order for both of you in restaurants," I said.

Jocelyn smiled. "He loves to tell people that. You'd think I was a sparrow with a broken wing that he found in the woods and nursed back to health. But there's a lot of truth to it. I was pretty messed up for a long time after you, uh—"

"Bolted?"

"Dumped me, is how I saw it."

"Ouch," I said. "It probably sounds weird, but I never thought of us in those terms: dumper and dumpee. It just never seemed to have anything to do with us."

"That's because you did the dumping," Jocelyn said. "Not to throw it in your face or anything. But you took the heart out of me."

"And Bill put it back?"

"Not at first. At first he just picked out the toppings on our pizzas. And made me laugh. Kept my interest. I had forgotten what it was like, to be interested in anyone or anything. But Bill is an interesting man."

We were almost out of town now. We approached a Chinese restaurant advertising a lunchtime hamburger special. I supposed they had to make certain concessions to their clientele out here.

"I'd kill for mu-shu pork right now," Jocelyn said, reading my mind.

"Me too. Or kung pao chicken."

"Szechwan shrimp, and spring rolls. Something sweet and sour."

"You could order for both of us," I said. "But that place looks closed."

"The Chinese," Jocelyn said. "No hurricane grit." She watched the restaurant go by, then reached down into the cooler and came up with a sandwich and a beer. "Do you mind? I'm starving."

"That's what they're for."

"Do you want anything?"

"I want two hands on the wheel, for the moment." The windshield was starting to fog up and I reached over and clicked the defroster onto HIGH, adding another layer of roar to the din.

Jocelyn took a bite of the sandwich, and a swallow of the beer.

"This is very Bill-like, you know," she said.

"What is?"

"You commandeering the situation. Driving on, come hell or literal high water."

"I said that you could order the Chinese food."

"I remember when that phase came to an end," she said. "I was pregnant with Billy, and Bill ordered veal for me."

"I *knew* it," I exclaimed. "I almost asked him about that. I remembered your policy on food that had once been cute."

"I threw up, right there at the table in a four-star restaurant. And after that I started ordering for myself."

"A turning point."

"Billy was a turning point in just about every way, really. Just looking at his face when he was born. It was the way we used to look at each other, you know? Just looking at this being, and this being looking back, and that was all that was necessary. Simple and perfect. And I thought then, for the first time, Well, maybe what we'd gone through made its own kind of sense, if it had prepared me for that love."

"Bill said you came into your own as a mom."

Jocelyn laughed. "You guys had quite the conversation, didn't you?"

"We went out to The Tiger Cage and had a couple of truth-serum margaritas."

"That Vietnamese seafood place out on Sandbridge?"

"You've been there?"

"Once, on a girls' night out. The owner is sort of a nut."

"That nut and I go way back," I said. "Nick is actually a hell of a guy."

"If you say so."

"He's sort of an acid test, in his way. Pass/fail. Bill held his own surprisingly well. Right off the bat, Nick tried to make him take off his tie, and Bill just looked at him and said, 'Bite me.'"

Jocelyn laughed. "Oh my God."

"Nick loved it. I was impressed, I have to say."

"Bill does have spine."

"Okay, that's my point," I said. "That's why I'm still driving. You love the guy." And, as she took a breath to tell me it wasn't that simple, "And don't give me that crap about unmarried people not understanding."

"You don't need me in this conversation at all, do you?' Jocelyn said. "God, it's eerie. You are just like Bill."

"There are subtle distinctions. Like, Bill is married to you."

"There's another motel up ahead," she said.

By way of an answer, I accelerated slightly and went into third gear, but this turned out to be hubris. Not only did the windshield go turbid with water again, the tarpaulin across the back window flailed one last time, then tore away and disappeared into the storm. The immediate sensation was of having driven into an automated carwash with the windows open. I had intended to keep driving until God gave me an unmistakable signal to stop, and I decided that if this was not it, I couldn't hold out any longer. I slowed until I could see again, then pulled into the parking lot of the motel.

CHAPTER TWENTY-THREE

In the motel's lot, the rain streamed into the cab as if we'd parked in a waterfall. I grabbed my poncho and hopped out to try to plug the gap. The physical reality of the storm outside the truck was a shock. The wind staggered me, and I had to set my feet against the boulder just to stay in place on the truck bed while I did the jury-rig on the back window. We almost lost the poncho to the gale several times, but with Jocelyn holding it down from the inside, I finally got the thing in place.

I climbed back into the cab, soaked to the skin, as the wind slammed the door shut after me. Jocelyn settled in her seat, using a paper towel to try to dry off. I noticed with some amusement that she had taken the keys out of the ignition to thwart any further attempts on my part to get back out on the road. That was okay with me. It really had been crazy, to be driving in this stuff.

"Admit it, Jocelyn, you're having a blast," I said.

She smiled. "It's not bad for a first date."

The motel's sign was directly in front of us, with big brown neon antlers framing the nightmare green of THE DEER LAKE INN. The office was to our left, the end suite of a series of half a dozen rooms in a shabby row. The parking lot was surprisingly crowded; a good storm was probably a bonanza for this place, the only time anyone ever checked in without a rifle.

"'The Buck Stops Here,'" Jocelyn noted, reading from the sign.

"I guess it does," I said. With further driving out of the question, I reached into the cooler and drew out a beer. The Bud was wonderfully cold after a full day on ice, which wasn't necessarily good, as I was starting to shiver in my wet clothes. Jocelyn seemed in no hurry to get down to business with the motel and I was grateful for that. We sat for a moment in silence, watching the storm make wild patterns in the pothole puddles in the parking lot. Behind us, the poncho rattled, but held. It actually seemed peaceful, relatively quiet, without the added din of the truck fighting the storm.

"When you said you and Bill would have made it, if Ariel hadn't died, what did you mean?" I said at last.

"It seems obvious."

"Not to me."

"We were fine," she said. "Better than fine, we were good. We're actually a great team, as parents. And Bill was so happy to have a little girl coming. We both were. We found out she would be a girl from an ultrasound at twenty-one weeks. The same day we found out that her heart wasn't developing normally."

"Oof."

"Bill was awesome. Never flinched. He was on the Internet from the moment they made the diagnosis, and by the time she was born, he probably could have performed the first operation himself. She had to have three; they did it in stages. We went up to the University of Michigan medical center for the operations; they're pretty much the state of the art. And in between operations, there was always something, infections, sat levels, always something. So we did a lot of time at the Children's Hospital of the King's Daughters in Norfolk. The poor kid spent most of her life in and out of pediatric wards. I mean, her favorite book was *Franklin Goes to the Hospital*. How sad is that?"

"What was her second favorite book?"

Jocelyn smiled. "*Franklin Makes a Mess*. She wanted to be a turtle when she grew up. She pronounced it 'tuhh-tuhl.' Tuhh-tuhl this, tuhh-tuhl that. When they came into the room to do an injection or something, she would duck her head under the covers and pretend she had gone into her shell. It would break my heart. But the funny thing was, she never let anything slow her down. I mean, you saw the picture— she was such an irrepressible *kid*, she just took it all in stride. The second they pulled the tubes after a procedure, she'd want to be off down the hall to find the playroom. I guess she figured, that's just how life was. She took it as it came."

"And Bill?"

"Right there every second. It was beautiful. I mean, God, he loved that girl. It wrecked his career, basically, he got passed over as a partner at the firm because he wasn't putting in the billable hours, but he didn't care. We took turns sleeping over, one of us at the hospital with Ariel, one at home with the boys. Bill had the whole place figured out after a while. He was better at dealing with her IVs than most of the nurses."

"I can picture that. He drives well with two margaritas in him too."

"Grace under pressure. I fell apart three or four times for every time he broke down. He was awesome. Right up to . . . the end." Jocelyn shivered abruptly and drew her coat around her. "God, it's freezing. I thought hurricanes were supposed to be tropical."

"I'd turn the heater on, but I seem to have misplaced my keys."

"Why don't we just check in?"

"I haven't finished my beer. I'm drinking as slow as a tuhh-tuhl."

Jocelyn was silent for a moment, then said, "Eli, I appreciate your concern for my, um, virtue. Or whatever. But—"

"How did she die?" I asked.

Jocelyn blinked, then blinked again; then she dipped into

her purse and drew out the truck keys. "Just for the heater," she said. "Promise. No tricks."

"Just for the heater. I promise. Only an idiot would try to drive in this weather."

She handed me the keys and I started the truck and got the heater going. With the engine still hot, the air was warm right away, a big relief. The goosebumps sharpened, then receded from my arms. Jocelyn undid the top button of her coat and took a beer out of the cooler for herself.

"You sure know how to show a girl a good time," she said.

"It's a gift."

She twisted off the cap, tapped her bottle against mine, and we both sipped. The puddles on the motel parking lot had begun to merge into a lake, like rock pools in a rising tide. It was late afternoon, but dark as evening. The lights on the motel sign flickered once, and then again, but stayed on. It was just a matter of time, though. The power lines were twanging between the utility poles like banjo strings.

As the temperature in the truck cab grew comfortable, I turned the heat down a notch. Jocelyn undid the rest of the buttons on her raincoat, scooted down in her seat, and put her feet up on the dashboard, like a kid.

"The third operation didn't get it done," she said. "Ariel had been a borderline case all along, as to whether the procedures would work or not, but it was close enough that she qualified for the operations, so we couldn't even try for a transplant until we'd tried the surgery route. She went on the waiting list after the third operation. That was in November. But she was home for Thanksgiving, and it was so sweet. Almost normal. I guess we had a bit of magic hope for the transplant, even though the waiting list was so long. Like, all we had to do was hang in there. But by mid-December Ariel's blood pressure was so high we had to take her back to CHKD in the middle of the night. It was the kind of thing that had happened before, and I think we sort of thought she'd get through it like she always did and we'd be home for Christmas. But she didn't get through it."

Jocelyn glanced at me, assessing my capacity, maybe, or looking for a stop sign. "It's weird," she said. "I haven't actually told any of this to anyone. It's like getting hit by lightning or something. Everything just stops, right there."

I thought of the endless night of my mother's death, and nodded.

"Bill was out of the room," she said. "He had gone to get us sodas. I was sitting by the bed and Ariel was dozing, and then she gave this little gasp, and woke up. And I knew instantly. I don't know how. I picked her up right away, IV lines and all. And she was just looking at me. She had eyes like Joshua, I don't know how to describe it, like mine and Bill's mixed—"

"A touch of the Hartley green," I said.

"Exactly. And we just looked at each other, and then she was gone. Just . . . gone."

The truck shuddered in the wind. I could hear the crane creaking, the jib twisting on its stripped gears like a wind vane. Jocelyn said, "When Bill came back into the room with the Cokes, he actually smiled. I guess it was a pretty peaceful-looking scene by then, except that the blood pressure monitor was honking every five seconds. I just looked at him and shook my head. And he stopped smiling and came over and put his arms around both of us. I could feel his tears dripping onto my head."

Jocelyn was silent a moment. "I wish we could have just stopped right there," she said. "It wasn't a nightmare yet somehow, and we were still together in it. But of course eventually the nurse came in to deal with the monitor, and she started crying right away. Everyone knew Ariel by then, she was a sort of CHKD celebrity, they'd all been rooting for her for years. And then of course people started streaming in, everybody with something to do and something they needed from us, and they all wanted me to put her down, and I said no way. I wouldn't let anyone touch her. Bill finally took out the IV lines and disconnected all the monitor wires himself. And they kept asking me to put her down and I wouldn't.

It wasn't like I had a plan or anything. I just couldn't do it. I was figuring they were just going to have to make a casket big enough for both of us, because I wasn't ever going to be able to put her down. And of course Bill was trying to talk me down and I started to get mad at him and finally they gave me a sedative, an injection, and the last thing I remember before I went under was Bill taking her out of my arms, and the tears streaming down his face."

We were silent for a time. It was dark as night by now. The lights burning in the motel rooms seemed like the lights of distant towns viewed from the sea.

"I guess I never quite forgave him for that," Jocelyn said at last. "I mean, the poor guy, right? Just doing what he had to do. He took care of everything after that, of course, I was a basket case. The obituary, the phone calls, the funeral, everything. The boys. Someone had to, and he did. It's not like he had a choice. But I hated him for it. Every little bit of life going on, every check mark on the to-do list: I hated him for it. It wasn't his fault. But that's the way it went down."

"He understood all that, I think," I said. "In his mind, you guys were back where you had started: he was ordering the food for both of you at the restaurant. That's how he saw the memorial too."

"But I wasn't hungry. That's what he didn't get."

"True. All he knew was that you had to eat."

Jocelyn shook her head. Not denying my point, just a quiet shake. "Bill's a good man, yes, everyone has been telling me that. And it's true. A good man, a good father, a good husband. A good friend, even. But all that goodness at this point is like gravel on my nerves. I'm rubbed raw with his goddamned goodness. Stop already, with the goodness." She looked at me, her eyes suddenly fierce in the weird brown neon glow of the motel sign. "The truth is, Bill is a man who needs to be in control. He needs to put the situation into order. He needs to do what he does best. But none of that means a thing when your child gives that little gasp and looks up at you to die. Control, order, goodness—meaning, even—

217

they evaporate. You are helpless, and the world stops. You pick her up and you watch her die in your arms. There is nothing anyone can say to you to put that moment back into a world where order, control, and goodness mean anything at all, nothing anyone can say that isn't fed by their own terror and helplessness, and their own denial of it. But Bill has never gotten that, not once. He's too busy being good. He's never had the nerve, or the soul, or the desperation maybe; he's never gotten to the end of his rope, or just been weak, or whatever the hell it takes, to really see it, to stop his beautiful goddamned earnest life-affirming projects for a single terrifying second and just live with the complete . . . failure, the futility, the obliteration of all that feverish order and control and goodness in the single moment when it would have actually meant something. To live for a single second with the emptiness of that."

I thought of Bill Sherman, with his futon and his badly cooked chicken pot pies, refusing to buy furniture in Ghent. "I think he may have caught a glimpse, actually, by now."

"What do you mean?"

"He told me that when he asked you about the separation, you said that you needed space, and time. And he asked how much space, how much time. And you said, 'Long enough for you to stop asking questions like that.'"

"You guys sure covered the waterfront," Jocelyn said.

"My point is: When was the last time he asked you?"

"A technicality," Jocelyn said. "Bill is nothing if not a quick study. He figured out the new game, and started making the right plays. That's all that is."

"Seems like Catch-22 to me, then. He's either too clueless, or too cunning."

"God, did he hire you as his agent or something, at The Tiger Cage?"

"No. He told me that I should call you."

Jocelyn looked at me sharply. "You're kidding."

"I don't kid about shampoos, or drunken heart-to-hearts," I said. "How do you think I got the hot line number?"

She considered that. "What did he actually say?"

"'You should call her.'"

"Meaning what? In context."

"Meaning, as I read it, that I was an undropped shoe in your life, and he wanted it to drop and be done with, for better or worse. Meaning that the only way you guys had a chance was for you to run it out with me."

"And what did you say?"

"I told him no fucking way. . . . Of course, I ended up calling you anyway."

"This is all very un-Bill-like, I must say," Jocelyn conceded. "I'm still trying to picture it."

"I'm not trying to paint the guy as a saint. He seemed pretty sure that I would fuck up with you. I suspect he's counting on that. But he definitely and repeatedly urged me to make the run at it."

"Very un-Bill-like," Jocelyn repeated. I could see her eyes flickering in the surreal brown and green glow of the neon, left, right, down, remembering moments, making connections. When she surfaced after a long moment, there was a trace of a smile in her voice. "You have a very funny way of trying to get a girl into bed, Elijah."

"It gets funnier," I said. "Was it Bill-like for him to tell us to check into a motel tonight?"

"Actually, I would have bet that he would prefer us to drown."

"Bill-like to leave the choosing of the stone to you?"

"Ah, but that's where it breaks down," Jocelyn said. "All that other stuff—okay, granted, he's wrestling with himself. Bless his heart. But that stone burns the bridge, whatever else is true. You saw the way he was about the sketch—he's been so dead-set on getting his precious memorial in place, putting the world back in its proper orbit with his hokey little lamb and his squared-off planes, in pastel shades. If I know anything about the man, I know that he's going to flip out when he sees that rock back there."

I hesitated, but there seemed no way around it. You can study the stone for hours, use a calipers to set your angles and your points, and weigh the stroke in advance to within a feather's touch, but there comes a moment when you just have to smack the chisel and see what flies off and what stays. "With all due respect, Jos, I'm not sure you know shit."

Jocelyn blinked once, and then her nostrils flared and her face went hard. It was an expression remarkably like Bill's at The Tiger Cage, when I had told him "Bullshit," though this did not seem an opportune moment to point that out.

"And you do, I suppose?" she demanded coldly.

"I know I'm not about to check into this motel and help you square off the planes on some half-assed idea of a wrecked marriage, just because your husband wasn't willing to pick out a coffin big enough for both his daughter and his wife."

Jocelyn glared at me for another moment, her dark eyes glittering in the neon. It was a shock. I had forgotten how angry she could get, how fast.

"Fuck you, Eli," she said at last, very softly. "Fuck . . . you." She turned to yank her door handle, hopped out into the middle of a puddle, and let the wind slam the door as she stalked away.

* * *

I gave her five minutes, then went after her. The motel's simple layout didn't leave many options, and I found her without much trouble, huddled in the lee of the ice machine at the far end of the back wing.

A steady stream of water was pouring off the roof just beyond her niche and I had to pass through it to get to her. It felt like wading through a chest-deep stream. Jocelyn, standing with her arms folded across her chest, was shivering visibly. As I stepped out of the cataract, she angled her body more toward the ice machine and ignored me.

I settled in to wait her out, giving her as much space as I could to minimize the painful sense of having cornered an animal. We were out of the direct rain here, but getting splattered by the cascade from the roof. At the edge of the weak patch of light cast by the light mounted on the wall, a large tree limb lay on the ground like a discarded match; beyond that a row of battered crepe myrtles flailed in the wind. Everything else was liquid darkness, whirling.

After a while, Jocelyn remarked, in a surprisingly matter-of-fact tone, "You must be freezing."

"I've been warmer," I conceded.

"You really don't need to stay out here. Why don't you just get back in the truck?"

"Not without you."

A crash in the near darkness startled us both—another tree limb falling, or maybe an entire tree.

"Do you remember that time we got caught out in the woods during a thunderstorm?" Jocelyn said. "We were about ten, I guess. I could feel the thunder in my chest. It was stronger than my heart."

"I remember the lightning more than the thunder. It seemed like everything turned transparent, like an x-ray, every time it flashed. Like time stopped."

"I was sure we'd get fried."

"Me too. But I remember being glad that if I had to die, at least it was with you. And also thinking that if only one of us died, I hoped it was me."

Jocelyn smiled. "Because you didn't want to have to face my dad?"

"No," I said. "Because I couldn't imagine living without you."

A siren started to wail somewhere down the street just then. It was going to be a long night for the emergency crews. The ice machine rumbled beside us, faithfully cranking out more ice. That would be a precious commodity, once the power went out.

"Look, it's only going to get worse out here for a while," I said. "Let's get back in the truck, Jos. You can be as mad at me as you want, with the heater on."

"I'm not mad at you," Jocelyn said. She gave me a look, quite stern, but with one corner of her mouth almost microscopically tucked. "I think I may hate you, though."

"Hate me in the truck," I said.

* * *

Back in the truck cab, I got the heater going again. As the temperature climbed toward somewhere close to comfortable, Jocelyn shrugged out of her raincoat and slid across the seat toward me. I opened my arm for her and she nestled under it, turned her face into my chest, and began to cry, quietly at first, but building into sobs.

I brought my other arm around to enclose her, as she wept and shuddered. Something, I wasn't sure what, had shifted and come loose, like a bank of stone lifted by a PneumoPillow. And now the air was bleeding out of the bag; the freed weight was settling, and I could feel it on my heart.

Jocelyn cried for a long time. At some point the motel's lights flickered and went dark, along with the streetlights and every other light in sight. In the sudden, blustering blackness, the truck rocked in the wind and the rain lashed at the tarp, and in the distance the sirens came and went. Jocelyn wept and wept, for what seemed an impossibly long time; and when she quieted, I realized from her breathing that she had fallen asleep. I turned off the truck's engine and reached to pull her raincoat over her, then settled back with her still in my arms, breathing in the scent of Asian pear and red tea, with a hint of freesia.

My sense of time had drowned long since, but the glowing hands of my watch crawled through the hours. Just after midnight, the storm eased; the wind dropped off with surprising swiftness and the rain thinned and then stopped entirely. The truck's windows were so fogged by then that I couldn't see anything outside, but I thought the stars might be out.

Jocelyn woke at the silence, lifted her face, and said sleepily, like a child waking too early, "Is it over?"

"It's the eye," I said. "One more round."

"You're okay?"

"Golden," I said. "Go back to sleep."

She turned her face obligingly back into my chest and was breathing steadily within moments. The rain and wind started again, and built, and raged. Jocelyn shivered once in her sleep, and I tugged the raincoat up, over her shoulder, and tucked it in.

As she settled, I felt something slide onto the seat between us. I reached down carefully and rummaged until I found the pewter crucifix. Apparently no chain was ever going to hold that cross. I slipped it into the raincoat's pocket, smoothed Jocelyn's hair once more and breathed her in, and settled back to wait out the rest of the storm.

CHAPTER TWENTY-FOUR

I didn't see Jocelyn again until the unveiling of Ariel Sherman's stone on the anniversary of her death in late December. Bill Sherman handled the interim details of the job by telephone, and mailed me the final sketch of the memorial after determining, to his obvious amusement, that I had no fax machine. I was able to learn that he had moved back into the house, but otherwise our brief talks were constrained by an air of professional courtesy so meticulous that it amounted to a barrier.

I took no offense at the coolness and distance; it made perfect sense to me that it was going to take a while for the dust to settle. In any case, the autumn went by fast and busy, what with putting the roof back on my shop after the hurricane, helping my grandmother get her garden turned under and her winter vegetables in, and working through the various jobs that came in.

On the morning of the winter solstice, I dressed in my best black funeral suit. I had gone back and forth over what to wear; I usually wear work clothes to the ceremonies I end up at, and stand way back near the back hoe. I thought that might seem disrespectful in this case, given the depth of my involvement, but I began to suspect I had chosen wrong as soon as I got to the cemetery at St. James the Apostle. Charlie's teenage assistant had failed to show up and I had to help Charlie lay out the bright green carpet of Astroturf and set up the awning and chairs beside the draped stone.

It was a cool clear December day, typical of Virginia Beach's mild winter, and I was sweating by the time we were done, even after I took my jacket off. The service had already begun by then in the church, and rather than bust in late on that and stand in the back mopping sweat off my face, I shrugged my jacket back on and had a cigarette with Charlie, nodding at the latest round of his strange-but-true stories while keeping one anxious eye on the church's entryway.

The ushers opened the door at last, and the small, intimate assembly processed out toward the gravesite. A step behind the vested priest and an altar boy swinging a smoking censer, the Sherman family walked as an indivisible unit, with Bill and Jocelyn holding hands, and each of them holding the hand of one of the boys. Billy, I noted, was carrying the purple roanoke sash that Little Mike had given Jocelyn at the Big Rabbit. Behind them were Jocelyn's parents and a dozen or so people I didn't recognize. The last one out of the church was Marietta Hartley in a wheelchair. She was ostensibly being pushed by a pleasant looking young man, but she kept slapping his hands away to propel the chair herself.

As the procession crossed the grass, I stubbed my cigarette out and put the butt in my pocket, then eased back half a step off Charlie's shoulder, trying my best to look like his assistant. It was clear to me by now that I should have worn work clothes. I was thinking of the last thing Jocelyn had said to me, when I had finally dropped her off at her home on Little Neck Road, just before dawn on the morning after the hurricane. She had met my eyes and said, "I'm not going to say 'Thank you' yet, because it sounds too much like 'Good-bye.'" And I had said, "Okay. And I won't say 'You're welcome.'" She had leaned across to kiss me on the cheek, then turned and gotten out of the truck to walk to the house. I put the truck in gear immediately, but was still unable to get out of the driveway before the front door opened and Bill Sherman stepped out onto the porch to take her into his arms.

The group reached the grave and arrayed around it. I noticed that everyone was carrying a single long-stemmed yellow rose. Bill nodded at me right away as he took his place beside the veiled stone, not quite curtly, but with a distinct air of fulfilling a necessary protocol in a timely fashion. Jocelyn waited a moment longer as everyone settled, then met my eyes across the grass and knitted her brows in a brief, rueful, almost apologetic moue, as if to say she had no idea how we should be acting. I gave a quick shrug in reply: Me neither. Farther down to their right, Marietta had spotted me too, and gave me a playful wink. I winked back, grateful for the simplicity of it.

The priest opened his missal and began to read from the 118th Psalm: "*Open to me the gates of righteousness: I will go into them, and I will praise the Lord. . . .*" Beside him, the altar boy's eyes streamed from the drifting incense; I could smell the frankincense even from my distant spot.

"*I will praise thee: for thou hast heard me, and art become my salvation. The stone which the builders rejected is become the head stone of the corner. This is the Lord's doing; it is marvelous in our eyes. . . .*"

Billy Sherman, standing in front of his mother, was still cradling the purple conch belt like the folded flag at a military funeral. Jocelyn herself seemed steady, calm, and dignified, her hands resting on Billy's shoulders, her eyes on the gravestone draped in its ivory linen pall. She was wearing an overcoat of soft black cashmere, buttoned all the way up to her throat, as if against a chill, despite the relative mildness of the day.

"*This is the day which the Lord hath made: Let us rejoice and be glad in it. . . .*"

Joshua glanced up at his father, a bit restlessly; I could see that he wanted to be done with all the ceremony and just lift the veil on the stone. Bill gave him a smile and the briefest shake of his head: Sorry, sport. Patience.

"*Save now, I beseech thee, O Lord: O Lord, I beseech thee, send now thy comfort. For thou art my God, and I will praise thee: thou art my God, and I will exalt thee.*"

"O, give thanks unto the Lord: for his mercy endureth forever."

"Amen," the small crowd murmured, and Joshua, at a nod from his father, moved to slide the linen away from the stone.

When Charlie and I had placed the monument the previous evening, I had felt a wave of dread, anticipating this moment. In the winter twilight, the manganese-tinctured quartzite had looked to me exactly like what it was, an unhealed wound of a boulder, torn from the edge of a cliff during a storm. I suppose my sense of the thing was colored by the image of it swooping toward me on the truck bed like the angel of death on a jib.

But now, in the late morning sun, the blood-red lump of stone glowed with an unexpected life of its own. It looked like nothing so much as a human heart—not the Valentine icon, but an actual human heart, the ventricular chambers perhaps a bit underdeveloped, cradled in the green grass.

Jocelyn's initial vision of unflinching rawness had been tempered somewhat: there were neither angels nor a lamb, and the bulk of the rock was untouched, but Bill Sherman had gotten his epitaph from Samuel Clemens, inscribed in modest Mistral handlettering on a planed facet that seemed made for it. The porcelain photo of Ariel Sherman had found a home in one of the boulder's recesses, a natural pocket like the niche for a statue in a church wall, and a small butane flame flickered below it like an altar lamp, fed by the invisible line I had run up through the boulder's heart.

And on the front of the stone, on the only worked surface, framed by the winter-stark rose bush and gleaming ruby-red after the polishing:

ARIEL MARIE SHERMAN
BELOVED DAUGHTER
FEBRUARY 22, 2003 - DECEMBER 22, 2006.

Bill Sherman glanced at his wife, who gave him a quiet smile and stepped to the stone to lay her rose in front of the porcelain photo of their daughter. Billy and Joshua did the same, and then Bill himself, and the rest of the crowd began to move, to take their turns.

As they did, Bill Sherman started walking toward me. I contained my initial crazed impulse to flee, and met his eyes as he approached. If there had been a trace of glee or triumph in his look, I suppose it would have been easy to hate him, but Sherman's expression was open, earnest, and even a little tender. It looked like I was going to be stuck with actually liking the guy. The fear of God was in him, as it was in me.

"I haven't had a chance to properly thank you," he said. "The stone is beautiful. If that's the word."

"I guess it will have to do," I said.

We stood for a moment watching the yellow roses piling up on the monument. Jocelyn was standing beside the stone like someone receiving guests, giving everyone a hug after they had laid their flower, and accepting their sympathies. She was crying, softly, but it was a weeping that had a quiet sweetness, and even a sort of radiance to it. As we watched, her mother laid her rose and turned to take her daughter in her arms, and the two clung to each other.

"I guess it took a hurricane," Bill Sherman said.

There was something in his tone, a note of wistfulness or pain, the thorn on a yellow rose. I hesitated, then thought, What the hell. The truth was, I wanted the guy to be at peace. "Listen, Bill, about that night—"

He held up his hand to stop me. "All I know is that you got my daughter's gravestone quarried, and got my wife home safely. And that's all I need to know."

"But—"

"It ain't broke, Eli," Sherman said. "Isn't that what you grandfather would say here? It ain't broke. Don't try to fix it."

I met his eyes and saw that he was sincere. "I believe that would be his advice, now that you mention it."

"'Nuff said, then." Sherman gave me a thin smile. "But if you don't mind, amigo, I think I'll pass on that next drink at The Tiger Cage."

"Fair enough," I said. "Amigo."

Sherman's cell phone rang just then in his pocket. He reached quickly to silence it, but not before I recognized the ring tone. It was "Nice Work If You Can Get It."

"I always forget to turn this damned thing off," Sherman said. "Thank God it didn't ring during the ceremony." And, apologetically, with a glance at the screen. "Damn, I should probably take this."

"Of course."

"Thank you, again, for everything."

"De nada," I said, and he stepped away to take his call.

* * *

I would have liked to get myself out of there right away, to find a quiet place to sob or throw up, but as I started to ease away, Marietta Hartley came wheeling across the grass toward me, steering her wheelchair among the gravestones as if it were a slalom course. I turned and moved to meet her halfway. She had aged quietly since I had last seen her, but she had one of those faces that only get richer with time, like the light in a Vermeer. And her jade-green eyes were still to die for, gleaming with playful intelligence. I bent to give her a kiss on the cheek and she took advantage of my posture to pinch my butt.

"You've done me a real favor, you know," she said without preamble.

"Oh?"

"Yep. Now I'm not the only one in the family who pushed through a scandalous memorial."

"We aim to please," I said. "Thank you for the recommendation, by the way."

"I knew you'd talk some sense into them somehow. Those cherubs were going to make me gag until the end of time."

"I can't take any credit, really. Jocelyn and Bill pretty much worked it out on their own."

"Well, it's beautiful. Powerful."

229

"Thank you. . . . You're looking marvelous."

"There's no point buttering me up, sweetie," she said. "The money's all going to the grandkids."

I laughed. I had forgotten how much fun the woman was. "How's your hip?"

Marietta shrugged. "It's put a crimp in my tennis game and that's it for the ballet," she said. "But I'm going to get a hip replacement. Better than new."

"Really? They can do that now?"

"Titanium," she said. "It's great stuff, it will outlast my teeth. And, let's face it, I've still got a few asses to kick."

* * *

People were beginning to move toward the parking lot; apparently there was to be a post-ceremony reception at the Shermans' home. Jocelyn and Bill were talking with a small group of people under a tree, and Billy and Joshua had wandered off into the farther reaches of the graveyard on some all-absorbing boy mission. The area around Ariel Sherman's grave had cleared out and I moved toward it quietly, trying for invisibility. Even from a distance I could see the polished face of the stone gleaming like a ruby in the morning sunlight. I wanted to see it one more time, heaped with roses.

As I walked up to the grave, I caught a flash of red in the trees beyond it: the last cardinal of the season, foraging in the winter-bare oaks, a flickering scarlet echo of the stone itself. One of the roses left by the mourners had slipped to the ground and I stooped to pick it up and laid it, not on the altar-like shelf in front of the picture of Ariel Sherman, with the rest of the flowers, but across from it, beside the single yellow rose that Bill Sherman had set before his homage to his daughter:

"Warm summer sun shine kindly here;
Warm southern wind blow gently here.
Green sod above lie light, lie light

Good night, dear heart, good night, good night."

You promise yourself you won't forget. Every time the holy hush comes, it seems like the only obvious thing, the green truth of the hills after morning fog, and it is possible to believe that all of life can be lived in that sweet quiet lucidity, and that everything you touch will be blessed by that. And then you blink, and wake to that silence afresh from the buzz that blurred it, and it's been—whatever it has been, days, seconds, years, lost time, time dreamed away, like the long sleep in a fairy tale. But the perpetual forgetting doesn't matter. To return to that silence, where love and death lie lightly on your heart in tender balance, at any time and in any place, is to know as if for the first time that nothing matters except the things that take forever. And to know, anew, that there is no work on earth except to hold your raw heart open to the aching day, and give that truth away to the grieving world.

"I thought you'd bolted again," Jocelyn said, beside me, and I turned in the seamless moment to meet her unplumbable eyes.

"I'm pretty much out of places to run," I said.

Jocelyn smiled. "Imagine that." She had undone the top button of her black coat at last, and I saw that she was wearing a butter-yellow dress beneath it, the shard of color like the first flash of petals within a splitting bud.

"Bill seems happy with the stone," I said.

"He is. He surprised me, completely." She gave me a wry look. "He still wants the lamb, though. And the cherry tree. I told him no way on the lamb. But I may have to give him the tree, next spring."

"I'm sure the lawn mower guy will be thrilled. But Charlie will have your back."

"Was he shitty to you?"

"Bill? Not really." And, as she looked dubious, "Maybe a tad. But very precisely. It was almost surgical. I felt like a tumor, but a benign one."

"I think he's a little upset that I went up to Hog Island last

231

week."

It took me a moment to catch up with that. "To the cathedral, you mean?"

Jocelyn shrugged. "I guess Bill thought I was hoping to run into you. But that really wasn't it—I'd probably have turned right around, if I'd seen your truck. I just wanted to see the place." Her smile had a touch of teasing in it. "The new scaffolding looks good."

"The old one ended up in the creek. Thank God we weren't still sitting on it."

"That wall is coming along."

"At the standard breakneck pace of a crippled snail. But I can't complain. In the old days, they would already have stopped working for the winter and covered everything with sheep shit and straw to keep the mortar from freezing."

"I liked being there," Jocelyn said. "It was . . . heartening, somehow. To think of you working on the place. I'll probably go back from time to time, if that's okay with you. To watch it grow."

"That's between you and God," I said. "I just work there."

Across the cemetery, Bill and Joshua were bent over one of the sprinkler faucets. They had taken off their jackets and ties, but Billy was still holding the conch sash. Joshua was filling some kind of container with water from the spigot. I considered giving a holler to warn them off drinking the irrigation water, then realized that Josh was almost certainly just taking some kind of sample. No doubt he was concerned about the effect of all these dead people on the ground water.

Jocelyn had followed my gaze, and we shared a smile at the two boys absorbed in their research.

"That's my cathedral," she said.

It was so true that there was nothing else to say. We stood for a time in a peaceful silence beside her daughter's gravestone. An unforeseen side effect of leaving most of the rock untouched was that the few polished spots shone with a heightened intensity, like portals, as if the stone was glowing from within. Beside the monument, caressing its edge, the Gloria Dei rose bush was the feeblest spray of thorned twigs; Charlie had already pruned it back for the winter. It looked a little sad today, but that was the nature of the season.

The last of the conversational groups were breaking up, and cars were starting in the parking lot. Bill moved to round up the boys. The clock was ticking, and Jocelyn looked at me and smiled.

"Thank you," she said.

I met her gaze. I wanted to kiss her. But I was always going to want to kiss her. "You're welcome."

She held my eyes one last moment, then turned and walked away, toward her husband—unbuttoning her coat, I could not help but note, as she went. I would have loved to see her shed that black cashmere and blossom in her yellow dress. But it was enough just knowing it would happen. As it was enough for her, it seemed, to know that those cathedral walls were going to keep growing, and that the rose bush at her daughter's grave would flower when summer came. Some things, including some human things, are more certain even than stone.

* * *

I finally got started on my grandfather's stone about a week and a half later, on a bright winter morning early in the new year. The weather had turned chilly at last, and the heat of the forge felt good as I sharpened and tempered my grandfather's best granite points. Mrs. Durka was heaving away at her organ next door, playing something extreme and bacchanalian. The January air was crisp and the cries of the gulls carried in from the sea on the breeze. The third and Final Notice Before Termination of Services had arrived from Dominion Power in the previous day's mail, but I had already sent them their check, and felt quite smug. My landlord Mitchell was also content; I was a mere two months behind on my rent.

I set a fresh pot of coffee brewing, and fed two cookies from Mrs. Durka's latest batch to the local racoon, who seemed to be growing quite fond of them as long as I supplied sufficient water too. I opened the west window to the breeze, and took out the trash—garbage pick-up had commenced again after serious negotiations and a good faith deposit toward payment of the bill. The coffee was ready by then and I filled my mug and arrayed the first round of tools I'd need on the workbench.

Beside the bench, my grandfather's stone rested on the big tree stump, already squared-off and polished smooth on the surface. A strain of unforeseen and gratuitous pink had surfaced in the granite's face during the grinding, like a whimsy of water or wind, which had given me some concern, but the final effect was lovely. I figured I would carve a good Celtic border, and an Old Testament angel or two around the stone's script, a few of the little touches my grandfather used to call foo-foo nonsense, but secretly delighted in.

For the text, which I had already inked on, I knew that my grandfather would have insisted on the simplest effect, and I had blocked out the name and the relevant dates like a child's grammar in less than a day, in straightforward Trajan. Edward W. O'Reilly had been born in August 1913 to a sky filled with meteors, and died in the quiet heart of the fall, his favorite season, in the fullness of his years, beloved by his family and his friends.

In the end, the epitaph had come to hand just fine as well, despite my anxieties. I had simply copied the text directly from the battered wooden signboard, carved in Big Jake Awahili's hand, that had hung over the shop entrance in Shenandoah Springs for decades:

"EXCEPT THE LORD BUILD THE HOUSE,
THEY LABOR IN VAIN THAT BUILD IT."

My grandfather would have liked that, the economy of it. And he'd always had a soft spot for the Psalms. He said that once they were carved in stone, you could hear the music of them for a thousand years.

ACKNOWLEDGMENTS

"Praise, the ocean," Rumi says, in Coleman Barks's marvelous translation. "What we say, a little ship." In the ocean of my gratitude, Laurie Fox is the one who taught me how to say anything at all from the rowboat of my writing. She shaped the first drafts of this novel in the early 1990s, and she was there still teaching me how to say it better through every one of the twenty-three drafts that evolved to the present version, as mentor, editor, comrade, true-blue friend, and the world's gutsiest courage-under-fire agent, straight into the cannons' mouths, again and again. Thank you, Larushka. The ocean alone knows how to say more.

A book going back this far owes its existence to more than the usual throng in the cloud of unseen witnesses and angels. A special thanks to Abbie Rabinowitz, for the walk through the neighborhoods of the Oakland hills in October, 1991, where we came upon the funky little mason's workyard strewn with unworked stone, lit with dappled autumn sunlight, that crystallized the book's theme.